# Advance Praise for *Catwalk*

"Nicole Gabor's coming-of-age tale of first love and high fashion is a MUST-read. Five stars!"

-Jennifer Byrne, freelancer for *The New York Times* and author of *The Lazy Girl's Guide to Life*

"*Catwalk* moves along as swiftly as a model on the runway and will nudge readers to question their notions of fame, glamour, and self worth!"

—Debra Moffitt, author of *The Pink Locker Society* series

"I loved going on Catherine's journey with her! I was rooting for her the entire time!"

—_lindsayreads, book reviewer

"*Catwalk* is an engaging read offering an interesting look at the fashion industry and what happens once the shiny veil is lifted."

—Reedsy Discovery reviewer

# catwalk

*a novel*

## NICOLE GABOR

BVP

Brandywine Valley Press

ISBN: 978-1-7368311-1-3

Text copyright © 2021 Nicole Gabor
www.nicolegabor.com

Jacket art: Lily Wilson at LilyCatherine Design

*For Mom. Thank you.*
*For Dearma. Here you go.*
*For Eric. We did it.*

# PROLOGUE

My parents stared at me from across the kitchen table, stunned. They looked as though I'd just told them that our 12-year-old lab, Holly, had died.

I watched the wrinkles on my mother's forehead get deeper and darker, and it seemed like she was aging right before my eyes. Was her hair turning gray? I once heard that former First Lady Barbara Bush's hair turned gray overnight from the shock and grief of losing her baby daughter.

But I was not dead, or even dying. I was alive, and in the flesh. And I had just told my parents that I, Catherine Watson, their only daughter — the one with the 4.0 grade point average who my stay-at-home mother hoped would become a successful career woman, and my father secretly wished would follow in his footsteps as a lawyer — was not going to college after all.

I was, in fact, moving to New York City. To be a fashion model.

As I spoke, my letter of decline to the University of Pennsylvania's College of Arts and Sciences was signed, sealed, and on its way to the admissions office. My mother cried and said that I was breaking her heart. My father yelled and said that I was ruining my life. Part of me feared they were right. To be honest, I couldn't believe I'd actually gotten up the nerve to send that letter. I'd always listened to my parents, did the "right" thing. Never cut class. Been teacher's pet. Made curfew. But I was sick of following the rules.

With my high school graduation just behind me, the idea of more school — only to be followed by an office job that would imprison me within four gray walls — was something that I couldn't succumb to yet, if ever.

I was ready for adventure, for excitement, for a life less … ordinary. And I had a hunch that plenty of people stuck to the safe roads, so maybe, just maybe, I could make it on a path where everyone else wasn't taking up so much space.

Of course, it did seem an odd choice. I'd always been so ashamed of the attributes that could, quite possibly, make me a model. Lanky and lean at 6 feet tall, I had a way of sticking out in the hallways, towering over most of the female (and many of the male) teachers. Growing up, I'd tried everything I could to blend in, to bulk up, to deny my stature: I drank milkshakes. Dressed in layers. Only wore flats. Avoided stretching in gym glass. Never stood next to the short boys in line.

But then, one day, something happened. My mother took me to Victoria's Secret in Philadelphia to pick out my first fancy grown-up bra for my birthday. I was eying the "extreme lift" padded pushups (which I was sure would jumpstart my love life), when a woman tapped me on the shoulder and asked if I wanted to be a model. Just like that.

"She just turned 14," my mother said, looking a bit puzzled and slightly irritated. "I think she's a little young, don't you?"

"She's perfect," said the older woman, who was in her sixties and dressed far more fashionably than my 45-year-old mother.

She couldn't possibly be talking about me, I thought. Is this some sort of practical joke? A sick, twisted joke? I looked around expecting to see some mean girls from school, but the place was virtually empty. I turned back around, feeling my face flush.

"You … you think I could model?" I stammered.

"I think you're wasting your talent if you don't," she said. "Here's my card. Call me when your mother changes her mind."

But she never did. And neither did my father. Despite all my begging and pleading. My parents said that high school was more important, that getting into college was more important. That anything was more important than "aspiring toward such a frivolous pursuit." So I did what any girl in my situation would do. I stomped up the stairs, slammed the door, and screamed and cried into my pillow. But for the first time in my life, I felt like something special. *Someone* special. And my parents were not going to take that away from me.

A few weeks before my high school graduation, I rooted through my old jewelry box and pulled out the tattered business card the agent in Philadelphia had given me. Much to my surprise, she remembered me and started me off in Philadelphia to learn the ropes on a smaller scale before pushing me toward the ultimate goal: New York, New York. I did a little bit of modeling here and there, and with babysitting money I began to build my portfolio. Of course, I kept this all from my parents, assuming that once I had pictures and a little bit of income, they'd take me seriously.

But you know what they (or at least my know-it-all dad) say about what happens when you assume: You make an ass out of *u* and *me*.

The news didn't go over so well. It took three days of the silent treatment (courtesy of moi) to get my parents to finally agree to support me in my New York dream (after all, at that point college was out for the semester, so what else could they really do?). The agreement hinged upon one stipulation: I had a year — 365 days — to achieve a certain level of success in modeling (success defined as steady work). If I didn't become the Heidi Klum of my generation, I was to continue with college the following fall. My romantic notions of reaching fashion stardom immediately fogged my inhibitions and, before I knew it, I agreed to my parents' proposal and managed to get an apartment and a roommate in Brooklyn, just a stone's throw away from Manhattan.

It all happened quite quickly, before I was able to process it fully. My agent called me one day to say that Jon-Michelle La-Roché, a girl who I had met in passing — and, really, one of the most sought-after models in our little market — was looking for a roommate in New York. Was I interested in rooming with her? My heart raced at the thought, believing that the whole coincidence was quite an act of fate.

Yes, I said. And that was it.

I was set to move in on August 15, just two days before I

would have started my freshman year of college. I'd made a left at the fork in the road, just before hitting the interstate, and there was no turning back now.

# 1

*Him: So you're going where?*
*Me: NYC*
*Him: How long???*
*Me: As long as it takes.*

I dropped the phone on the bed and looked at my disaster of a room, desperately trying to piece together something cool from the lame selection of jean shorts, Polo shirts, and Old Navy tees I'd pulled from drawers.

The phone rang (playing Taylor Swift's "Welcome to New York" for inspiration) and I knew it would be Benji. There was no chance he was letting me off the hook with the bomb I'd dropped seconds earlier. I dug the phone out from between my 200 stuffed animals — those kept multiplying even though my grandmother knew I'd stopped playing with them over a decade ago — and answered.

"Hey ... can't talk now. Am totally late. My bus leaves in two hours and I haven't finished packing yet."

"Who's this? I'm looking for Catherine. You know, the girl who lives at home with her parents and whose idea of adventure is walking to Wawa at 10 p.m. for a blue raspberry slushie?"

"Benji! I don't have time for this! Listen, can I call you from the bus?"

OK, so I was being a bit evasive. But evasive is good. I mean, aren't girls supposed to be mysterious every once in a while?

Aren't we supposed to keep them guessing? I could hear my mother's voice in my head: Catherine, it's not nice to tease your boyfriend. But Benji wasn't my boyfriend ... exactly. He was just a "boy" who was also a "friend," who I just happened to kiss a couple times (OK four times to be exact, but who's counting?). So what did I owe him? I wasn't obligated to update him on every little twist and turn in my life.

"So, when were you going to tell me?" he said, the sound of his voice changing from playful to slightly awkwardly serious. "After you'd been receiving mail at some New York address? And what about school?!"

That, right there, was the reason I conveniently "forgot" to tell Benji about my plans. Sure, he knew I wanted to move to New York City someday. He just didn't know that "someday" was, like, a week from Tuesday. I resisted telling him because I was sure he would object. After all, "Benjamin Darling III" — as his mother insisted on calling him in her high-pitched northeastern cant — had his act together in the more traditional sense. He was going to be a senior at Villanova University and on track to become a high school English teacher. The minute I told him about my outrageous decision I knew he'd launch into a sermon that would sound a lot like my dad's. And, to be honest, I couldn't stand one more soapbox speech after hearing them all summer long.

"School can wait," I said. "Besides, I'm only 18 — I have the rest of my life for school." I braced myself and waited for the avalanche of judgment.

But there was no lecture. No speech. Just ... static. And then more static.

"Hello? Are you still there? Are you breathing? Do you need CPR?" I asked, half joking, half serious.

"Wow — I'm just surprised," he said, his voice cracking a bit. "That's a really bold move, Catherine. I hope it works out for you."

"That's it?" I said, slightly miffed. I guess I expected him to put up more of a fight. Or at least lecture me on the virtues of higher education. Or maybe act like he might miss me in even a teeny, weenie way. "You're not going to tell me I'm being a complete idiot? That I'm making the biggest mistake of my life?"

"No, I'm not."

I replayed the conversation over and over in my mind on the cab ride to the Greyhound bus station. I insisted that my parents not drive me there, because I knew my mother would get all dramatic and emotional at the gate and be totally ridiculously embarrassing as if I was moving to Guam or something. Besides, they'd be up that weekend to deliver the rest of my stuff. I knew I could have waited till then, but the anticipation was killing me.

At the bus terminal, I began to feel queasy, like I was going to hurl right then and there in front of a group of Japanese tourists who already had cameras at the ready in case I made a viral spectacle of myself. I sat down on one of those 1980s plastic stadium chairs that were bolted to the ground and tried to keep my cool, looking out the window and thinking about unicorns and rainbows and puppies and anything other than moving to a big city all by myself.

A station attendant's voice blasted through the loudspeaker, further setting me on edge. A northbound bus from Washington to New York Penn Station had arrived.

AGH. This is it. My ride.

*Breathe, Catherine. Breathe.*

I stood on Jell-O legs and dragged my suitcases over to the outdoor boarding area where the driver was taking tickets. As I waited — reminding myself that I could always hop back on the bus and, in two hours, have a home-cooked meal and my raggedy old Barney pillow for comfort — I noticed a mob of people gesturing toward something from behind. I turned to look, just as the tourists started rolling their cameras and clicking away.

Inside the waiting area, a guy was pressed up against the window, sucking face with the glass. His body turned and contorted into crazy positions as he smooched the pane. At first, it was hard to get a good look, but then I noticed the farmer's tan, the light-brown locks, the deep-set blue eyes and comical expression when he pulled away (looking quite pleased with himself!).

Oh. My. Gawd. You've got to be kidding me: BENJI!

When he saw that he'd finally gotten my attention (more like, my mortified reaction), he grabbed a poster off the ground and held it above his head. In bold black letters, it read:

## DON'T FORGET THE LITTLE PEOPLE.

Beneath it, a tiny red arrow pointed down, toward his head.

I burst out laughing, unable to maintain my cool. A security guard came up from behind Benji and not-so-politely motioned toward the exit. I quickly turned away — so as not to be associated with this little display — and handed the driver my boarding pass, which was now drenched in sweat from my cold, clammy hands.

I boarded the bus, still feeling like I might collapse at any moment. But at least now, I could breathe again.

117 Leonard Street was a lonely tenement on a forgotten block dotted with shuttered row homes and burned-out garages in the Williamsburg section of Brooklyn. The apartment building, once teetering on the brink of demolition, received a facelift from anxious real estate developers looking to revive the "Burg" as hipsters — who flocked to the borough in droves — called it.

Across the street from the apartment building was a liquor store (which I soon discovered sold more than just alcohol after hours), a junkyard with a chained-up pit bull, and, a few blocks up, public housing.

As I struggled down the street with my belongings, after a nerve-wracking cab ride in which the driver got lost and dumped me five blocks from my destination, the locals' eyes were on me. They followed me from block to block, as I strived to keep my bearing — and my nerve. From a nearby playground, someone shouted, "Yo, spaghetti legs!" I cringed. Even 100 miles from home, I couldn't escape the nickname that had tormented me since childhood.

I finally reached the fourth-floor apartment and hesitantly

knocked. An old-fashioned peephole slid open to reveal a flutter of thick caterpillar lashes sweeping across a penetrating eye.

"Jon-Michelle? It's me, Catherine."

Silence ... and then a look of recognition. Thank god.

"Oh, hiii, Catherine!" she said, pulling the door open, wearing a teeny lace camisole with matching hot pants. "I wasn't expecting you till later!" She smiled and her lips revealed a full mouth of perfectly placed Chiclets.

Inside the apartment, white, freshly painted walls met newly laid hardwood floors. The midmorning sunlight streaked through three floor-to-ceiling windows. I watched as the beams riveted across the floor in a dizzying kaleidoscope. The spacious, airy room gave the appearance of modern sturdy craftsmanship rather than what it really was — a thin veil of plaster masking a structural oddity. Stepping forward, I tripped on a board that jutted out.

"Be careful, the floors are really uneven," Jon-Michelle said, pointing to a plant that was sitting on the ground, cocked to one side. "And watch your head in the doorways, they slant! I swear, this place was built by elves on acid!" she said, rolling her eyes. "Welcome to the funhouse!"

From the bedroom, a beefy 20-something in boxer briefs, and nothing else, emerged. Jon-Michelle introduced him as Eric. He was your typical blond-hair, blue-eyed pretty boy and, as I guessed, a model as well.

"Want the grand tour?" Jon-Michelle asked me, waving Eric off as he tried to wrap his arms around her waist.

The kitchenette, a tiny two-by-four at the end of the room, was equipped with a new stove, refrigerator, and a flimsy butcher block on wheels that teetered from side to side when you stepped at various spots on the floor. On the other side of the room was a wrought-iron daybed — my new sleeping quarters. The small adjacent room was Jon-Michelle's room. In it, there was a gigantic sleigh bed that fit flush to the walls, making it nearly impossible for anyone to walk around it. The solid oak structure had been a gift from a former boyfriend, she said. It had a matching armoire cramped in the corner that hovered over it like the Leaning Tower of Pisa.

In the bathroom, the tub appeared freshly mounted, with powdery white clay collecting at the bottom of the basin and a sparkly, silver-plated showerhead that hung above. I looked at myself in the mirror. My pale skin seemed opalescent, almost blue under the LED lights that sprung from the cabinet with copper plugs and wires popping out like broken jack-in-the-boxes. I studied my sallow reflection, searching for a sign of strength. My cheeks were flushed but a coolness ran over me. I pushed my mousy brown locks away from my face, and stared at my reflection. This was it: my new life. The tomorrow I had been waiting for.

"Isn't she adorable, Eric?" Jon-Michelle said, as she came up behind me. "When we met, I just knew she'd be great for high fashion." She turned and whispered to me that Eric had just finished up a campaign for Hollister.

"You'd do great in Japan," he said to me, flashing his hundred-dollars-an-hour smile. "They dig girls with pale skin and large, exaggerated eyes. Like Anime."

"She'll do just fine here," Jon-Michelle said, tapping my shoulder.

It sort of felt like an out-of-body experience to have Jon-Michelle, a certifiable cool girl, take an interest in me — a person who, until now, had never quite been able to overcome my second-class social status.

Being a late-bloomer (and, well, clumsy "spaghetti legs") meant I pretty much lost out on most normal teen milestones — like dates to dances, invites to co-ed parties (after all, what boy wants to grope a double-A cup in the dark during 7-minutes-in-heaven?), and, of course, eating lunch with the cool kids in the cafeteria. By the time I finally started to "blossom" as my mother put it, it was too late to climb the social ladder — the girls had me labeled and the boys weren't interested. They liked the short, cute cheerleader types with the big boobs and the bleached blonde hair. And the tattoos.

(I thought about getting a tattoo once — one of those little Chinese characters that said "peace" or "love" — but my mother would have cried herself into a nervous breakdown and my father would have grounded me for life.)

So I just flew under the radar, hanging out with the quiet, nerdy types from my AP classes, but secretly forming crushes on the brooding poets or depressed Goths, whom, I imagined, were equally misunderstood.

That's why when Jon-Michelle showed an interest in me (in, of all things, *rooming* with me), I was a bit wary of her motives. What was in it for her?

"She's my next project!" Jon-Michelle chatted away to Eric.

Eric shot me an "Is she serious?" look.

I shrugged my shoulders.

"Oh, come on, she's new to New York. I'm going to give her all the dirty details of how things work up here."

A veteran of the modeling world at just 21, Jon-Michelle knew what designers were looking for. Perhaps she thought of me as that somewhat awkward ugly duckling (let's face it, my Lauren Conrad á la Kohl's wardrobe could use a little help) who might someday become a beautiful (or, at least, less awkward) swan. At least I hope that's what she thought.

"Just tell me what to do," I said with an awkward laugh, half-kidding. If Jon-Michelle wanted me as her pet project, so be it. I was gonna need all the help I could get.

I dragged my bags into my closet of a room and started to unpack my things, listening to the two of them talk about how someone might go about getting a New York agent (which, Jon-Michelle promised, she'd explain later in laymen's terms). About a half hour into the discussion, Eric realized that he was late for a shoot. He ran back into the bedroom and threw on a pair of skinny jeans and a graphic Rolling Stones tee before coming back to plant a long, wet kiss on Jon-Michelle's lips. I tried not to gape as she returned the gesture with a long, wet kiss of her own.

After he left, I turned to her, slightly confused. "Eric's nice, but I thought you said your boyfriend's name was Ian?"

"Oh, it is," she said, with a mischievous grin. "Eric and I are just friends." Oh, right ... silly me.

# ✦ 2 ✦

Moving to the Big Apple marked the first of many firsts. First cab ride. First apartment. First roommate. First night out in Manhattan.

That night, Jon-Michelle and I took the L train (another first) into the city. On the subway platform, people couldn't take their eyes off of Jon-Michelle. She wore a tiny gunmetal asymmetrical dress and stilettos, legs up to her neck. She walked ahead with an air of indifference, her eyes staring straight ahead with a sort of blank purpose. I marched in step, trying to keep up while sneaking sideway glances at my own reflection that coasted by in the train cars that passed.

My hair was in a boho side braid (thank you, my friends at *Teen Vogue*, for the how-to) with a fringe of bangs framing my face. I wore my favorite quilted leather miniskirt, a hand-me-down from my cousin, who worked at a boutique in Philly. The skirt was adorable, with patches of suede and rawhide, but it was so short that you could see my thigh gap when I stood still. My dad would have killed me had he known that I was walking through the subways of New York City, nearly at midnight, in a 12-inch skirt that barely covered my butt.

While stepping off the train at Union Square station, we were flashed by a man urinating in our path.

"Asshole!" Jon-Michelle spat at him in disgust. Fear being my immediate response, I worried that the man would yell back or lurch at one of us as we passed, but thankfully he barely even noticed us.

We arrived at our destination, a club in the meatpacking district of Manhattan, at 11:45. There was no sign to mark out the old, abandoned warehouse. People just knew where to show up. I worried that we (meaning "I") would be caught trying to get into a club that served alcohol. Having never been invited to drinking parties (much less had a "beverage") in high school, I wasn't quite sure how to appear nonchalant about the whole thing.

"Are you sure I can get into this place?" I asked. I held my breath while a cop car slowly crept by us as the driver, a face like a boxer, threw us a suspicious glance.

Great. What would my parents say about my next first: First arrest?

"You sure about this?" I said to Jon-Michelle, panicking.

She laughed. "You're so cute."

"What?"

"Catherine, models never get carded in New York. We basically have a free pass."

A few minutes later, her friend Theo, a DJ, showed up with a few other guys. Jon-Michelle greeted them with double-cheeked kisses before introducing me.

"S'up," one said, with a nod of the head. I gave a half-hearted smile, trying to appear nonchalant, like I sneak into nightclubs all the time.

We walked around to the back of the building, where a man was peering out of a contraption that looked like it belonged in the front of a Depression-era speakeasy. Theo waved and the man opened the door for us, pointing to a doorway at the end of a pitch-black corridor. We walked in single file, struggling to see a foot in front of us, before we reached the doorway, illuminated by a red glow from within.

The door opened and I was blinded by the saturation of color and light. When my eyes adjusted, it felt like stepping into an exotic wonderland. There were vines climbing up to a 50-foot-high domed copper ceiling. Red and purple satin draperies hung from rafters, falling into lazy piles on the floor. People lounged on velvet couches, topped with beaded silk throws and overstuffed pillows. The floors were busy with oriental rugs and ornately woven mats of gold and silver. As we moved through the room, off to a dimly lit spot in the corner, I felt like a coveted concubine floating to my master's chamber by way of magic carpet. Candles spotted the room like jeweled confetti and gave everyone an unearthly glow.

Our table was stacked with crystal ice buckets overflowing with champagne and bottles of vodka with impossible-to-pronounce Russian names. Theo opened the first bottle of bubbly and poured it into a crystal flute. "Cheers," he said in his British accent, handing a glass to me.

"Oh, I'm fine. Thanks," I said, still feeling like I could be kicked out at any minute.

"Oh, Catherine, relax," Jon-Michelle said, taking the glass out of his hand for herself. "You'll be fine. I promise."

I looked around and realized that the place was packed. It was probably silly of me to think that anyone was watching what I was doing. Besides, I didn't want Jon-Michelle to think she was rooming with a total nerd, either ...

"OK," I said. "Maybe just one glass."

I held on to the glass for a while before tasting the clear bubbly. It stung my tongue and left a metallic aftertaste like days-old ginger ale. This is what everyone is raving about? I didn't like it, but, not wanting to appear more out-of-place, I drank it anyway, feeling the cool liquid burn my throat as it made its way down.

Nearby, a man with a sitar and a synthesizer conjured up music that married ethnic chants with techno beats. The bittersweet wail of a woman at a microphone and the constant pound of a far-off drum drove Jon-Michelle onto the dance floor.

"Come on," she said, grabbing my hand.

After a couple of seconds out on the floor, Theo appeared with more drinks. I took one and gulped it down quickly, just to get it over with. His friends joined us and then one of the cuter ones named Vincent handed me another drink. He slipped his arm around my waist.

Vincent had thick black locks that fell down over his ears and stuck to the nape of his neck. I could see beads of perspiration dotting his cheeks and could smell the soap on his skin, the alcohol on his breath. He pulled me closer as more people crowded the dance floor. The room around us became heavy with sweat and fatigue. I tried to get rid of my drink, but the dance floor was so packed with bodies that I couldn't move. Vincent tipped the glass to my mouth and I swallowed.

As the dance floor got smaller, people pushed from every direction. I felt skin on skin: slippery, warm, and wet. Ahead, in a panel of mirrors, I saw Vincent and me, with my long brown braid whipping around, spiraling through the flashes of light. I watched myself in the middle of the chaos, suddenly part of this harem of the exquisite, the elite. Vincent put both arms around me, pressing me close, and we spun around and around. *This is it. This is what it's like to be young and beautiful in the greatest city in the world.* I closed my eyes, and let the music move through me.

When I opened my eyes, people with glow sticks were spinning all around us. The room turned with them, faster and faster, crowding us. Bumping us. I began to feel dizzy, hot, suffocated. I needed to stop, to breathe. But my body wouldn't stop; it just kept moving with the music. I jerked around, turning with the room and getting dizzier and sicker with each revolution.

That's when I saw her. Out of the corner of my eye, I saw a girl standing on the periphery. She was watching me. She was alone. Abandoned and afraid, like a sulking child on a subway platform. She watched me as I passed her by, over and over, with every rotation.

"Who's that?" I yelled to Vincent over the pounding music, pointing in her direction. She was staring at me.

Vincent looked around. "Who? Where?"
He didn't see her. "Come on, don't stop," he said, pulling me closer. "Why aren't you dancing?"

"I don't feel good." I pushed him away and turned to leave. But the girl was there, standing next to me. I turned around, and she was there, too. Her glare seared into my brain, a pain shot to my temples. My eyelids flickered; my head throbbed. Fighting off the nausea, I tried to focus on her blurry image. Her hair dangled in strings, covering her eyes. We stood, face to face. She looked hurt. Who was she? What did she want?

I reached out to touch her, and my hand hit the glass. Startled, I looked up and pounded my fist into the mirror. She stood there, before me, but also in every mirror, every pane of glass, every doorway, every flash of light, cloned in multiples.

It was me.

I pushed through the crowd. Faces came toward me in peculiar shapes, people yelled, the room spun on its side like a top. In the hallway, on the way to the bathroom, I kept bumping into walls that turned at odd directions, like a maze of uneven corridors in a haunted house. Was this what being drunk felt like?

The small mint green tiles on the floor of the co-ed bathroom reminded me of the old showers in my junior high school that no one used anymore. I found myself down on the floor, looking hard at those tiles. I tapped my finger on a whole row of them. They were ice cold. I almost pressed my hot face against them, but I didn't dare because the girls who fixed their hair were staring at me.

I pushed the stall door open and walked in on someone. No, strike that. I pushed the door closed because the people walking in on me were saying, "Are you all right?"

Hoping that they wouldn't see me, I closed my eyes really tight. But the girls kept laughing and I wanted to see what was so funny, but I didn't dare get away from the toilet because I was throwing up. I watched as the clear vomit flew like a waterfall over my chin and into the white basin. I tried to be quiet, but I couldn't help it. My boots made black streak marks on the floor. I was crying when I felt the sticker stuck to the back of my thigh. It was spongy and foamy. I pulled it off to see its two little green men with exaggerated eyebrows and mischievous grins smiling up at me. Now they were dancing on the green tile, mocking me, these little leprechauns. Where did they come from? A hand reached under the door and grabbed the dancing men off the floor.

"This yours?"

I looked down at a pair of neon yellow sneakers with bright blue laces. With all of my strength, I pushed the door open and saw a blurry, long-limbed figure towering above.

"Those things can really mess you up." It was a man's voice. "You all right?"

"What things?" I asked, wiping my chin with my sleeve.

"Lucies." he said.

I squinted, feeling like my eyes were going to fall out of my head from the shooting pain in my temples. "What are they?"

"You know, Lucies ..." he motioned with his hands, waving the two little men through the air. I looked up at him. The green tile from the ceiling began dripping down onto his head. It ran down the side of his face like green Elmer's glue.

*This is not happening. This is not happening.*

"An LSD patch," he said under his breath, while peering down at me in peppermint camouflage.

Ohmigod.

"Hey, are you all right?"

Ohmigod.

"You OK?"

"Um ..." I looked up with apprehension, relieved to see that he was himself again. "Yeah, I am now ... I think." He helped pull me up. I staggered, feeling like my legs were coming unhinged at the joints.

"Guess that's not the kind of trip you were looking for," he said.

I shook my head. "Not sure where I got that ..."

"Take this," he said, handing me a Dixie cup of water.

I drank three cups and walked over to the mirror. My braid had fallen out and now was just a sweaty, knotty, mangled mess. I combed my fingers through it and wiped the mascara from under my eyes. I always cried when I threw up. When I was little, my mom used to pat my back and stroke my head when I was sick. It was the only thing that would make me stop crying.

I turned to face him, seeing him clearly for the first time. Shaggy, chin-length hair. Big eyes. Rough skin. Five o'clock shadow. Beautiful teeth. "Thanks ..."

"Seth," he interjected. Smiling shyly now, looking more like a boy now and less like a man. "I'm friends with Theo. He sent me in to see if you're all right."

"Oh, umm, where's Jon-Michelle?"

"She's wasted."

"Well, uhh, thanks. You really didn't have to help me out. I'm really fine," I said. My eyes brushed the floor; I finally felt a wave of embarrassment.

"Hey, listen, don't worry about it. My friend once got screwed up on one of those things and he was fucked up for days."

I wanted to respond, but my stomach kept churning. I lunged towards the sink. "Sorry," I said, "I'm ..."

His fingers, gently touching my hairline, gave me goose bumps. I didn't get sick; I was just horrified. What an introduction.

In the cab, on the way home, we had to pull over a few times so I could throw up again. We had all crammed into a cab: Jon-Michelle, Theo, Vincent, Seth, and me. I remember thinking that on a normal night I would have been mortified that four new people I barely knew, two cute guys included, were watching me puke my brains out. But right then I was so sick that I didn't even care.

I awoke parched and shivering on the daybed in the apartment. My tongue felt like sandpaper. Ashtrays and empty beer bottles were scattered on the floor below me. I picked up a water bottle and chugged. My head was still throbbing, but at least I was no longer seeing double. The window in the kitchen was wide open, letting in a cool rush of air. It was pitch black, except for a red light coming from the alarm clock. It said 4:59.

"Jon-Michelle?" I called out, feeling strangely vulnerable. I paused to listen and heard music playing, voices coming from outside.

"Jonnie?" I yelled again, using the nickname she insisted I call her. I was suddenly feeling a bit abandoned and also a tinge jealous, like I was missing out on something.

"Yeah, girl, we're up here," she called out. I poked my head out through the kitchen window and looked up. She was standing about 12 feet above me, on the roof.

"Are you feeling better?" Jonnie asked. "Come up, we're

hanging out. The view of Manhattan is amazing from here."

A little hesitant, I climbed out onto a rickety fire escape and clung to a rusty ladder that led to the roof above our apartment. The sky above was clear and black, except for a few twinkling lights that lined the Williamsburg Bridge, a few blocks ahead. A gust of wind hit me and spread a rash of chills down my arms and legs. It was August 16th, what would have been the last day of summer vacation. A knot of fear tightened in my chest.

Everyone was lying on a torn-up stretch of Astroturf. The stench of marijuana crept up over the building, stinging my nostrils. It was my first time ever seeing that stuff. I peeked out of the corner of my eye, pretending not to look, and saw piles of little green leaves, all shriveled up, on white rolling paper. There were a few lighters lying on the ground.

"You want some?" Theo asked.

"No thanks," I said, pretending like it was no big deal. Like I had been around that stuff a million times before.

"Man, that really sucks what happened to you tonight," Theo said, taking a drag off his joint.

"I bet someone slapped that patch on you on the dance floor. I've heard of that happening before," Jon-Michelle said.

I looked at Vincent. He didn't seem to be too concerned about my wellbeing.

"There's some crazy shit that goes on out there," Theo added, quickly.

"Yeah, man," Vincent shook his head in agreement, pursing his lips. I looked at him, but he averted his eyes.

Jon-Michelle motioned for me to join her on a lawn chair and whispered in my ear. "Sethie took good care of you."

"Really?" I said, still trying to remember what happened after the cab ride home, but nevertheless feeling slightly flattered by his chivalry.

"He carried you up to bed and tucked you right in. I think he even gave you a goodnight kiss," she said, loud enough for him to hear.

Seth looked up. "Nope, sorry ... I save those for when a girl is actually conscious," he said, his grin exposing a crooked little smile.

My cheeks burned. He was adorable. My knight in shining armor.

I laid my head down on the rough mesh, and my gaze met the Manhattan skyline, beyond the bridge. The lights glowed like a child's Lite-Brite, with yellow, orange, red, and green dots. It was my first moment of clarity.

All those lights, at my command.

With one finger, I chose which light to turn off and on. I closed my left eye and held up my thumb, covering the Empire State Building, the United Nations, and the Brooklyn Bridge. Then I held up the palm of my hand and cupped the island of Manhattan. It was there, within my reach. I closed my palm and tightened my fist.

# ✦ 3 ✦

In the shower I scrubbed myself clean, trying to rid my body of the filth from the night before. A mixture of cigarettes, alco-hol, vomit, and the confusion of the night swirled in my head. I granted myself the pleasure of sitting at the base of the tub, letting the water beat down on me. The drops proved cathartic, allowing me to banish the images that cycled through my brain: that steady look in Vincent's eyes, him putting his hands all over me, the horror of my reflection, the patch, little men dancing on the tiles ... feeling duped somehow, foolish.

Lightheaded and weak, I felt the weight of my bones soar exponentially when I raised an arm or lifted a leg to dry off. As I climbed out of the tub, the lump in my throat slunk down into the pit of my stomach with dread of what was to come. Jonnie had gotten me an appointment with an agent at Icon, her New York agency. His name was Clive Loreaux, "the man who's launched a thousand faces." If someone was going to make it happen for me, she said, he was.

I laid out my go-see outfit, the skirt suit that I wore to visit my agent back home. It was tailored and conservative and of-fered me clean, straight lines. It projected the image of someone who had it all together — an image I certainly could use at the moment. But staring at the gray and charcoal pinstripes, it made me feel cheated, aged beyond my years. This wasn't the image I wanted to project here in a new city, where nobody knew me, and nobody expected anything from me.

"Leave the blazer at home," Jonnie said. "Trust me, you won't need it."

In the lobby of Icon, I looked out the window, watching taxis, buses, and ambulances roll by, observing all the commotion in eerie silence. A dreary day unfolded before me as a rain cloud descended on 32nd Street. Passersby took shelter under awnings and covered bus stops. I fidgeted with my hair, twisting the ends round my finger, over and over, a nervous habit since childhood. The elevator opened and a woman of Amazonian proportions emerged. In a New York minute (which I assumed is however long it takes for someone to give you the onceover), she pinned me to the wall with her beady eyes, checking my hair, skin, face, breasts, waist, hips, and legs just before brushing past me, her Rapunzel-length locks whipping across her back. Deciding to get the rest of the assault over with, I entered the waiting room and took my seat as Jonnie walked ahead to meet with an agent.

It was a large, minimalist space, with bleachers to sit on and a cement slab floor. The walls sported framed magazine covers and posters of models dating back to the late '70s. Girls filtered in and out of the office carrying portfolios under their arms like badges of beauty.

A model's portfolio, or "book"— as those in the biz casually referred to these pictorial shrines — is essentially her resume. Jonnie said that in New York a girl could show up to a go-see with puke in her hair from a drinking binge the night before, but if her pictures looked good, so did she. The selection of photographs in a model's portfolio, then, was absolutely critical to her success. Ideally, one's book included beauty shots of the face, body shots of the figure, and photographs of one's range, showing versatility. Some girls were perfect for commercial work, like catalogs and magazine ads. Others were "editorial" types, prime subjects of art-house magazines and haute couture clients. I guessed that I was more commercial, not exactly the edgy type, but I knew that to be a true success, I had to pull off both genres.

"Catherine Watson?" a voice called, jolting me out of thought. I stood up.

A tall, sleek Italian woman named Isabel with coarse, curly black hair and wiry black eyeglasses shook my hand and asked me to follow her. We walked into a conference room that overlooked Penn Station on 33rd Street. On the table were stacks of composite cards — the calling cards of the modeling world — dispersed in tiny stacks. I handed her mine.

"6 feet tall, 34-24-34. Size 4?" She looked at me suspiciously.

"Depending on the designer," I said, and the time of the month.

"Brown hair, green eyes," she said, eyeing me. "You're a little pale, though. Not in a good way, either. You should get some color."

She reached for my book and I quickly searched for an evacuation route. *What a HUGE mistake. What are you thinking, Catherine, that your rinky-dink pictures could compete up here in the fashion mecca!?*

I tried not to make excuses as she skimmed the pictures. First page, a headshot of me in a fuchsia top, which I'd thought quite cleverly highlighted my fair, rosy complexion rather than drawing attention to my unstylish avoidance of the sun.

"Your arm looks funny here," she pointed. "You should consider getting it airbrushed." I looked at the small crease in my upper arm. It was barely visible.

Next page: "Too commercial."

Page after that: "Consider pulling this."

The subsequent page was a quarter-body shot. I wore a bikini top under a wrinkled peasant shirt. It was a black-and-white photo that my art-student cousin had taken over the summer at the Jersey Shore. My hair was damp and curly from the saltwater and fell loosely around my face. It was one of my favorite pictures because it was relaxed, not posed, and looked natural.

"Amateurish," Isabel said. She flipped through the rest of my book with the enthusiasm of a housewife reading a circular in the checkout line.

When she asked how old I was, she said I was too old to be

starting up in New York. "Most girls your age are already estab-lished before they come here," she said. "Why did you wait?"

"Oh, I was in school ... just graduated, with honors," I said, smiling. Graduating at the top of my class had been a virtue I was quite proud of, but after seeing the vacant expression on Isabel's face, I quickly realized it wasn't a sought-out attribute here.

"Wait right here," she said, grabbing my book and heading out of the room.

On the table before me was a lookbook — a collection of models' headshots. Jon-Michelle was there, flanked by some hottie she did a leather jacket ad with in *W* magazine. She was just as breathtaking in print as she was in person. Her thick, dark brows rounded out a jaw line I thought only Brangelina's kids could've inherited. Her eyes, pools of honey, illuminated her face at all hours of the day or night, regardless of how much sleep she'd had the night before. Underneath her petite but strong nose lay two luscious mauve lips. Her skin was olive; hair, chestnut brown. In the photo, she smirked at the camera the way she always did, like she was holding on to a secret we mere mortals could never be privy to. Her allure, something she attributed to her exotic Colombian roots, was undeniable.

I looked up to see the seductress standing before me, in the flesh. "Clive's coming," Jonnie said. "Don't let him spook you."

Her agent, Clive, a middle-aged man who walked in relevés, entered the room. He approached me with the cadence of a cat before pouncing.

"Honey," he said, shaking his head. "I've looked through your book, and I'm sorry but I just don't know what you have to offer us. We are an established agency, for established models, like Jonnie here, who has worked since she was 13 ... have you tried acting?"

Jon-Michelle stood awkwardly in the doorway. "Clive," she offered, "how about she goes out with me, just for the day?"

"I don't think so," he said, eyeing me curiously.

"Well now, Clive, she is quite skinny. It might be wise to let Victoria or Agnes have a look at her," Isabel protested, with a sudden and inexplicable change of heart.

"Victoria's in Italy preparing for fashion week," Clive hammered in staccato.

"Well, Agnes, then?" she persisted.

I was being tossed around the room like a hot potato.

Clive shot Isabel a look, with one of his perfectly arched eyebrows nearly jumping off his face to whip her into submission.

"It's OK, really," I said, trying to appear unharmed by the assault to my ego. "I do have other agencies to see today. Thank you for your time."

"Honey, you don't have to get defensive," Clive said, slowly backpedaling his words. "You're just not really what our clients are looking for right now. It means nothing about you personally."

"I understand," I said, caught in a moment where I wanted to dig a hole down through the center of the earth and crawl out in China.

Isabel and Jonnie threw each other a sympathetic look that Clive intercepted.

"I guess I'm outnumbered!" he yelled, throwing his hands in the air. "Have it your way, then. Let Agnes see her."

Clive stormed out of the room.

"Agnes is our runway booker," Isabel said. She flashed me a look of pity and walked outside.

Great, now I was a charity case.

Agnes was a plain woman of about 40, with a long, bony British nose and poker-straight platinum hair. Like Clive and Isabel, she was cloaked in black.

"Have you done runway?" she asked.

Does the junior department at JCPenney's count? She pointed me out to a chaotic hallway, amidst gaggles of girls and bookers, chatting and yelling about casting calls and photo shoots. Once I appeared, the chatter ceased, and everyone gaped — no doubt waiting to see a wanna-be fall flat on her face.

Agnes handed me a pair of strappy sandals to slip on. My heart raced as I wobbled slightly in the initial pacing. But my jumpy nerves forced me to walk briskly, my feet shooting forward, one in front of the other, as I shifted my hips from side to side. I neared the end of the stretch, stopped, lingered there for a moment and made as "fierce" a face as I could (à la Tyra Banks on *Next Top Model*), then turned quickly to return to my starting point.

"Fine," Agnes said. "Come into my office."

My heart leapt.

She agreed to send me out for the week. The biannual Fashion Week shows were coming to New York in about a month, and go-sees were happening everywhere. Agnes made sure to let me know that this opportunity was just a one-time thing. But if I got booked for any of the shows, Icon would represent me.

She motioned for my book, pulling out every picture but the first. "We don't have time to get you test shots, so just use this for now," she said. Then, she walked out to the copy machine, photocopied about 50 pictures of my headshot, took half the stack and placed it on a shelved wall of composite cards, and returned with a roll of stickers that said Icon, complete with phone number and address.

"Place these on your headshots," she instructed.

Jonnie and I walked out of the offices of Icon, and, surprising myself, I planted a giant kiss on her cheek. Even though it was a torrid, rainy day and thunderstorms had descended on the city by this time, I felt like in my little world — by some utter miracle — a perfect little bud had sprouted. And I would do all I could to nourish and protect it.

Week one of go-sees in New York City went something like this:

Hair?
Bleh.
Makeup?
Wrong.
Hips?
Too big.
Boobs?
Too small.

Walk?
Too rigid.
Smile?
Crooked.

I was too editorial, not editorial enough, too commercial, not commercial enough, too old to start in high fashion, too young for beer and cigarette ads. Would I consider escort work?

The biographies of the girls I competed against went something like this: tearsheets from every major magazine; photo shoots in Japan, Italy, and France; hair commercials; reality show appearances; fashion influencers with millions of followers; Miss America or Miss USA contestants; engagement rings the size of sailboats.

And the hair? Perfect. Makeup? Flawless. Hips? What hips? Boobs? Victoria's Secret-worthy. Walk? Patented.

Each starlet who straddled the runway was even more striking than the last. Transformed, it seemed, from the torn T-shirts, messy hair, and mismatched thrift-store pieces they shuffled in wearing earlier that day. I stood next to them in line, my dour pinstripes depressing everyone in the room, looking like I'd just stepped out of a horrible corporate training video from 2001.

At go-sees, while standing among these 7-feet-tall glamazons, I shrank smaller and smaller, like Alice in Wonderland, until the Mad Hatter, wearing a pashmina and smoking a Parliament instead of a pipe, called out my name, took one long, sorry look and screeched, "Neeeeext!"

By day five, Jonnie managed to avert yet another fashion tragedy by taking me shopping in SoHo. She wouldn't be seen with her "little sis" on the subways anymore unless I kicked it up a notch ... or four. I was guided through the subtle nuances of fashion, which changed on an almost-hourly basis in New York. Square toe or round? Chunky heel or wedge? She knew. We picked out the must-haves of the season: cropped black leather jackets; painted-on skinny jeans; shrunken baby tees; aviator sunglasses; dainty earrings. I paid for it with birthday money and, oh, the small fortune I'd saved up to pay for college textbooks (sayonara, psychology 101!).

Later, we hit her wardrobe, a feasting ground for the fashion addict made up of couture pieces, one-of-a-kinds, vintage dresses, and fashion freebies she had attained throughout her career. Not having an older sister, I had been deprived of the sheer joy of pillaging the closet of someone older with better taste and more money. I slipped into one of her gems — a vintage Missoni jersey dress, circa 1990 — and imagined her sun-kissed Colombian mother wearing it to a Bogotá country club, sipping piña coladas, as her children's nannies tended to them, poolside.

"Wow, your mom must have been a diva," I said, running my hand along the dress' plunging neckline and chain-link belt that hung low on the hips. "But I don't think I have the cleavage for this." Strike that. I didn't have cleavage, period.

We were figuring out what to wear to an invite-only club Seth had asked us to, at a place where one of his friends was spinning old-school records. Very New York underground, it seemed. Jonnie had been talking about the place all week. I was excited to go, but also a little nervous considering what happened my first night out in New York. Hopefully, this time I could keep creepy guys with fast-moving hands away from me.

I turned to show Jonnie the dress. "What do you think? I'm not sure I can pull it off. Your mother must have had an amazing body."

"She was a model too, you know." Jonnie said. "Did I ever tell you that?"

"No, how cool!" I said. "I wish my mother would have done something interesting like that. She never really had a career."

"Yeah, well, I think my mother preferred her career to ... oh, I don't know. She was just never very motherly, let's put it that way," she frowned at herself in the mirror, pulling a piece of lint off her dress. "And ... unfortunately ... my mom was never very successful as a model, either. I think that's why she wanted me to model so badly — sort of like to make up for it."

"Well, I'm sure you've made her proud," I said, trying to make her feel better.

She smiled, "... yeah, I guess. After my parents divorced, she remarried and moved to California. We only see each other like once a year now."

She turned to me, "I'd give anything to be closer to her, like you are with your mom."

It surprised me to hear her say that. I'd been so embarrassed by my parents' constant pestering since I'd moved up here. On any given day, I was bombarded by nonstop texts from my mother, who was even wondering if I ate dinner, and to make sure I wasn't lying, what had I eaten? Before I left, I made her promise not to download Life360, and even after I couldn't be quite sure she wasn't tracking my every move.

"Trust me, it gets old," I said, looking back at myself in the mirror, and realizing that I'd not even felt homesick for one minute since I'd gotten up there. Did that make me a terrible daughter? Or had I finally gotten what I'd been wanting for all along — a chance to start over, a redo, a refresh.

Jonnie reached over and pulled on the straps of my dress so the neckline came up higher. "There, I think that's better. Seth's gonna love you in this!"

"Stop! ... *Really?*" I asked, feeling a flutter of excitement.

Jonnie had known Seth for a while. She said he was quiet and sort of the mysterious type — like you didn't know if he was being aloof because he was shy, or because he had "secrets."

"I think you'd make a cute couple," she said. "Him, the distraught, depressed-poet type; you, the perky, sweet little suburban girl."

"Don't get carried away," I said, pulling my hair up in the mirror, figuring out if it would look better up or down. "Plus, you don't even know if he likes me."

"Oh ... believe me — I know!" she blurted, barely able to contain her excitement. "Theo told me. Seth thought you were cute ... said you reminded him of someone."

"Cute!? While puking my guts out!?" I said, now feeling the butterflies in my stomach go frantically wild.

Taylor Swift's voice sprang from the other room, and I turned to get the phone, but Jonnie pulled on my shoulder while pinning up the straps of my dress. "Let it go," she said, assuming it was Ian, her on-again, off-again, who she was presently "off." Ian insisted on calling my phone when he couldn't reach Jonnie on hers.

A few minutes later, we listened to the message on speaker, but it wasn't Ian:

"Catherine? Hi, it's me ... just wanted to see how you were doing up there. Hope you're settling in."

I stopped messing with my hair and paused to listen.

"Hey, are you a famous model yet? Cause, ah, I thought I saw you on the cover of *Cosmo* the other day. Yeah, it sure looked like you. Well, I hope you're having fun up there. Call me when you get the chance. Bye."

"He sounds cute," Jonnie said. "Is that the guy you told me about?"

"That's the one."

"The one you dated?"

It occurred to me that I may have exaggerated a tad — or slightly more — when I told Jonnie about my relationship with Benji. It's not like we were serious boyfriend and girlfriend, at least, not in the way that Jonnie had had serious relationships (take, for example, the fact that Benji never brought me a diamond Tiffany tennis bracelet or paid for my European vacation).

Benji was, technically speaking, the first guy I sorta dated — if you didn't count dorky Lee Quigley, from church sleepaway camp, who used to kiss me in the dark during nighttime nature walks. Benji and I hooked up a bunch of times, but certainly never did *it* (because, of course, I was saving myself for THE ONE.) But this little truth wasn't exactly something I wanted to advertise around town — after all, Jonnie was a girl who had men (not boys, but full-grown, beard-sprouting, I-can-drink-legally-and-apply-for-a-mortgage men) crawling out of the woodwork to get a better glimpse of her.

I flipped through the pictures on my phone and found a slightly blurry but cute shot of Benji and me at the aquarium — the only shot of him acting normal that day and not trying to make himself look like a blowfish — and held it up to show her.

"He *is* cute!" she said.

I couldn't disagree. Benji was cute in that nerdy sort of Clark Kent way. He was a prep who always wore crisp khakis with the center crease expertly ironed, and golf shirts that I imagined were stacked neatly in Gap-style tri-folds within every drawer. Even though he looked quite vanilla on the outside, beneath that veneer was a closeted goofball yearning for attention.

We'd met over the summer in the Old City section of Philadelphia. My parents let me take the speedline into the city with my older cousin and her boyfriend to see an arthouse flick at the Ritz Theatre. But after waiting for admission in the pouring rain and then being turned away from a full house on opening night, we ducked into a warm, fiery pub that glowed from across the street. There, we waited out the storm. I remember smelling the cool musk of timber and rainwater. The old oak bar was stained with crescent-moon rings and worn down in places where patrons had etched their names into the soft, wet wood. We found a spot near the entrance and stood there, watching the rain pelt the passersby on 2nd Street, who were soaked but still looking for their Friday night fun.

I walked down the length of the bar to find the restroom, weaving through a crowd of frat boys and bachelorette party girls snapping selfies in matching tees, and noticed Benji. I stopped, or perhaps everything around me stopped, because I remember nothing of the noise, the women, the college boys, the music, the thunder outside. There was no sound, no commotion. Just him.

He was telling a story. As he used his hands to talk, he made exaggerated gestures with his long fingers and opened his bright eyes wide enough to illicit an "ah-ha!" from the onlookers.

When the audience burst into laughter, the look of gratification on his face made my chest cave and my heart beat erratically and, my god, my stomach flipped like a 6-year-old's on Christmas morning. He looked startled, caught by my sudden interest, and then quickly looked away. On the way back from the bathroom, I prepared myself to walk by him with a little more restraint. But he wasn't there. I quickly scanned the room, hoping I hadn't missed him leave, when I saw him talking to my cousin Aleta and her boyfriend, captivating them with his presence.

Benji and I pretty much saw each other every night from that point on. His charm was undeniable. My mother loved how he would pick me up at the house, "like a gentleman," instead of casually meeting me at Starbucks or the mall. He would come by and bring his mother's baked breads and cookies, and his dad's bottles of wine for my father, which only added to their adoration. I did love all the attention ... at first. But after a while, it sorta started to scare me. Benji could be so serious and so grown up about things.

He was on the fast track and had his whole life planned out: Married by 30, a principalship by 35, two kids, two dogs, two-car garage. It scared me half to death.

"What happens if your wife doesn't want kids?" I asked this over-achiever one day, as we were sitting on benches along the Schuylkill River after taking an early morning jog in Fairmount Park.

"She will."

"How do you know?"

"Because I won't marry her if she doesn't."

"Oh, yes, that makes things much easier. So you're willing to have your American dream at the expense of true love?"

He looked at me strangely.

"What are you talking about, Catherine?"

"I mean, if you fall in love with a girl, and she doesn't want that typical life, then you'll just leave her?"

It irritated me how Benji had it all figured out, like he was ready to step up for his prize for having mastered it all — the grown-up job, the five-year plan, the unwavering resolve — at barely 21. He would often look at me quizzically from across the table, wondering why his powers weren't working.

But, to me, following that traditional path meant being sucked into early adulthood to carry out a paint-by-numbers existence. And deep down, I think he secretly agreed. He told me once, on a late-night phone call, that he wanted to be a filmmaker ever since seeing the Harry Potter movies as a kid. He'd even made a few shorts with his father's old-school 18-millimeter camera. But when I pressed him about his career choice, he insisted that film was just a hobby, and besides, he said, "What's the point in trying to make it in a career with such a high failure rate?" His words didn't sound too convincing, though. It was like he was mimicking what he'd heard someone else (his father?) say to him. That's why I'd been hesitant to tell Benji about my own aspirations.

I snapped back from my daydream and noticed Jonnie was still looking over at me, impatiently, waiting for an answer. "Um, hello!" she said. "The guy? A boyfriend?"

"We sorta had this thing over the summer, but it's over now," I said, realizing that we were, in fact, better off as friends. That's the one thing I liked about Benji, he let me sorta take the lead with things and when I was starting to get freaked, he eased off on the boyfriend thing.

"What does he do?" she asked, walking over to the full-length mirror to check out her ensemble, flash her trademark pout.

"Well, he doesn't *do* anything quite yet. He's going to be a teacher."

"A teacher?" she gasped. "Oh god, why would anybody want to teach?"

"I don't know. I guess to help people," I said, feeling slightly annoyed by her shallowness. "He's that kind of a guy ... a Big Brother and all."

"But do those people make any money? Like what do they make a year, 40,000 dollars?" She looked me up and down and handed me a lipstick. "Red lips look great with that dress."

"Um ... I never really thought about it," I said, wondering what the big deal was.

"Seriously, sweetie, if you're into the professional type, don't waste your time with a schoolteacher," she said. "Find a guy who works down in the financial district. Wall Street is crawling with those assholes, and they love models. They pull in like 200,000 dollars a year."

"A year? That's waaay more than my dad makes, and he's been a public defender forever," I said in disbelief.

"Yeah, most of these guys were the biggest geeks back in

high school. Now that they're loaded and living in a penthouse in Tribeca, they'd do practically anything to get a beautiful girl to fuck them."

"Jonnie!" I shrieked, slightly horrified by her language but also, I confess, a teeny-weeny bit thrilled by the prospect of men — successful men like that — clamoring over a girl like me. Catherine, the girl who, up until Lee Quigley came along, was practically invisible to those of the opposite sex.

"It's true," Jonnie said, holding up the picture of Benji and shaking her head. "Just don't limit yourself, Catherine. You're in New York now. You'll have the pick of the litter."

I grabbed my phone, staring down at the blurry picture of us for just a moment, before pressing "delete."

# ✦ 4 ✦

Seth lived in a very ritzy part of town, just blocks from Central Park and the Natural History Museum. Pulling up to a high-rise with gold awnings, I half expected a white-gloved doorman in tails to escort him out.

"Wow ... how can Seth afford to live here?" I asked.

"It's his dad's place, he's like some big record executive," Jonnie said. "He signed a bunch of boy bands in the early '90s and made a fortune."

Seth emerged wearing a pair of skinny jeans, with the hems falling over his vintage, Brit-style leather ankle boots, and a lightweight black turtleneck that clung to his wiry frame. He opened the door and whispered, "Hey you, feeling better?" before sliding into the cab. He squeezed next to me, pushing his knobby knees against mine. His hair, black as kohl, hung messily about his face. A few strands fell into his eyes. My heart fluttered: He could have been the fifth Beatle. I breathed in the faint odor of Dove soap. *Mmm.*

"Mind if we swing by my stepmom's place on the way?" he asked, once he had settled in. "She's having a little party, and I told her I'd stop by. It'll only take a few minutes, she lives off 59th."

"Fine," Jonnie said, rolling the window down to light a cigarette. "Want one?" she asked.

"Nah, I quit," he said.

"So you prefer pot to Parliaments?" I asked, sounding a lot less playful than I'd hoped. But, oh, how he would be perfect were it not for this little drug thing I despised!

He turned and gave me a confused look, "I'm straight edge," he said, furrowing his eyebrows. "I don't smoke anything."

"Oh, but I thought you were smoking the other night ..." I said, feeling slightly chastised.

"Nah, my friends do it, but I stopped that stuff a long time ago," he said, shifting in his seat.

Jonnie flashed me a look, like "Don't believe it."

I stared back at him, and her eyes followed.

He lifted his palms, "What is this, the Inquisition?"

"She just wants to know what she's getting into," Jonnie said.

My face flushed. Oh, god. Oh, god, oh god. She could be so ... *forward*.

"Well, I'm not sure you're such a good influence," he said, watching Jonnie hand me a cigarette that I attempted to puff on without choking. "Little Miss, you shouldn't mess with that stuff," he said, pulling it out of my lips. "I take it you're a lightweight."

"She's a virgin," Jonnie said, botching a French inhale. "Don't taint her."

I shot her a horrified look. What the heck was this girl revealing?

"Her body is a temple," she said, looking at me with a little smirk. "Right? Sort of like a Buddhist?"

"Um ... sure," I said, trying to recover from this near-hives-inducing moment.

"Not too many girls around here are like that," he said, looking out the window.

I wasn't sure, but from the sound of his voice, it seemed like he thought that was a good thing.

Seth's stepmom had a 7-foot-high waterfall in the middle of her living room. The apartment was on the twentieth floor, the penthouse of an Art Deco office building that had been converted into lofts.

In the elevator, Seth explained that his stepmom was actually his *former* stepmom — who had been married to his father when he was little but who was now married to Jake Eisenhower, the vice president of programming at HBO. I guessed the divorce was amicable.

"I just want to stop by and say 'hi,' otherwise she'll get on my case," he said to the once-impatient Jonnie, whose demeanor changed instantly the moment she realized she was going to a party hosted by someone so important. "Maybe I can pick up a few bottles of Stoli for us to take to the club."

"Oh, of course, take your time!" Jonnie gushed.

We entered a plush white entryway and were immediately ambushed by a woman bedecked in Chanel from head to toe.

"Sethie, darling, you made it, honey!" said the woman. She placed a pink-lacquered lip on his cheek. He stiffly pulled away, as Jonnie suddenly squeezed my upper arm.

"*Holy shit!*" she whispered. "*Holy shit!*" she repeated, Seth's stepmom approached us.

"And who are these lovely creatures?" she said, hands clasped together.

"Catherine," I smiled, extending my hand to greet her. "Nice to meet you."

"Jon-Michelle La Roche," Jonnie said. "I think we've met before. Gail, right? Gail Halloway, the stylist? We worked together a few years ago on a *Vanity Fair* shoot."

"Oh, yes! Jon-Michelle, of course," Gail said, her eyes faintly disassociated, looking like she was still trying to figure out who she was. "How are you doing, sweetie?"

"Great. I'm with Icon now."

"Excellent, darling. I'd love to see your book ..." she said, looking over our heads at people entering behind us. "Oh, Philippe just arrived. Please excuse me."

"Philippe?" I said, turning to Jonnie in disbelief. "As in, Philippe whose ads are plastered all over every *Vogue* magazine?"

"That's the one," she said, as we began to walk through a roomful of established fashionistas.

"And you can bet he's not the only designer here," she said. "Gail Halloway is one of the most famous stylists in the city. She's worked on movie sets, dressed celebrities, models ... I had no idea Seth was *related* to her. How dare he keep this little secret from me!"

I scanned the room to find Gail lookalikes fabulously fooling Father Time with their gravity-defying bosoms and taut complexions. They wore clothing fashioned for the very young but carrying price tags only the post-30 crowd could afford. Most of them had more money invested in their diamond-encrusted, French manicured fingertips than my parents had spent on my entire Catholic school education.

"That's Esmeralda, one of the first Calvin Klein models," Jonnie said, pointing to a beautifully coiffed older woman draped in a light mohair cape.

"And that's Perri Pileggi, the photographer," she said, motioning to a small man in black sunglasses, with an open collar exposing a tuft of chest hair.

The Hollywood celebs started filtering in.

"Roberto," Gail squealed. "It's so good to see you! I heard about Cannes!"

I watched, with my vision obscured by the crystalline fountain in the middle of the room, as the image of the movie producer and his entourage morphed into exaggerated proportions, with arms and legs springing out like Silly String.

"Here you go, darling, pass around," Gail said, handing me two glasses of champagne. "We are toasting Roberto's latest film festival success."

"Seth, darling! Where are you?" she called out. I looked around for Seth, but he was gone, probably off raiding her stash of alcohol somewhere.

By now the room had become smaller, with everyone touching elbow to elbow, arms raised only slightly with painted smiles and startled expressions.

Gail clinked her highball with a butter knife and muttered some inaudible phrases, pierced with deference and praise: "genius," "master," "phenom."

Someone said Roberto should run for president, and the room burst into laughter.

At that moment, it hit me. I was a mere mortal in a room full of demigods: actors, actresses, bygone legends of the stage and screen; men and women who had traipsed down red carpets all their lives, whom the rest of the country — no, the world — had pined for, had paid to know the secrets of. Here I was standing among them, cavorting with 21st century royals.

And I felt smaller than ever. My short, uneventful life had left so little impact on the world. I mean, by my age, some of these giants had already starred in movies, written novels, won Oscars. I felt like an impostor standing among them. I tried to silence the little voice inside of me screaming, "Who do you think you're fooling? You're not one of them! You'll never be one of them!" And then I caught sight of myself in the mirrored curio cabinets and saw what everyone else saw: a slim, unusually poised young woman who, thanks to another woman's dress and makeup artistry, might pass for one of them.

"My god, its Remi Fosgate come to life," a voice called out from behind, and an older gentleman with white hair walked over. "Frank ... Frank, come here. Doesn't this young lady look like Remi?"

"Why, yes, Cal, yes she does," the man said. "Don't tell me you're related?"

"Um, sorry? ... no, I don't think so," I said, wondering whether this was really a middle-aged ploy to talk to a younger woman at a party. I scanned the room looking for Jonnie, who had by now attached herself to a friend of a friend of Pileggi's, the man who she would be slowly inching toward for the rest of the night. "Who is she?"

"Fosgate? Oh, she was going to be the It girl of the '90s. She was a real rising star in fashion," he said.

"And Frank would know," said Cal. "He photographed her for years."

My antennae perked: *It girl. Fashion. Photographer.*

Wait — did a New York fashion photographer just say that *I* looked like an It girl?

"Yeah, back in the day, Gail, Philippe, Remi, and I worked

together on many projects," Frank said.

My heart began pounding so loudly in my ear at this point and I could barely focus on what these two were saying. Focus, Catherine, focus! Act nonchalant … like important men tell you this all the time! *All. The. Time.*

"What happened to her, Remi?" I asked, breathlessly. "If you don't mind me asking…"

"Oh, she died, tragically. Terrible shame. Just as she was beginning to make it in modeling, too. I mean really make it. She was on the brink of signing a 100,000 dollar contract. That was a lot in those days."

*Yikes.* "How awful," I said, finding my voice again.

"Yeah, poor thing. She had a young son at the time," Frank said, reaching into his pocket to retrieve his ringing cellphone. "I'd better take this," he said, pulling out his business card. "Give me a call sometime."

He slipped the card into my palm and I thanked him, trying to keep an appropriately chill facade intact, while on the inside I was SCREAMING AT THE TOP OF MY LUNGS.

I stood by the window for a bit, fantasizing about how to share this news with my no-doubt skeptical parents, but quickly realized that I probably looked silly standing in the middle of the room all by myself, with nothing to do and no approachable person left to talk to. Bathroom break!

A waiter by the antipasto station said the closest restroom was at the end of a long corridor, on the other side of the sprawling apartment, third door on the left. As I navigated through a maze of rooms, each one seemingly ripped from the pages of *Town & Country,* I tried to keep a poised posture and loose strut, attempting to appear fearless in the face of the fashion elite who possessed the power to make or break.

The bathroom door was closed.

"Third door down on the left," I repeated to myself and knocked on the door. No answer.

"Hello?" I placed my hand on the doorknob; it turned. I entered what turned out to be a full-sized bedroom. Wrong door. But it was such a charming room, decked in shabby chic décor, that I couldn't resist taking a peek. No one was around and no one would see me, I thought. I stopped in front of the mirror to check my hair, which Jonnie had straightened with a clothes iron on the bathroom rug of our apartment after her flat-iron died. My hair now appeared to be at least two inches longer and fell to the middle of my back. As I put on a second coat of lip gloss, a series of photos on the wall caught my eye.

Most were of Seth's stepmom posing with various celebrities: Naomi Campbell and Kate Moss, Miss America 1991, George Michael and Madonna; Calvin Klein and Ralph Lauren. I stared in awe. This woman had lived the life. There were even older pictures, ones of her in the late-1970s, when I guessed she was just beginning her career. In one photo with two other girls, Gail wore a cool head wrap, à la Erykah Badu. The caption below the picture said, "Debbie, Remi, and Gail — Studio 54, New Year's 1986."

*Ohmigod.* I looked at the photo more closely. Was this the Remi I had just heard about? At first, I didn't see any resemblance between her and me. She was super skinny and looked like most typical models up here. But in other pictures I noticed some familiarity. Same skin tone, same eye color, her hair was a lot lighter than mine but we had the same dark, bushy eyebrows. Her two front teeth stuck out just slightly below her top lip, which, on me caused terrible buck teeth until I was about eleven, but on her seemed sexy enough to be appealing.

Suddenly, the door swung open and Gail entered.

Oops.

"Hi, um, sorry, Gail," I stammered, "I was told the bathroom was in here, but I —"

She said nothing, walked past me, and fell onto the bed.

"Gail, are you all right?" I walked over to her and heard her murmuring something under her breath. It sounded like she was saying, "Gimmizziishew" over and over. Her eyes were wide open, and she was staring at the ceiling.

She kept mumbling the same words, like she was in a trance. I started to feel all hot and panicky. *Um, what is going on?*

"Gail, I'm going to go find Seth, stay right here." I said.

"Phi-lippe!" she yelled. "Phi-lippe."

Oh, god. OK. She wanted Philippe, only the most intimidating person she could possibly steer me toward in this whole place.

I dashed outside and found Philippe, the master of cloth, sipping a martini at one of the many bars dotted throughout the apartment. He was sitting next to what looked like a miniature palm tree. "Um ... hello, Philippe," I said, poking my head through the branches in the most awkward position.

It took a few meek tries before he stopped talking and turned to me in disgust, for I had interrupted his conversation with another, very important-looking man.

"And what do *you* want?" he demanded in a deep, dark Italian accent, looking me up and down with a sweep of the eyes.

"Um, sorry, hi. Gail, um, our hostess, is in her bedroom and she has asked me to come get you."

He wrinkled his forehead.

Oh, god, that came out all wrong.

"She's not feeling very well," I slowly mumbled and smiled at the older man standing next to him.

"Ah, excuse me." Philippe said.

I led His Highness back to the bedroom, where Gail was on the bed. By now, she was sitting up trying to stop a nosebleed.

"My dear, let me get you a tissue," Philippe said, while peering sideways at me very oddly. I watched him open a bottle of prescription pills and hand her two little white tablets, along with his handkerchief.

"This will help, *mi bambino*," he said. Gail swallowed the pills sans water, and then blew her nose until it ran clear. Some blood fell onto her shabby chic duvet.

Even though I was standing there among two fashion icons, it seemed the wrong time to, ah, promote myself, shall we say. In fact, I seriously wanted to get the heck out of there. I had walked into a private moment that I wasn't supposed to witness. Gail still seemed drugged or something. Things were just a bit too *weird*.

I started to leave, but Philippe held his palm up.

"Forgive me for being so rude earlier. I am Philippe Borghetta. And you are?" he said as he helped Gail up from the bed.

"Oh, I'm Catherine, Catherine Watson," I said, flattered by the sudden interest. "I'm here with Seth, Gail's ...ah ... stepson."

"Sethie brought two very beautiful girls with him tonight," Gail said in lucid prose. "Why don't you look at this one, Philippe? Frank thinks she looks like Remi."

I felt the adrenaline rush into my veins once again.

"Yes ..." he said, his voice changing to become a bit more high-pitched, a bit less Dracula. "Who are you with? You are a model, no?"

Before I could answer, Seth opened the door. "There you are, Catherine. I've been looking everywhere for you and Jon —"

He stopped mid-sentence and looked at Gail.

"Oh, this again," he said and sighed, picking up the bottle of pills off the table and throwing them down. "Thought you were clean?"

*Good god. Get me out of here.*

"Of course, Sethie, sweetie. Of course I am!" Gail said, as she flattened out her rumpled top. "Those are just my blood pressure pills. Promise! I was having another one of my spells, but I'm feeling better now."

"Let's go," Seth said, taking my hand in what felt like an overly heroic (and adorable) gesture.

Gail continued as we moved toward the door. "We were just having a talk with your girlfriend here. Maybe you can give Philippe her comp card," she said, appeasingly. "He may have a place for her in his fall show."

*WHAT!?!?!?*

Ignoring the awkwardness of the moment, I let out a stunned "*Really?* You really think *so*?"

Philippe smiled with a rather frog-like grin.

"Great," Seth said, halfheartedly, as he ushered me toward the door.

"She is lovely," Gail said, trying to stall him. "We think that your new friend — Catherine, is it? — bears a striking resemblance to your mother, Remi."

# 5

"She was *discovered*! Discovered by Philippe!" Clive, my new agent (yes, *agent!*) at Icon, chimed into the phone as I walked into his office to get my daily appointments in late-September.

"Yes, she is booked for the spring show and Philippe's fall print campaign … Fashion week? Booked solid!" he said, winking at me. "Sorry, honey, she's in high demand. But for you, maybe we could work something out. Say, time and a half?"

Time and a half? *Ohmigod.* I still couldn't believe the turn of events here. This man was talking about *me*, Catherine Watson, and not some other incredibly fortunate girl.

Pinch me. Smack me. Punch me!

"Oh, she can't walk out of the house for twice that! … I know, I know, but I'm telling you, she's gonna be huge! Remember Fosgate?"

The last three weeks had thrust me into an alternate universe, where star-studded cocktail parties, casting calls, go-sees, and nightclub openings revolved around me like constellations. I tried to play along and not think about the catalyst of this sudden success — that fact that I was running around with the son of the dead woman I supposedly resembled. Given its Freudian implications, it wasn't something I really wanted to dwell on.

Sitting there, waiting for Clive to get off the phone (yes, Clive of the "we have no place for you here" notoriety), I let my mind wander, reimaging for the three-hundredth time the scene in the Icon offices when, weeks earlier, Philippe's personal assistant called up to ask if I was available for the showing of his spring collection at Fashion Week.

Jaws dropped, eyebrows arched, and coffee cups tumbled, no doubt. Wasn't I that forgettable girl they had dared to take a chance on to appease their star, Jonnie, only days earlier? My god, yes.

Then miraculously and all at once, as if a fairy godmother had sprinkled dewdrops and glitter into the eyes of all who gazed upon me, I became the most enchanting creature, one worthy of the Icon name. Before I could ask for it, I had a portfolio with my name emblazoned on the cover, a new iPhone filled with go-see appointments, blond highlights framing my face, and hair extensions that would make the Kardashians jealous. I, Catherine Watson, had been "made." *AGH!*

But perhaps most unbelievable of all, I had a new name: Cat. "It's hip, modern," Clive had said.

Catherine, on the other hand, was what he called "stuffy, boring, old," a person his mother would watch on PBS. There's no denying that. In junior high, I tried shortening my name to Cate, but at the time Cate Winters (the most popular girl in 8th grade) was already a Cate with a "C" and there was no way a peon like me was going to steal her nickname. So, since Cate with a "C" was ruined for me, "Cat" seemed a welcome change.

It was all part of the branding process, Clive said. "Babe, you exude youth and innocence. It's refreshing! I can read the headlines now: 'Plucked from Obscurity!'"

Not *completely* true, but evidently we weren't going for truth here.

"We're gonna make you the girl next door, the one out in East Bumblefuck driving all the boys crazy with her kitty cat eyes ..."

I was excited, but somehow listening to a balding, fat man say "kitty cat eyes" made me want to puke.

"So, I know you've got the good girl thing down pat, but you're going to have to get a little naughty."

"Naughty?" I said, hoping I misheard him and this wasn't really the premise for a Hallmark movie.

"Step it up a bit," he said. "Nice girls with no edge get nowhere in fashion."

He handed over the contract — about 10 pages of tiny text. I flipped through it, trying to absorb all the information in the five-minute window he had allotted for this purpose.

"It's standard," he said. "We get a cut from each job you take, you take home the rest."

I'd never had to sign something so official-looking before.

"Is it nonbinding?" I asked, having heard my father talk about contracts before and trying to appear in the know.

"Look, it's what all our girls sign," he said, slightly annoyed by my dilly-dallying. "Do you need more time? 'Cause you gotta run if you're going to make your go-sees in Midtown."

A part of me wanted to hold back. I knew I should go over the contract with my father, but Clive wouldn't have gone for that. That was part of the "little girl" mentality I was going to have to shed. I held my breath and signed on the dotted line.

"Mom, Daddy's not home, is he?" I whispered into the phone.

"Why, yes, dear. He's right here ... *Bill!*" she called, pulling her mouth away from the receiver.

"Noooo! No, Mom, psssssss ... Mom. I don't want to talk to him," I said, still whispering. "I want to talk to you. About my modeling contract."

"What's this I hear? Modeling contract?" my father said, slightly bemused.

Too late.

"Why, sweetie, that's wonderful!" my mom said, having just picked up the receiver in the other room. "When do you sign?"

"Sign?" my dad's voice went up an octave. "Don't tell me you signed anything before letting me take a look at it."

"Dad, it's totally legit, I promise. This is a well-known agency."

"Did you take it to a lawyer?" he went on, ignoring me. "Did you have someone review it? You should have counsel review anything before you —"

"Dad, that's so lame. Nobody does that. Besides, it's completely fine. Girls do it all the time. Anyway, I'm not going to question it. I mean, I should be *thanking* them. Do you know how hard it is to get a modeling contract in New York City?"

"I want you to fax me over a copy of that contract tomorrow morning."

"Dad, no."

"Sweetie, dear, listen to your father. There's a lot about this modeling business that we don't know about. We're just trying to protect you, to keep you safe."

"I understand, Mom. But I am an adult now, and I am on my own. I can't have you always holding my hand, always coming to my rescue — or telling me what to do."

Unbelievable. My parents were supposed to be happy for me, excited even, that I had accomplished my goal in just one short month. But all they could do was focus on what I didn't do. Oh, yes, of course, I forgot to ask all the appropriate questions: What happens if I get sick? Is there health insurance coverage? Disability?

Disability? What am I, a 58-year-old man?

"I'm not working at some stupid office like you, Dad!" I quipped before hanging up. It was dramatic, yes. And I'll admit, maybe even a little *too* harsh — I knew they were my parents, after all. But I was trying to prove a point. I wasn't a little girl anymore, and my parents were just going to have to assert their authority elsewhere.

My first runway show in New York City was held during Mercedes Benz Fashion Week, just the most intimidating venue to take your first turn on the catwalk. Celebrities were *everywhere*: backstage, in the audience, standing next to me in line waiting for a complimentary gift tote or a free bottle of Fresca.

I spotted designers, photographers, influencers, Hollywood celebs, society It girls made famous by Page Six, ladies who lunched, and intimidating Nina Garcia types bathed in black with discriminating stares that pierced through you with their oversized black sunglasses. Such was the woman who peered up at me as I attempted to enter the gates at Lincoln Center nearly

10 minutes late, after fighting through a crowd of design students who loitered on West 65th Street.

"Your pass?"

Pass? What pass? No one said anything about a pass!

"Um.... I'm a model," I said. "I'm with Icon." I held up my book.

"Sure you are," she said to me, as she let a few girls slip by the entrance. "Step aside, please."

"But I'm doing Philippe's show today," I said, looking down at the time on my phone and now beginning to shift into panic mode.

"Ah-huh," she said, eyeing me like I was some disheveled design student who was attempting a break-in. "I need to see your pass."

Shit. Shitshitshit. So typical of you, Catherine! Being late to your *first* show! And for Philippe. *PHIL-LI-PE!*

"I'm sorry, but I wasn't aware I needed a pass," I said, trying to sound as calm and direct as possible. "But if you please let me in, I'm sure we can get this whole thing straightened out, I just need a moment to ..."

Ignoring me, she pulled a curtain aside to let some members of the press go by and I caught my first glimpse of an official showroom, with its wide, wooden runway that seemed to stretch out for miles. Harsh white lights flooded the room. Wires and cables netted the floor like cobwebs below the pine-piqué chairs that sat staunchly, like soldiers, waiting to hoist the next bony bottom. A sick, anxious feeling grew in the pit of my stomach as I thought about how I should probably be practicing on one of those runways at this very *moment*. AGH!

Thinking that my fashion career was over before it had officially begun, I dug back into my purse to reach for my phone, petrified of what Clive would say when he found out I was late. But fortunately the fashion gods were on my side, because before the line began to ring I heard a familiar voice: "Cat! Where have you been?"

Thank (the fashion) god! It was Gail.

*Holy crap, it was Gail!* Why am I always in the wrong place at the wrong time when this woman is around?

"Is there a problem here?" she said, shooting the gatekeeper a disquieting death stare.

"I'm ... ah ... unauthorized," I said, motioning to the little woman, who by now was turning 20 shades of pink.

"This is one of our new girls, Cat," Gail said, narrowing her eyes and digging a blood-red, lacquered fingernail into my shoulder. "She's been handpicked by the House of Philippe to show his fall collection, and she's permitted to walk within these halls. If you have an objection, take it up with Philippe himself!"

Now that's how you do it.

Around us a crowd of publicists, low-profile journalists, and onlookers trying to sneak into the shows stopped short to listen, with a chandeliered ear, attempting to get their first dose of morning gossip. A hubbub murmured through the crowd, and a few onlookers scratched in their notepads, eyeing me up and down.

I awkwardly thanked Gail (kiss, kiss) and skidded through the halls, my heels gliding across the glassy floor, until I reached the last venue, where my morning show would take place. I darted behind tall, white canvas curtains that separated the front of the house from the back and entered a maze of clothing racks, veering around frantic faces running to and fro to stitch a seam or pad a bra or change the color of someone's lips.

"Manuel! She's here!" The runway director yelled over my head as I blew in a whirl, trying to pace myself so as to appear like I was right on time and not, for lack of a better term, fashionably late.

But the director stopped me to give that head-shake, eye-roll "you're irresponsible" look that teachers give when you show up late to class. But at least I wasn't (really) in trouble. He guided me toward a little man in tight jeans and a shrunken T-shirt, who was armed with a boar brush and a hair dryer. Perched on his head was some sort of tragic identity crisis. It was short, it was long. It was a mullet.

"Sit here, Mamita," Manuel said, as he pushed me toward a vanity. I sat down, happy to be free from the anxiety-inducing moments just seconds earlier. I looked in the mirror at him and let out a nervous chuckle.

"You lookin' at my hair, skinny bitch?" Manuel said, raking the brush over my head.

"No, no," I said, slightly embarrassed by his tone. "I love your hair. It's, um, very ... trailer chic." Ohmigod. Did I just say that? What is *wrong* with you, Catherine?

He looked up at me in the mirror, trying to assess my failed attempt at humor.

"In a good way," I added. Yup, I had done it. I had really done it. This boar brush was going to be up my butt in a few seconds.

"Trailer chic? Trailer chic?" he said. "You're damn right it's trailer trash. It's punk-ass-in-your-face-tater-tots-and-fuck-me-pumps hot." He gave me a wink in the mirror. I began to breathe again: Manuel and I were cool for the moment. I just needed to keep my mouth shut.

By then, Gail had entered the backstage area, yelling at the models who were congregating around the breakfast tray "like vultures." She walked over to me, complaining about the other girls, who she criticized for not being weight-conscious enough.

"Really, look at this," she said, scanning the room. "We gave all these girls a talking to just last week, and there's Sydney eating a bagel with cream cheese. *Cream cheese!* It will be hanging off her thighs by midday!

"Cat, sweetie, make sure you stick to just raw vegetables this week. Maybe a little bit of soy for protein ..." she continued, giving me a distracted once-over.

"Yes, of course," I said, not really thinking about the reper-cussions of an all-veggie diet to my regularity. "And what about fruit? Fruit is always good."

She looked at me, plain-faced. "People in concentration camps didn't have fruit, did they? Did they?"

My jaw must have still been on the floor when Gail left be-cause Manuel muttered, "Oy vey. Don't listen to that crazy lady. Just do your thang, girlfriend."

I sucked my stomach in the whole time I waited in line for makeup, trying to touch my belly button to my spinal cord, as Agnes had showed me during a "good-posture" lesson. For tip-top form on the runway, she said to envision a string coming out of my head, pulling me up from my crown and aligning all my bones and vertebrae. Shoulders back, hips forward, and for dramatic effect, a slight arch in the back. Who would have believed there was actually a skill to what appeared to be the most natural action on earth?

Standing behind the other girls, many of whom I recognized from Jonnie's piles of fashion magazines, I listened intently, catching tidbits of information about which photographer was a pervert, who was addicted to diet pills, who was sleeping with who. They whispered things in each other's ears, then, like a gaggle of girls on the playground, burst out into tremendous laughter. And just like on the playground, there was the Queen Bee, a platinum blonde named Fiona, who stood in line regaling us with tales from the diary of a married man; the playground tramp, Natasha, who walked around half naked, pretending not to distract anyone with her bare breasts; the jock, who stood next to her wardrobe rack, getting in the last few yoga stretches; the pseudo-intellect, sitting on the floor in the corner of the room immersed in some trendy read; and the quiet, nerdy one (me). No sooner had I begun to think I'd successfully flown under the radar then I was outed, front and center.

"Cat, is it?" the Queen Bee buzzed from the front of the line. "Clive's new girl, right?"

All talking petered out.

"Yes, I ... I am. I just signed with him."

"Yes, we've heard *aaaall* about you," she said. "So, how do you like working for Philippe?"

"Oh, great! I love it ... but truthfully haven't really done much yet. Or anything, actually."

"Oh, don't worry, honey, you *will*," the playground tramp said, invoking roars of laughter from the girls around her. "Philippe is a very, ah, demanding, shall we say."

Not sure what she meant by *that*, but I wasn't going to let her know.

"How old are you?" the Bee asked, stifling her amusement.

"Eighteen," I said, feeling my face get hot and trying to fight off the pangs of yesteryear creeping up my throat. Why did she want to know?

"Well," she said, looking around the room and making eye contact with the others. "It's just that I thought Philippe liked them a little more experienced on the runway... and in the bedroom."

She was trying to freak me out, I knew it. This was a classic cool-girl thing to do. But whatever she was alluding to, I couldn't imagine that sort of thing went on in this day and age, *especially* with reputable agencies like Icon or fashion houses like the House of Philippe. And besides, Philippe was like 100 years old (OK, probably closer to my dad's age, but that may as well be 100!), so I seriously doubt he'd be interested in me. So I ignored Fiona's comments, playing it off like I didn't hear her. But on the inside, it did make me wonder.

Later that morning, my role as social outcast was outshined by a bitchy Brazilian girl who couldn't speak English and screamed foreign obscenities into her cellphone, pissing off all the other divas (who would not be outdone). While waiting for my dresser to appear, I watched each of these girls, those who were the most popular ones in high school, who always had comebacks at the ready, and, of course, who never suffered from a lack of male attention. Even girls younger than me were already blessed with the inherent knowledge of how to act, what to say, and how to move in front of an audience or a camera. Next to them, I felt transparent, invisible. Those who did see me, like the makeup artist who eeked in disgust because I had never plucked my own eyebrows, knew that I had no right to be there. It was an all-too-familiar feeling.

Seven minutes to curtain. *Argh! Where did the time go?* My personal dresser appeared. She was a design student from NYU who hung on my every word and marveled at my long fingers and toes, like I was from another planet. I wanted to shake her and tell her, "Look at me! I'm one of you! This isn't real!"

Five minutes to curtain. Do I have to pee? OMG. I do. I do have to pee. God, why, oh, *whyyy* did I drink that whole bottle of orange juice? OJ always makes me pee! Well, too late to do anything about it, now ...

Three minutes to spare. Boy, it's crowded in here. Is there like an emergency exit or something? No, seriously, is there? What if there's a fire!?! I would be trampled to death. By 5-inch Jimmy Choos. Please God, please God, don't let me get trampled to death by 5-inch Jimmy Choos. Sneakers, maybe ...

The hubbub of the crowd on the other side of the curtains grew louder, and soon we were lined up like school kids, categorized by color, in muted reds, yellows, and pinks for spring. A short, chubby man with a headset on was watching the show from a backstage monitor and gave each girl the signal to go. Panic came to me in waves as I tried to remember which side to walk down on.

*Right, no left. No right! Definitely right! AGGGH.*

As I prayed to the fashion gods to not let me tinkle on the runway, and to help me walk without tripping in my ankle-breaking platforms, I heard a familiar voice from behind. The man with the headset tapped my shoulder and before I launched down the runway Manuel shouted, "Go, you skinny bitch!"

Jolted by that burst of adrenaline, I stormed down the runway, facing a crowd of hundreds, my legs flicking sharply like the stroke of a match. Cameras flashed and heads bobbled. I felt all eyes on me ... and it felt a*MA*Zing. Like some kind of drug. At the end of the runway, I saw my reflection in the mirrored panels that lined the room. It was me, but it wasn't. It was someone else. *Something* else had taken over. I was an actress playing a part. As I turned again and again, I felt energized by this surprising confidence. I smiled. I laughed. I *owned* that runway. Through a transformation of hair and makeup, I had the courage to become whatever I wanted, whoever I wanted, someone who Catherine alone didn't have the courage to be.

At the finish of the show, we floated down the runway in feathered evening gowns, fluttering about like fairies dipped in pastel print. Philippe joined us to receive the applause and mark the opening of Fashion Week. He emerged from behind, with a bouquet of watercolor lilies on his arm. As he walked past, he grabbed my hand and pulled me up to the front of the runway.

The other girls looked on with envy. Philippe blew kisses to the crowd, and as the lights dimmed we turned to exit the runway.

# ✦ 6 ✦

The New York Times> Fashion & Style> Blogs

On the Runway/
ALL THINGS FASHION

**Unknown Model Turns Heads at Fashion Week**
*Insiders say the 'fresh face' is just what industry needs*
By STACY GOLDBERG

While sales of couture collections have slumped lower than a cowl neckline these past few seasons — turning off buyers with the return of unforgivable Lycra leggings, shapeless tunics and hair of the '80s that reminds us of a cocaine binge we'd rather forget — fashion addicts this year were anxiously awaiting the signal from designers that a new era in fashion had begun.

And while designers like Calvin Klein, Michael Kors, and Christian Siriano may have had a few hits (and misses) with their more modern take on sportswear, it was the tenacity of a virtual unknown model who opened Philippe Borghetta's show and returned, again and again, throughout the week, pumping life into the tired old looks and leaving buyers with something other than the clothes to talk about.

They call her Cat. She's a six-foot-tall, willowy waif with legs up to her neck, chestnut hair, vibrant green eyes, porcelain skin and a refreshingly unaffected sense of self. On the runway, she has fun with the clothes, at times laughing and smiling on the catwalk — a cardinal no-no in the holier-than-thou modeling code of ethics. And yet her presence seems to have melted away the icy stares of the fashion elite sitting in the front row, who say her spirit is infectious.

"She's refreshing," says Anna Wintour of Vogue. "It's what fashion should be all about — not taking itself too seriously."

The magazine's editor-at-large André Leon Talley says Cat is a throwback to the late '70s, the Christie Brinkley era, when designers like Halston were more playful with their silhouettes and models knew how to enjoy the clothes. Lately, Talley says, fashion has become "frighteningly dull," with advertising, not art, driving design.

Industry insiders say Cat is not only a joy on the runway but also off, being affable, friendly and easy to work with. Her unexpected arrival is leading many to wonder from where on earth (or otherwise) did this sprite emerge?

Word is Philippe Borghetta picked her out of a crowd on Fifth Avenue, right in front of his design studio, Borghetta Enterprises. Sources say he's hoping the 18-year-old will help jumpstart his floundering brand, which enjoyed much success in the late '80s, when Remi Fosgate, another fresh-faced, raven-haired nymph, took the scene. The design house has fallen on hard times since the mid '90s, when grunge-era heroin chic ruled the runway and more tailored looks took a backseat ...

My phone had been blowing up all morning. It was an endless barrage of calls and texts from family and friends and random people, strange men — who had somehow discovered my cell number off the Internet — calling themselves agents or saying they were "in the biz." On social, I had 79 new friend requests, most of whom were either complete unknowns or someone claiming to be the cousin of a friend of a friend.

It was my moment. My big moment. It had happened so easily, I thought. Was it really supposed to be this way? So ... effortless? I looked at the pictures of myself online and in the newspapers, admiring them like they were photos of someone else. On the runway, I'd forgotten my "fierce face." It was just so much fun

— more fun than I expected. I just couldn't keep a straight face up there. I was sure I was going to hear it from Gail after the show. But to my surprise, she ran up to me, grabbing my cheeks between her bony hands, and said, "They loved it! Keep it up!"

Clippings from Fashion Week had been mailed to me from all over the continental U.S. Cousins in Florida. My uncle in Boston. Benji even sent something. It was an article from *The Philadelphia Inquirer*.

He wrote: "Catherine takes over the world!" in bold black marker above the headline. He had attached a short note, saying how honored he was to know a celebrity (hardy har), and could I please send him my autograph so that he can sell it on eBay to the highest bidder? Such a dork! I skimmed the story and noticed the reporter had managed to interview my (OMG!) high school English teacher along with my track coach.

My heart started beating out of my chest as I read their descriptions of me: "shy," "quiet," "kind of a loner." Homecoming was just around the corner, and I cringed, feeling those old feelings bubble up inside of me. That girl was but a shadow of who I was now, who I was becoming.

I wondered how many people I knew would see this, would come to know what had happened to Spaghetti Legs. I hoped at least one of those Cate Winters-types who had made my adolescence so painful was reading it right now. I could just imagine the texting thread ripping through my hometown at that moment: "Catherine *who?* HER? WHAT?!"

My cellphone rang, and Clive told me that *Glamour* wanted me for its December cover, *Vogue* and *W* had me scheduled for a layout next month, and Philippe wanted to shoot the catalog for his spring collection in Aruba.

Aruba? I was speechless.

"You're on your way, baby," Clive said before hanging up.

I put the phone down. Then, with my stomach turning cartwheels, I decided that I would, in fact, attend the homecoming celebration at my high school this year.

*Ah, sweet revenge.*

## ✦ 7 ✦

*"Big. Black. Boots.*
*Long. Brown. Hair.*
*She's so sweet …*
*with her GET BACK staaaare!"*

I was serenaded in the kitchen of my apartment while chopping veggies by none other than Seth, who sang the lyrics to his favorite Jet song as it blasted from my Jambox. We were getting ready for the Thanksgiving dinner that Jonnie and I were making for a few friends and neighbors, on the night before the big day.

*"Uh, be my girl.*

*Be my girl.*

*Are you gonna be my girrrrl???"*

His hair fell into perfect curls over his right eye as he pounded on his air drums and sang out those last two lines of the refrain. He eyed me with a trademark rocker pout.

I laughed, giving him my playful "Wouldn't you like to know?" look as he switched to air guitar.

We'd spent the last few weeks together. Seth had come with me to most of my shoots. He said that he didn't mind. He was used to being on the set of those things, having accompanied his mom as a little boy and, later, his father, when one of his musical acts made it big. I enjoyed having the company, as one could wait hours between takes or wardrobe changes.

"Pass me a strawberry, Jagger," I directed.

Seth reached for the basket and pulled out a heart-shaped berry, lifting it to my lips.

In the beginning, we hung out just as friends. But during the past few days, we started to let our guards down. I was feeling less self-conscious about us being seen together, and Seth, well, he was finally beginning to come out of his shell.

"Can you teach me to chop like that?" he asked, as I sent a carrot flying across the room, having cut it with the wrong knife. I burst out laughing. He smiled and encircled me with his arms from behind.

"Get a room!" Jonnie said playfully while walking into the room to check the Tofurky (a vegetarian wonder that tasted better than it looked) baking in the oven.

Since we had no dining room table, we had to improvise. I laid down a pretty burgundy tablecloth on the hardwood floor, and Jonnie placed wine glasses and festive-looking paper plates we picked up at the dollar store. For dramatic effect, she sprinkled a few leaves around the settings.

We'd invited a few of Jonnie's friends to dinner. While eating, we went around in a circle as each told funny stories about their first Thanksgiving in New York. I couldn't believe how many people hadn't been home to see their families. It was like they left home, came to New York, and never looked back. I was the only one who was going home the next day. Even Seth, who lived with his dad, wasn't spending the holiday with him.

As much as they'd been driving me crazy the past few weeks, I couldn't imagine not seeing my parents on Thanksgiving. Besides, even if I tried to shake them, they'd be up on the next train, overnight bag in hand.

"OK, kids," Jonnie said, after most of the plates were cleared, "pin-the-waddle-on-the-turkey time."

Pin the waddle on the turkey was a drinking game Jonnie had concocted. You had to take a shot of Grey Goose vodka (what else?), turn three times while blindfolded, and then stick a cardboard cutout waddle onto a turkey we'd drawn on poster board. It was a hit!

"I used to play this when I was little," I said. "The nonalcoholic version, of course."

Back then, I never would have imagined playing a bastardized version of the turkey game. As a kid, I'd taken one of those corny church youth group pledges vowing to abstain from alcohol. But then, of course, that was before I found out that not all alcoholic drinks tasted like communion wine, and many — especially those at New York fashion after-parties — tasted a lot like Trolli Peachie Os or Country Time Lemonade.

"I wish we'd done family things like that once in a while," Seth said, as we watched people stumble around the room blindfolded.

"Believe me, you don't," I said. "It got to be ridiculous. Every Thanksgiving, my mom would come up with a 'game' or make me write a story about the Pilgrims. Other times we'd have to go around the table saying what we were thankful for, corny stuff like that."

Secretly, I kind of liked that part about saying what you were thankful for. We had stopped doing that a few years earlier, but I still continued, in my own way, to say a little prayer for all blessings each year.

"So what are you thankful for this year?"

I rolled my eyes.

"Sorry, can't let you off the hook with this one," he smiled.

"Well ..." I said, trying not to jinx my luck while realizing that I did, in fact, have a lot to be grateful for at the moment. "I guess I'm thankful for ... meeting you."

"Oh?" he said, visibly enjoying every second of my awkwardness.

"Yes, well, as you know, without you, I never would have been rescued from the bathroom of that nightclub ... I'd probably still be stumbling around trying to find my way home!" I laughed.

"Face it," Jonnie said, eavesdropping on our conversation, "You're her knight in shining armor!" She covered her mouth, as if shocked by her revelation, and then ran away, cackling like a witch.

My face tingled, my cheeks hot. It was true. He was sort of like my white, um, dark, brooding knight.

"I can't take that credit," Seth said bashfully. "I'm sure someone else would have helped you out."

"Well," I said, "You can take credit for helping launch my career. If I hadn't met you, I'd probably be living back home with my folks right now."

After dinner, people went up to the rooftop, and Seth stayed downstairs to keep me company while I cleaned up. I was washing dishes at the sink when I saw him reach down to the floor, pick up what was left of the vodka, and down it in a matter of seconds.

"Seth, we have glasses, you know." I said.

He looked surprised. "Oh, no thanks. I'm fine."

"Are you OK?"

"Sure."

"I thought you didn't drink," I said calmly. "What's that about?

"I don't."

"Well, then why are you? Not that I mind, of course," I said, trying not to come off as the beverage police. After all, I, myself, was drinking. But — wanting to avoid a repeat performance of my first night out in New York City — I was sticking to my self-imposed two-drink limit.

Seth smirked.

"That's sweet that you're looking out for me," he said, rising to his feet. He slid his hands into his pockets and leaned against the wall, kicking it with the heel of his sneaker. He hesitated as if he wanted to tell me something. "Well, guess I'd better jet soon," he said after a few seconds.

"What? Why?" I asked, taken aback. It wasn't even 10 o'clock yet.

"It's late."

"Isn't this the time your night usually starts?" I asked playfully, feeling a bit bolder thanks to the drink in my hand.

I reached over to comb my fingers through his hair and leaned into — *Ohmigod! Am I doing this? Am I really doing this?* — kiss him. He didn't seem to care that my French kissing style was sloppy and unrefined (nor did I after almost two Long Island iced teas) and helped direct me with the velvety smooth strokes of his own delicate tongue. After a few minutes, I pulled away coyly, pleased with myself. *So this is why people drink! It's like you can still be you — only braver!*

But before Seth could enjoy the brave new Catherine, he started to inch toward the door.

"Listen, Cat, that was nice ... really, it was," he said. "But I gotta get going."

The look on my face must have been one of near-humiliation, because he quickly followed up with, "Honestly, it's me ... not you. You're great ... it's just that I don't want to bog you down with my crap right now."

"What ... what are you talking about?" I stammered, still feeling a bit embarrassed about throwing myself (and my spit) at him, but probably not as much as if I'd been totally sober.

"Nothing. It's just ... I'm going through some rough stuff right now. Family stuff. Life stuff."

We heard someone climbing down the fire escape. It was Theo, a latecomer to the party. He poked his head through the window, "Man, you got a lighter? Mine's shot." His eyes were bloodshot, and he looked as high as a kite.

"You'd better be careful," I said to him, as he listlessly swayed back and forth. "Watch yourself on that ledge."

"Watch yourself, young lady," he said, pointing to Seth. "This guy's a real conman."

"Get the hell outta here, dude," Seth said, as he handed Theo a book of matches that was on the counter.

Theo lingered a little longer, his eyes cold, watching me. I thought it strange for him to talk that way about his friend. There was no humor in his tone. Seth laughed weakly and slammed the window shut.

When he was gone, I asked, "What's that about?"

"Oh nothing," he said, looking back again toward the door. "... Theo's spent."

"Yeah ... guess you're right. So," I said, frowning, "Still gotta go?"

"... I just don't want to spoil your good time tonight."

"You'll spoil it if you leave," I said.

We stood in silence for a few moments. I started to think that things had been going so well with us, maybe too well. Up until then, everything had fallen into place. It was too good to be true — I knew it. I waited for the other shoe to drop.

"Cat," he said, picking up a bottle of wine. "What would you say if I told you tonight was the first time I've had a drink in four years?"

"I'd say, 'Wow.'"

"And?"

"And, 'Why not?' You're straight edge, right?"

"Not exactly."

"What do you mean?"

"It's a little complicated. I'm straight edge because I'm a recovering alcoholic."

It took a few moments for the words to sink in. I couldn't really comprehend what that meant. The buzz I had began to wane, and now I was easing back into reality.

"I started drinking when I was in my early teens," he said, still holding the bottle in his hands. "Well, when I was 12 actually. My dad was married to Gail at the time. She stashed alcohol all over the place. Me and my friends would drink at a playground before school, and then we'd go to school drunk off our asses ..."

"So, why are you drinking now? Aren't you afraid that —"

"That I can't control myself and I'll fall off the wagon?" he said, mocking my vigilance.

"Well ... yeah. Isn't that what can happen?"

"Not to me. It can't happen again. I've been to rehab, AA. I've sat through all that psychology; I know my limits." He picked up the bottle of wine again and stared at it.

"Seth, don't ..."

He looked at me, put down the bottle, and said, "I can stop."

"Just like that?"

"Just like that."

He walked over to open the window and poured the rest of the wine outside, onto the pavement.

"Why did you do it?" I asked, sitting on the daybed.

He sat down next to me and put his hands on mine. "Why did I do it ...," he repeated in a sing-songy voice. "I did it because I'm a self-defeatist. Because I'm really good at messing up really good things."

"But what are you messing up?"

"Look, Cat, I like you. A lot. In fact, I can't stop thinking about you lately. But I'm scared I'm gonna screw it all up. I don't know, I guess I took a drink because I was feeling ... nervous."

"Nervous? Why?"

He shrugged his shoulders, and a little smile crept over his face. *Oh.*

"Me? I make you nervous?"

"A little."

He told me what was bothering him. He'd gotten in a fight with his dad, who, he said, was never really around. He was always traveling for his job and spending time with his young up-and-coming musicians. Ironically, he spent more time with them than he ever did with his own son, he said. And when they did see each other, Seth's dad always yelled at him for his "lack of direction."

"My dad's always waving his money over my head, like it means something," he said. "He's always telling me that the kids he works with barely had a pot to piss in growing up, and me ... well, I have everything any kid would ever want."

From the looks of him, you'd never know Seth was privileged. He said he never wanted to become one of those hypocritical, spoiled rich kids who dressed punk and blasted rap music like they knew what life on the streets was about. And of course by graduation day, they had cleaned up, pulled out their ear plugs, signed up for their post-graduate degrees, and started shopping in the Brooks Brothers catalog. He said he knew he was different. He wanted to be different. Two years back, he'd done the college thing but it only lasted a few months.

"I was too busy skating down in Union Square and getting high all day," he said.

"My dad put a stop to all that when he sent me to rehab. It

was good for me. After that, I became straight edge, but I didn't go back to school. It was a waste for me."

"Do you still feel that way?"

"Sometimes. Like, I just want to get away from all the preaching and live for myself. See things for myself. Besides, how the hell are you supposed to go to school and prepare for some kind of future when ..."

"When you don't even know who you are? What you want out of life?" I could relate. Maybe that's why I decided to come to New York after high school. Going the traditional route and choosing a college, a major, an internship, and what to do with the next 40 years of my life — day in, day out — were decisions that I couldn't dream of making. I needed time ... time to help me understand who I was and who I wanted to be. After all, I knew deep down, in my heart of hearts, the modeling thing couldn't last forever.

We sat quietly. I leaned against Seth, resting my head in the nook between his chin and chest, my head rising and falling with his breath. I turned on the Christmas lights that Jonnie had strung around the ceiling. The white lights appeared like tiny starbursts in the pitch-blackness. I wondered if, this time, Seth would try to kiss me.

"Cat, do you know how my mother died?"

*Wow. Was not expecting this.* God, this guy is really pouring his heart out to me.

"Um ... I heard she was sick," I said, wondering if he would be angry that I knew that much.

"She was, for a while. My dad told me it was some chronic illness. But she was always depressed. Even as a little kid I could tell."

"I'm sorry."

"Don't be. She was trying to get better. On meds for her depression, but mixed it with some other drug and took too much," he said. "Overdose."

At the sound of that word, I froze with fear of saying the wrong thing. I reached down and grabbed his hand.

"It was hard, at first, seeing my dad cry and stuff. Then there were the press reports that just ripped her to shreds. I think that's what made him so negative. He would get so angry that he'd punch holes in the walls. It was a crazy time."

When Gail came into their lives, he said, she helped to settle things down, but not for long. His dad was never the same. The marriage didn't last.

"It must have been so hard for you," was all that I could eke out. I've never been that close to death, to knowing someone who died.

He didn't say anything for a while. Then, as if caught in a day-dream, he blurted out: "You know, people say you look like her. But not to me. I mean, no offense. You're beautiful, but you're Catherine. What you do have is this sort of innocence that was there, inside of her. She wasn't a big-city girl, either."

I pulled myself closer to him; I could feel his heart beating beneath my chest. *Ba-boom, ba-boom.* It pounded harder as I crawled up onto his body, forcing him to lie back on the ground.

We kissed as he slowly reached his hand up and under my tank top, and I — hesitant at first, for Benji was the only boy I'd ever let do that — let him move it up, slowly, to unhook my bra. I looked up to face him, to see his eyes in the gray night. His expression was open ... accepting.

We kissed for what seemed like a few short minutes but was, in fact, an hour.

Just before falling asleep, I pulled a blanket up over him, feeling strangely protective. He needed someone to comfort him, to help him. Could I? Maybe I could love him like no one ever has. I wanted to. At that moment, I wanted to fold him into me, to tuck him inside of me. I wanted to save him like he saved me on that first night.

# ✦ 8 ✦

"There she is, Miss A-mer-ica!" my Mom sang out as I walked through the front door. A "Welcome Home" banner hung over the archway to the family room, with a dorky picture of me at my high school graduation perched atop the table beneath. On the wall in the hallway hung newspaper clippings and modeling pictures of me that had been framed and matted.

I turned to my dad, who — looking balder, grayer, and slightly more disheveled than the last time I saw him — had just picked me up from the bus station. "Thanks for the warning," I said.

He shrugged his classic "Women!" shrug.

"Surprise!" My grandmother said in usual delayed response, her petite frame inched toward me, with arms extended. My mom hugged and kissed me next with sticky gravy fingers and walked back into the kitchen to wash her hands. "Are you hungry?" she called out from the other room.

"Nah," I said, reaching down to pet my dog Holly, who proceeded to lick my whole face with one stroke of her tongue. "I'm just tired. I'll probably take a nap."

"Well, you have clean sheets on the bed."

"Thanks, but ... um ...," I said, as I stood in the hallway. "Can you please promise to take these pictures down tonight before our cousins come over? It's embarrassing."

"I will not," she said, indignant.

I was always amazed at the level of one-upmanship, even among family members. As much as my mother loved her sisters, she would never pass up the opportunity to brag. I'm sure by now they were sick of hearing about what "Catherine was doing" in New York.

"Remember when your cousin Suzanne was in all those pageants?" she said, walking over to straighten a photo. "Well, wait till she gets a load of you!"

It was hard to believe that this was the same woman who cried hysterically because I was "ruining my life" attempting to become a fashion model. But now that I'd had two spreads in fashion magazines that she'd actually *heard* of, an agent, and more than a few thousand dollars in the bank, she was singing a MUCH different tune.

"I'm sure Suzanne really cares about what *I'm* doing, Mom," I said, sighing as I shuffled up the steps. "She's married with three kids."

I walked into my bedroom, turned on the light and threw my stuff on the bed. The familiar bubble-gum pink walls looked faded and worn, like they were going to flake off at any moment.

I opened my drawers, making room beside clothes I hadn't worn in years, relics I had yet to part with: threadbare hoodies, field hockey socks, boxer shorts I'd slept in, and summer camp T-shirts worn once. I shoved my new clothes inside the white wooden bureau — the kind in every little girl's room, with the curlicue accents on the edges and knobby handles. A matching desk and canopy bed with a white eyelet skirt completed the set. I remember how excited I was when it was delivered on my 7th birthday. I felt like a princess. When my parents weren't around, I would reach up onto my tiptoes and pull down the skirt, wrapping it over my head and around my body, prancing around the room like a bride.

But standing in the middle of that room now, I felt like I was trapped in a Candyland board game.

Everything looked much smaller than it had just months before. Strange how I'd never noticed this before, but the room was a time capsule. The porcelain china dolls, perched on their shelves, still held the poses I had left them in years ago. The mirror had photos wedged into its side from my 8th-grade trip to Florida and sophomore cotillion (to which I painfully went stag, stuck watching everyone *else* slow dance to the corny-as-hell but, admit it, *totally romantic* "You're Beautiful" by James Blunt). On the walls still hung my boy band posters, with a fine film of dust, that were beginning to fade. It was an unsettling shrine of youth.

"Mom, I thought you said you were going to redo my room after I left?" I asked when I went downstairs for lunch.

"Oh, yes, honey. But I haven't really had the time. Your father's been so busy at work, and I've been helping him. Plus, I like looking at all your old stuff."

"That's a little creepy ... it's like someone died up there."

"What a morbid thought," she said, with a quizzical expression. "I'll get to it soon enough."

I sat down at the kitchen table. "Where is everyone?"

"Your father is at the drugstore. Mom-Mom's napping. You hungry?"

"I might make a sandwich or something—" I said while scanning the circulars that were scattered on the table. But before I could finish speaking, she was up, her apron swinging from side to side, scurrying around the room like a little elf. "What are you doing?"

"Making you a sandwich."

"I can make it myself," I said, knowing she had been slaving over a turkey since dawn.

"Don't be silly," she said.

My father breezed through the door and threw his coat onto the armchair in the living room, which my mother proceeded to hang up. By the time he sat down at the kitchen table, a cup of hot tea was placed in his right hand.

"Now that's service," he said with a wink. He looked down at his cup. "Lyn, I told you I don't like this herbal stuff. I can't drink this," he said gruffly and pushed away his cup to the edge of the table.

"Sorry, Bill," my mother said, taking it away. "Dr. Levin says you shouldn't drink so much caffeine with this new medicine you're on." She placed two yellow pills on the table for him with a large glass of water.

"Let me worry about what I'm drinking," he said. "Dr. Levin doesn't know everything."

"Yes, dear," she said, sighing.

"I'm starving," he said. "Think you can reheat some of those leftovers from last night?" He picked up the newspaper and started to read.

Feeling like I was watching my mom endure the shackles of a 1950s conjugal nightmare, I snapped. "What's the deal here?"

Both of them looked up at me in surprise.

"What, honey?" my mother said with a worried expression, the lines surrounding her eyes deepening as she grappled with a bottle of vitamins.

"This ... this entire display! Dad — can't you help yourself? Mom's been cooking all day, and all you've done is make her wait on you since the second you walked through the door!"

They looked at me like something had just crashed through the ceiling, shattering their perfect little dysfunctional utopia.

"What has gotten into you lately, Catherine?" my father asked. "I think all this modeling stuff is going to your head. You may act however you like up there with your friends in New York City, but here at 225 Oak Road, you will respect your mother and me."

I looked at my mother, expecting her to take my side, to defend me, but she just heaved a long, heavy sigh and shook her head.

I stomped back up to my room. Something about being home again made me revert to feeling that old childhood angst, like when my parents would argue with each other or something upsetting (or totally embarrassing — like when I lost my bikini top in the ocean at the Jersey Shore) would happen and they just wouldn't understand. We weren't the perfectly charming family I had cherished growing up. I guess I just never really, *really* stopped to think about it.

My father was a bit of a male chauvinist. He had always expected my mother to drop everything for him. In the past, it just was the way things were. That was *normal*. My mother scurried around the house putting out fires while he shouted dissatisfaction from his lofty perch. He worked. She didn't. It was hard to believe my parents had fallen into this cliché, but it was true. Not until I was on my own in New York had I really been around women my mother's age who weren't absorbed in day-to-day domestic tedium, putting everyone else's needs (even the dog's) before theirs. These women were not only holding down jobs but were also very successful at what they did. They accomplished things. Great things. They were actresses, designers, photographers, journalists, stylists.

"Mom, didn't you ever want to do something more exciting with your life?" I said later on that afternoon, after we'd all cooled down. I was helping her slice apples for a Waldorf salad she was preparing.

"Well, your father took me to Europe before you were born. That was a memorable experience."

"Mom, that was before I was born — more than 18 years ago. Besides, that's not what I'm talking about. I mean, didn't you ever want to become something ... other than a stay-at-home mom?"

"Raising a family and running a household is the most rewarding job in the world," she said, sounding like she hadn't quite convinced herself yet.

"I know, Mom, it's a wonderful job and all. But didn't you ever want ... more? To accomplish something .... *great*?"

"I wanted to get married and become a mother, and that's what I accomplished. Now you are accomplishing great things, and that makes me happy, too."

"Fine, Mom. But what ever happened to teaching?" My mother taught elementary school when she was in her 20s.

"It was nice for a little while, but when I had you I decided that being a mother was more important. Besides, your father was making enough money at the time, so I didn't have to work."

Didn't *have* to?

"But Mom, didn't you grow up during the '70s? Wasn't going to work — being able to use your brain just *like* a man — the whole point of the feminist movement? I mean, weren't women like you fighting for that opportunity?"

She stopped chopping, hesitated a moment, and looked up. At that moment, the distance between us from across the kitchen counter felt like it stretched for miles.

"Catherine, when you're a little bit older, you might find that some things that you *thought* would make you happy do not actually bring you true happiness. Sometimes, the things that are most worth fighting for are the things you already have."

Our kitchen and dining room was set up for 20 guests that evening. For the first time I was seated at the "adult" table, a privilege I had begged for throughout high school, resenting being squeezed in at a flimsy card table in the corner somewhere between five whiny cousins. But now, I wished I were back at that rickety old card table babysitting a bunch of brats rather than fielding 20 questions from their overbearing parents. Why had I decided to put college on hold? How long did I think this modeling thing would last? Does it pay?

"She's doing very well," my mom said. "They're calling her the new It girl. Aren't they, sweetie? They've never seen anyone like our Catherine up there."

"Mom, please."

"And, next week, she'll be flying to Aruba. *Aruba!* For a swimsuit shoot. Can you believe it?"

Yes. It was true. And *I* still couldn't believe it. Philippe wanted me — ME — to model for his next campaign. And on-location! Is it possible to be thrilled and terrified at the same time?

"I'm not sure I like that idea, of my little girl being photographed like that," my dad grumbled.

"It's actually not a swimsuit shoot," I cautioned. "We're just modeling regular clothes." Had to keep these two under control. There was no telling what tales they'd spin.

"Suzanne, honey," my mom continued, oblivious, "Did you see Catherine's new pictures in the hallway?"

For god's sake! Besides the embarrassing, overzealous parental pride, the expectations thrust upon me, here and in New York, were something I wasn't sure I could live up to. I still felt like I was playing a part, pretending to be someone I was not. This trip to Aruba would be the true test. I would be working long days on the beach with nothing but a photographer and natural light. There was nowhere to hide.

First course: the Waldorf salad. I was slightly disappointed to find this new recipe was made with iceberg lettuce, the old, floppy, tasteless, nutrition-deficient lettuce leaf I'd grown up on. I guess I'd gotten pretty used to (and partial to) salads in New York that had kale or spinach or even arugula.

"What's the matter, honey? Isn't salad what models eat?" my mother said, after noticing me pushing the salad around on my plate.

"She's not eating, she's not eating!" my aunt gasped.

"I'm fine." I took a tiny bite. Thanksgiving had always been my favorite holiday. But today, nothing, not even my mother's marshmallow-topped yams, looked appealing. I stared down at the good china. The dishes I would inherit one day. They were a beautiful Lenox setting with gold rims. *Eternal* they were named. Eternal, I thought, named for the life of one who owned it — eternal monotony, eternal banality, eternal obscurity.

"Before I forget," my aunt Diana whispered in my ear, "I have something for you."

She got up from the table and returned with a shopping bag. She always had the best taste in clothes. For a short time, in her twenties, she was a model for Wanamakers in Philadelphia. I was excited to see what item from her closet she had decided to bestow, having promised since childhood to pass down her favorite possessions to me. She placed the bag in my lap. From it I pulled a white T-shirt with puffy paint and rhinestones dotted in the shape of the Statue of Liberty.

I held the shirt up over my head, eliciting "ooos" and "ahhhs" from the crowd.

"Puffy paint is making a comeback," Aunt Diana said matter-of-factly.

"Right," I said, holding up the piece to hide the redness of my face.

"It sparkles in the light," my grandma said, reaching for her glasses.

"You like it, honey?" my mom asked.

"Um, yeah. It's very, um, colorful."

"I saw it and immediately thought of you, up there in New York doing your thing," Aunt Diana said, with a shake of shoulders and a jangle of jewelry.

"Was this yours?" I held onto the hope that maybe this was one prized possession from her '80s heyday that just hadn't quite stood the test of time.

"Oh, no. I got it at Frank's. You know, that new discount place that opened up on 73?"

Frank's? To my knowledge, my aunt had never stepped into a discount store in all her life. My mother was always complaining how the women on my father's side of the family were incredibly extravagant. His sister only ever wore designer clothes and certainly never shopped sub-retail. How fortunate for me that *now* — when I could use some nicer things — she decided it was the perfect time to start.

By the time dessert rolled around, most of the men had left the table. The "girls" were left to drink coffee and clean up the dishes. Aunt Diana decided to grill me ("What's this your mom says about some boyfriend you have up there? Some famous model's son?"). I tried to shush her, saying that she'd gotten the story wrong (like I was going to reveal my innermost thoughts to the equivalent of the familial Twitter feed) when my mother interrupted to bring up her second favorite subject (besides me) — Benji.

"He wants to see you this weekend," she said.

"Mom, you've got to be kidding me. Why are you even talking to him? I told you, I don't like him like that anymore."

"So go out with him as friends," she said. "He's a nice boy."

Nice boy. Nothing new. My mother had been in love with Benji since our 4th of July picnic, when he charmed the fam with his patrician good looks and boyish charisma. Ever since, she wouldn't stop talking about him.

"So, are you going to call him back or what?" she said, jolting me out of thought.

"Why is this so important to you?" I asked, annoyed by her

relentless preference after I'd told her, in private, about my new-found beau.

"Oh, Catherine, if I were you, I'd stick with the model's son. I'm sure he's going to come into money one day," Aunt Diana said with a catty laugh.

"He's probably loaded already. His father's a record exec," her sister, my Aunt Linda, cut in.

Great. Seems everyone here got the memo.

"Well, Catie-Lou?" my mother said (this is what she called me when she desperately wanted me to see things her way).

Before I could answer her, she was up to fix the television in the living room, making it possible for my father and uncles to watch their football games. She apologized to the table, saying, "Bill never knows how to work the new smart TV."

The "no signal" sign bounced around the screen and now I could hear my father muttering under his breath, "Damn it, Lyn."

I stared down at my dessert plate, at the *Eternal* setting. There was a blemish on the china pattern. The gold had chipped away on one of the edges.

*That's it.* I stood up.

"Where are you going?" my mother said as she reentered the room, coffee pot in hand. "You never told us if you were going to see Benji this weekend."

I looked at her. My face was hot with emotion. "How about not playing matchmaker for once, Mom? How about worrying about your own life? Your own marriage?"

Her face sank, and I realized that I had gone too far. As soon as it was out of my mouth, I regretted it. Everybody froze, and all that was left was the hum of the television in the background.

"I'm ... I'm sorry. I didn't mean it that way. It's just that—"

"That's enough, Catherine," she said firmly, cutting me off and trying to recover from the embarrassment, her face frozen in a superficial smile.

With tears brimming, I wove through the dining room and kitchen and ran upstairs to the bathroom, the only place in the house where no one could follow me. I sat down on the hard, plastic toilet lid and stared at the floor. It was my house, my family, but everything seemed so ... different. Even the house, the beautiful house that I had always been so proud of, looked old, dated. Out of style. The curtains, the ones hanging in the living room that my father and mother had fought over because they cost twice what he had expected, the beautiful gold drapes with the roped tassels, looked less important than I remembered, less opulent.

I wished I never came home. I wished I hadn't seen the shrine in my room, my mother's attempt to hang on to the last shred of my childhood, and this once-gleaming house that now looked like a bad retro-throwback. The things I had treasured diminished in light of New York. And my parents. My poor parents. They were middle-aged. They were getting older. They were like a shadow of what they once were. It was hard to tell if they were truly happy or not, but I wondered if I had never been born, whether they could have had a more exciting life. Maybe my mother could have been someone.

# ✦ 9 ✦

I went out with Benji that weekend. Just as friends. I hadn't really planned on it (purposefully, to spite my mother), but after 48 hours of being cooped up in the house with my parents and nap-taking granny who repeatedly fell asleep mid-sentence, I was ready for an escape.

"Catherine, you have a visitor," my mother rang out in delight. I had fought with her about not playing her coy little game where she would greet the "suitor" and call to me from the foot of the stairs so that he could watch me, in all my glory, descend the steps. But it was no use; she was dead set on making me feel like tragic little Laura from *The Glass Menagerie.*

Walking down the stairs, I could see Benji had dressed for the occasion. He was wearing a pair of gray wool pants and a brown, gray, and maroon argyle sweater, with a tip of a crisp, white collar peeking out. Impressive, I thought. He'd done his fashion homework — argyle was everywhere for men this fall.

My mother was telling him about an old Sears in town that was about to be knocked down, and he pretended to be deeply interested. But in between "oh nos" and "reallys?" I caught him trying to take a peek at me.

"Hi," I said, once the conversation had ended and my mother had gone up to her bedroom pretending to have something to do.

"You look beautiful, as usual," Benji said, giving me a kiss on the cheek. "Hermès," I said, doing a little curtsy and turning to show him the new skirt and matching tunic I had gotten for free at a photo shoot.

"Nice," he said. He looked taller and thinner than I remembered, more gaunt. His big blue eyes were stoic, and there was a maturing five o'clock shadow where before there had been peach fuzz.

"Growing a beard?" I said, scrunching up my nose.

"Huh? Oh ... no. Well, maybe. I just started student teaching, and I need something to make me look older than the students," he said. "Besides, it's Movember."

"Well, I like you better clean shaven. Makes you look..."

"Like I'm 10?"

*Wholesome* was the word I was thinking of. But, yes, he was right. Seeing this handsome boy with facial hair was like looking at a little girl with lipstick on. It just didn't go.

"Exactly."

"Oh, so you spend a few months in New York as some snazzy model, and suddenly you're the expert on fashion?" he asked, smirking, with one eyebrow cocked.

"Who says *snazzy* these days?" I said, grabbing my purse. "Next thing I know you'll be taking me to the drive-in for some Cokes. Let's go."

As we headed to the door, my father made his obligatory appearance, as he did with any guy who came to the house, from meter-reader to boy-next-door. He gave Benji a firm handshake and cool look as if to say, "I know where you live." It was embarrassing and totally unnecessary. Let's leave it at that.

We took the Ben Franklin Bridge into Philadelphia. The city looked beautiful at twilight, with the sun setting in the distance and the Comcast Center standing erect, like a gleaming sword staking a claim to the city. Philadelphia was really a microcosm of Manhattan, with its Chinatown, its "Little Italy" in South Philly and the beautiful parks at Rittenhouse Square and Washington Square. And it made me miss my new home. Nothing could compare to walking through Midtown at rush hour, as people push past you with a sense of urgency, a sense that anything can happen. I sighed, looking out the window, sad that I was missing out on New York.

"You're quiet," Benji said.

"Yeah, I'm tired. I've just been so busy. I mean, crazy busy. I haven't even had time to call my parents, much less my *friends*." I felt I had to let Benji know exactly where we stood on this whole date-like event.

"Oh, don't worry about it. I've been busy myself."

"School stuff?" I said, pulling out my compact.

"Yeah, but you don't want to hear about it," he said. "It's not as glamorous as jet-setting around New York."

"Oh, come on. Sure I do," I said, putting on a coat of lip gloss. To be honest, I was curious about college life and the 9-to-5 drudgery that Benji now had. "What's it like to be a student teacher, to be on the other side of the ... um ... podium?"

"Well, it's a desk and not a podium. It's high school, not college. And it's a lot of grading papers and preparing lesson plans."

He started talking about a pop quiz he gave to the students the day before, and I realized just how far apart our lives were. I couldn't imagine preparing for a real job. It sounded incredibly ... grown up.

"Enough about me," Benji said. "I didn't spend the entire month on the cover of fashion magazines."

I perked up.

"I've heard of that guy, Philippe," he continued. "My sister likes his clothes, I think."

"Yeah, he's a really big designer."

"And he likes you *why*?" he asked with a poker face.

Benji was a joker. He loved to tease me because he thought I took myself too seriously. The first few weeks I knew him, we'd stay up late talking on the phone for hours, him cracking me up with funny stories about his high school pranks on teachers, or about the times he and his brothers would go camping and scare their friends with ghost stories. He said I was the only person who really got his jokes. They were dorky but cute, in a way. Cute because he wanted to make me laugh. And, unlike any other guy who'd ever given me the time of day, Benji was just so easy to talk to. I never felt uneasy or embarrassed or self-conscious in front of him, because I felt like, deep down, he got me on some sort of level.

It kinda made me a little sad, knowing that I didn't have him to talk to up in New York. My New York friends, even Jonnie, tended to be, well ... a bit more guarded, I guess. *Cooler,* one might say.

We parked on Second Street and walked to a nearby restaurant in Northern Liberties. When the waiter came, I ordered the tofu kabobs (Jonnie's vegetarian influence was rubbing off on me), and ignored Benji's strange look. He ordered chicken fingers, a side of curly fries, and a Guinness. When it came, I took a sip.

"You drink now?" he asked.

"Yeah ... sure," I said, trying to act nonchalant about the whole thing. Of course his raised eyebrow (old school, à la the "Rock"– one of his many dorky impersonations) said it all: Benji was not impressed by my sudden, somewhat superficial decision-making, especially since he'd been well aware of my childhood "pledge."

"Ah, of course," he said. "You can't be a New York model and not drink a cocktail. That's almost as scandalous as mixing brown and black."

I decided not to tell him that brown and black was actually considered chic nowadays, and instead pleaded with him (using the puppy dog eyes I usually reserved for my father) to order another drink, for me. He made me thumb wrestle for it and promise that, when he came up to visit me in New York (um ... yeah, whenever *that* was happening) I would buy him a drink.

"So, have you been going out a lot up there?" Benji asked when the food finally came.

"Well, yes, in the beginning, especially after I met Seth—" Oops. Did I want to go there just yet? I didn't.

"Seth?"

"Oh, this guy Jonnie introduced me to ... who I'm sort of ... seeing."

"Oh?" His eyes widened; he seemed a little taken aback. "That's cool."

"Yeah." I smiled. We'd discussed all this before we broke things off, how this summer we were just "having fun" (his words exactly) and not making any sort of commitment. Benji masked whatever surprise or disappointment he was feeling and kept up the same look of interest. "Go on."

"Anyway, his mother was Remi Fosgate, the—"

"Yeah, I know who she was. She was never very pretty for a model — kinda weird looking."

"Really? You think so?" I asked, caught a little off guard by his harshness. Especially since people said I looked like her. "Well, regardless, she was very in-demand at the time. My bookers and people who knew her back in the day are saying we have a similar look."

"Definitely not. You're better looking."

"Well, thanks, but with makeup and hair and—"

"So, does this guy Seth have an Oedipus complex or what?"

"What?" I said, almost choking on my tofu chunk. "What are you talking about?"

He looked agitated. "Well, it's just that you supposedly look like his mother and now he has the hots for you? That's kinda creepy," he said, taking a gulp of his beer.

I sucked on my drink straw. "The hots? It's *not* the hots." God, this guy used the dorkiest lingo. He talked just like my dad.

"Didn't Remi what's-her-name die?"

"Apparently so ... want some?" I said, offering him some of my kabob to quickly change the subject.

"I think it was drugs or something. An overdose, if I recall. Now that's a surprise!"

"A surprise? What do you mean by that?"

"I mean, I'm not surprised that some model died of a drug overdose. Doesn't that happen on a regular basis up there?"

"Well, if you're the type of person who believes in stereotypes, then yes. But *I'm* not snorting cocaine at the moment, so I don't think you need to worry about it."

"Oh, give me a break, Catherine. I'm not talking about you. I know you're smarter than that. I'm talking about the majority of girls who get into that business."

I rolled my eyes, getting increasingly more annoyed. My face was burning up, no doubt from alternating between sips of Benji's gross-tasting beer and whatever weird, fruity concoction he'd ordered for himself (me).

"Come on, Catherine. It's common knowledge for Chrissakes!" This was the first time he'd ever raised his voice to me. Even in the crowded, noisy restaurant, people around us heard him and stopped to stare.

"So you think that my friends up there are druggies?" I whispered through clenched teeth. It bothered me that he was suddenly passing judgment on a whole industry without knowing anything about it.

"Well, I hope that you wouldn't get involved in that kind of stuff or with people who are doing that kind of stuff."

How dare he!

"Oh, and if I did, you wouldn't like me anymore?" I pressed him. "I modeled a string bikini at a fashion show the other day. Does that bother you? I guess I'm a slut now."

His eyes got wider. "You're joking, right?"

I wasn't.

"Let's just say, Catherine, *Cat*," he accentuated my nickname with a false sense of superiority, "I expect more class than that from you."

I looked at him firmly. "Excuse me, I'm feeling a bit ill. I have to go to the ladies room!" I said, preparing to stomp away from the table. But when I rose, I swerved a little and almost lost my balance, making my exit far less gratifying.

In the bathroom, I blotted my face and applied another coat of lip gloss. Unbelievable. Goes to show how no one really knows what goes on behind the headlines. If Seth had been here with me, he would have punched Benji right in the face. I regained my composure and headed out again, figuring I was ready to cut the night short when I saw a few people Benji had been talking to walk away from the table.

As I walked over, Benji mimicked me, trying to lighten the mood, no doubt. He protruded his pouty lips and squinted his eyes, strutting his shoulders from side to side. "Is that how you walk down the catwalk?" he asked, laughing.

"Is that why you wanted me to go out tonight? So that you could show off to your friends that you know a model?" I couldn't help myself. I was getting angrier by the second.

"Whoa," Benji said, cocking his head to one side. "Aren't we a little high on ourselves?"

"Well, is it?" I pressed, a bit louder than intended.

"Catherine, I think you've had too much to drink tonight. You're overreacting–"

"Answer the question!" I screeched, knowing full well that I probably had drank too much, and that I probably did sound like a raging bi-atch right about then, but unable to do anything about it.

"Of course not," he said. "I asked you to come out tonight because I wanted to know how you were making out up there. You know, I had a good time with you this summer and just wanted to see if you liked the whole New York thing. But listen, I'm sorry about what I said about your friend's mom. If you're happy up there, that's all that counts."

"Well, I am. I love it. I would die if I had to come back here."

He raised his brows. "Not good enough for you?"

"It's fine for some people. No offense to you, but I want more. I want to travel. I want to do something worthwhile, to make an impression."

"You've certainly made one," Benji said, raising his hand to flag down our waiter.

The waiter gave him the bill and Benji started to tell me my half of the bill: $42.50, excluding tip.

"After all, you are making more money than I am now," he said. "As you're well aware, we poor future schoolteachers won't have much in the bank."

Fine. I asked for it. If we are in fact just being friends, then we should definitely go Dutch.

I reached into my purse and started pulling out a few bills from my wallet, but Benji stopped me with his hand.

"Save it," Benji said. "It's on me. Save it for your New York party life."

# ✦ 10 ✦

"Can you move? You're blocking my sun," the voice said. I heard it, but felt like it was coming from a million miles away. My mind was elsewhere, thinking about how strange Benji had acted over the weekend.

At the end of our night together, we sat in the car in my parents' driveway, listening to whatever was on the radio in total silence. I apologized for overreacting maybe a *teeny* bit. He said he was sorry, too. Neither of us knew what the proper protocol was for saying goodbye to a friend, formerly a boyfriend or girlfriend. I decided to do the mature thing, and leaned over to kiss him on the cheek. It felt weird, remembering all the times he'd kissed me softly, gently, on the lips. Times that, for me, made me think that maybe I wasn't just a skinny freak, a girl who no boy liked, and maybe somebody who someone actually wanted.

A tiny part of me questioned whether I'd made the wrong decision by breaking things off with him. But then I thought of Seth, of lying in his arms and hearing those family secrets that he'd told no one else — and it quickly put the regret out of my mind.

"Ah-HEM! Hello? You-hoo!" The voice bellowed again, this time louder. "Catherine ... Cat ... whatever your name is!"

"It's Cat," I said, moving out of the way for the prima donna Fiona, otherwise known as the Queen Bee. Yes, she was back in my life, her sting stronger than ever.

We were into our second day of shooting in Aruba. It wasn't my first time on an island (I had been to St. Thomas in 8th grade with my parents), but it was my first time traveling alone. I had a mini-meltdown the night before, thinking I'd miss my flight, never find my hotel, or be mistaken for a pasty jellyfish on the beach. But so far, so good. I managed to get here by myself, and find my way around the tiny island thanks to a very helpful hotel chauffeur named Pepe who, while he didn't speak much English, was happy to take me anywhere I could point to on Google Maps.

On this particular afternoon, we were on a yacht off the coast of Baby Beach. (I know, tough life.) The Caribbean blue sea twinkled like a thousand tiny mirrors. White, cotton-wisp clouds spiraled above like pinwheels on a painter's canvas. It was the closest thing to heaven on earth. Well, except for a few minor disturbances...

"I'm melting out here! Can we get some fans?" Fiona asked the photographer's assistant. "It's, like, manual labor standing in this heat!"

We had been shooting all morning for Philippe's spring catalog. The feel they were going for was very Duran Duran, circa the *Rio* album. You know, that '80s sound that everyone's dads used to listen to when they were still young and had all their hair. The storyboards for the photo shoot depicted an exotic woman who lived in San Tropez, Buenos Aires, or somewhere on the Caribbean. She had a nanny for each child, a country club membership, personal jet, lots of chunky bling, 200K followers, and a wealthy husband who could provide multiple residencies. This was what we were supposed to portray on film. It was all about projecting the fantasy — that elusive ideal that every woman wanted but (as I was coming to find out) few in real life actually had.

"Put these on," Gail stood before me holding a pair of "chicken cutlets," gelatin-like falsies that I inserted into my strapless bra. She pushed and pulled my breasts from side to side, finally relying on masking tape to get just the right amount of cleavage. Fiona, with platinum pigtails curling up in the 100-degree heat, a redhead named Natasha, and I were dressed as sexy sailor girls. We wore blue pinstriped, boat-necked tees, high rise white hot pants with 4-inch, cork-wedged sandals à la Ralph Lauren.

Up ahead, Britton, an appropriately named model from Wales, sat at the helm of the vessel (which was no further from the dock than the anchor would allow). He wore linen pants, an Easter egg-colored polo shirt, and an ascot that framed his Nordic face. Britton feigned interest in his yacht guests for the camera but appeared to enjoy the attention of Benito, the sultry Spanish makeup artist, more than anyone else.

We stood like marionettes while a photographer's assistant plied and pried us for nearly three hours. First we were posed to look like sailors standing at attention, our pointy 1930s-style brassieres poking through our blouses. Then we were regrouped into a quasi-lesbian effect, our legs intertwined and arms strategically placed on one another's waists and bottoms. Finally, we were sprawled out on lounge chairs with mojitos in our hands. Midway through the shoot, my leg started to go numb.

"Get her to move her leg out to the left, and raise her arm a little higher," the photographer, with a dangling cigarette permanently attached to his lower lip, told his assistant. I wasn't sure who he was referring to until the assistant walked over to me and pulled my leg out.

"I'm Cat," I said, thinking the photographer didn't know my name.

"I don't care who the hell you are," he said, taking a drag off his cigarette and blowing a cloud of smoke into my hair as he stopped to recharge his camera. This was Perri Pileggi, one of the most in-demand photographers of the moment. Philippe had flown Perri to Aruba that morning to get his "signature close-ups." As I spoke, the assistant shot me a death stare, shaking her head furiously as if I had just committed a crime.

"Not like that!" Perri yelled at her once again, ripping the cigarette from his mouth and flailing it about, narrowly missing her cheek. "Her ass needs to be closer to the other one. Can't you do a fucking thing right?"

We took a break for five minutes while the camera crew set up the next scene. I got a bottle of water from the cooler, but as I sipped it, Benito gave me an evil look and complained about how he was going to have to retouch my lipstick again. Fiona and Natasha appeared near death in the sweltering heat. They had been out the night before. I heard them stumble into their hotel room, which was adjacent to mine, at 4 a.m., loud and drunk, laughing at the top of their lungs.

"Time!" the assistant yelled as we regrouped, resuming our sticky, sweaty positions.

"Let's get this right," Perri said. He smiled, appearing for the first time to be tolerable to bear. He walked over to Natasha and whispered something in her ear. She laughed weakly, then he went on to Fiona, then me, one by one. I couldn't imagine what was so clever, but when he got to me, he announced that I needed to hear this the most. This quite amused the others. Perri bent down into my ear, his breath a bizarre mix of cigarettes and Altoids, and placed his hand on the small of my back. He whispered in a rasp, "Now, look like you want to be fucked."

I froze, feeling like I had been punched in the stomach. His hand continued its downward path and reached my butt, squeezing hard. "Can you do that for me, huh?" he muttered.

Before I could muster up the courage to react, Fiona leaned up against me, her body trembling, swaying back and forth, mumbling "I feel sick," before finally collapsing on the deck.

Within seconds, Natasha ran to the side of the boat and threw up into the water.

Gail's scream could be heard miles away.

"Oh, my gawd!" she gasped, throwing her hands in the air. "They're dropping like flies! They're dropping like flies! We're never going to get this shoot over with!"

"Shit!" Perri yelled, stamping out a cigarette beneath his foot and stepping over Fiona's sweaty body. "Now we'll lose that natural light!"

I bent down, trying to give Fiona some of my water, straining to pull her up onto a lounge chair. "Can someone help me, please?" I asked, staring up into Gail's empty face.

"She'll recover," she said, walking away in disgust. "She always does."

There was a message from Clive on the hotel line when I got back to my room that evening. My cell had been on vibrate all day, and he no doubt had been impatient about reaching me. At first I didn't notice the phone blinking, because I was delirious with exhaustion after shooting for 15 hours. I flopped down on the king-size bed, ready to get lost in the soft down duvet, plush as a mountain of feathers. Through the drapes I could see the ocean in the distance and almost smell the mist rising off the water. The sun, having not relented all day, finally began to relinquish its power and set behind a cool, black ocean, still as ice.

In the shadows, the little red light flickered and became visible. I sprang for the phone in sleepy delirium, thinking that, perhaps, Seth had tried to reach me in my room. But when I heard the voice, my heart sank. Clive was insistent that I join Philippe, Gail, and the others for dinner that night.

I got up, stumbling in the dark. It was nearly 9:30 and I rushed to make the 10 o'clock dinner reservation. I had been asked earlier that evening, but declined, thinking everyone would naturally understand I needed some rest. Silly me, assuming beauty sleep was a priority! I slipped on a black strapless dress and 20 minutes later found myself sitting in the hotel lounge.

"What a pleasure!" Philippe said as he kissed me hello, pretending to be surprised by my presence, as if he weren't the catalyst for Clive's call. I feared that Perri wouldn't be far behind, but fortunately he'd already left the island to shoot a bunch of Brazilian girls down in São Paulo. In his place was a familiar-looking man, a photographer, who I soon realized was Frank, the man who said I looked like Remi Fosgate at Gail's party. We talked about finally setting up a photo shoot together. He seemed friendly and much less intimidating than the other men who joined us — friends of Philippe who spoke very little English.

As we stepped into a limousine that pulled up to the hotel, I realized I was the only female present. Gail was "under the weather," Philippe said, but assured me we'd be joined by Fiona and Natasha later. *Oh, joy*. The car took us to a restaurant at the end of the island, at the California Lighthouse. The Lighthouse stood on a cliff, overlooking the ocean at a gut-wrenching height above sea level. Tiki torches lit our pathway out to a private roof deck, which gave a breathtakingly frightening view of the ocean. I tried not to look down or think about the fact that we were virtually suspended over water, precariously teetering over our impending doom.

Fiona and Natasha appeared, looking fresh-faced and flawless. They turned heads with their fabulously messy hair, kohl black eyes, and plump, glossy lips.

Fiona ordered a drink from the waitress, then sat on the lap of an Italian man who had been watching the shoot on the boat deck earlier that day. He was Philippe's so-called silent partner, Anton. He beamed as Fiona placed her arm around his neck and lit one of his cigarettes. "Oh, you are starting early tonight, my little bambino," Anton said with a thick accent, pulling her closer to him. "I think you are getting too big to sit on Papa's lap."

*Papa's lap?*

The waiter appeared and Philippe ordered appetizers for the table: oysters, snails, squid, portabella mushrooms stuffed with crabmeat, and caviar. He was unimpressed with the drink selection and ordered bottles of Dom Pérignon from elsewhere on the island to be delivered to our table.

As we waited for our meal, I looked on in mortification as Fiona unbuttoned Anton's shirt, revealing a salt-and-peppered patch of curly chest hair, and buried her face in his collar. The fish eggs in my stomach churned at the sight of this girl kissing a man who was at least three times her senior. Hopefully it was all a ruse for free drinks ... she couldn't be seriously interested in him, *could she?*

The champagne arrived. Philippe filled our glasses and made a toast to "beautiful women, beautiful food." He then said something offhanded in Italian, which sent the Italian men at the table into hysterics. A few seconds later, Frank, the only American man at the table, leaned over and asked, "So where are you from? New England?"

"New Jersey," I said. "But, thanks. I'm flattered that you can't trace my Jersey accent."

He laughed. We talked. He told me that after graduating college in the early 1980s, he apprenticed in New York and got his big break with Philippe. He was cool to talk to, just a nice, normal guy, without an ounce of pretension (a rarity in this business, I was finding).

I began to relax and even enjoy myself a little, agreeing to a second (or was it a third?) glass of champagne. The more I drank, the less the tart taste bothered me and the more the tingly bubbles tickled my tongue. I leaned back in my chair, listening to the convergence of accents: Italian, British English, American English, even a little French, and I suddenly felt very cosmo-politan. Why on earth had I initially passed on this invitation? Wasn't this what high-fashion models — "haute girls'" — were supposed to do? Dine in fancy restaurants? Be out-and-about with the "beautiful" people? At this moment, I realized that there were hundreds, no, *thousands*, of girls just like me who would kill for this experience. Who might even do anything — *ANY*thing — to be here, to stay here. And it was me. Fate had chosen me.

And I felt a little embarrassed. I had almost settled back into my old ways. Being the loner, the one who tried to follow the rules, and who, by default, alienated herself. These days, I would not let that part of me hold myself back.

I downed the rest of my champagne. Then I moved onto champagne cocktails, with Jonnie's "flirtini" (a mix of champagne, fruit juice, and vodka) at the top of my list.

Natasha passed around the newly minted fake IDs that they'd gotten on the island, so that everyone could admire the hand-iwork. I figured they were both much older than I – say, 23 or 24 by the way they acted – but was surprised to find out they were all only about a year older. A *year*! Natasha and Fiona were much more experienced than I in the ways of the world (well, at least on certain subjects, it seemed. Like those involving men. But I guessed that wasn't too difficult).

"Oh, dahling, put that thing away," Philippe scolded Natasha. "You won't need it here, or in Europe, either." Or in New York City, I discovered. Jonnie was right about models pretty much getting away with *anything*. I hadn't been carded once since my arrival, and it didn't seem like anyone (my agents included!) seemed to care. Truly a perk!

The second course was served, and a mariachi player came by us, strumming on a tiny guitar. He asked couples to join him on the deck, and Anton lifted Fiona's hand and led her out to the dance floor, her laughter trailing behind her as they left. I felt a hand touch my shoulder and I looked up: It was Philippe. And he was not going to take no for an answer.

I stumbled a little on the way to the dance floor. He held me close, helping me keep my balance by pressing his chest against mine, his cheek against my cheek. It felt a little weird, like dancing with someone's grandfather (in fact, I probably was). His hand in mine felt rough, wrinkly, and hairy. To be honest, had I not been feeling so tipsy my creep meter would have been sounding off like a car alarm. He whispered something into my ear and I laughed, not really because what he said was funny, but because I just felt good.

*I,* Catherine Watson, was *dancing* with Philippe. The world-famous Master of Cloth.

My phone began to vibrate and I reached for it in my purse, but he stopped me, firmly placing his hand over mine, saying, "No, no ... you are mine for the night!"

"Of course," I said, feeling like I had just committed a social faux pas.

When we got back to the table, Philippe pulled up a seat next to mine, placing his arm on the back of my chair. At first, I thought nothing of it, but then slowly began to feel a little self-conscious. To any stranger in the room, it would have looked like we were a couple. Dancing with him was one thing, but I didn't want him to think that I was (gulp) gonna sit on *Papa's lap.* I started to move my chair away, but he only followed, leaning in closer.

Our glasses were continually filled for the rest of the night between courses of tapas. I tried to maintain a steady buzz, but Natasha and Fiona got infinitely inebriated, roaring with laughter at anything and everything that was said at the table, even if it was in Italian.

Amid talk about business, the table got quiet long enough to watch Natasha and Fiona on the deck. The pair spiraled around each other, holding hands and swaying in the breeze like lazy flowers being pushed from side to side. They began to touch each other, running their hands down each other's backs, wrapping their arms around one another's waists.

Philippe took a long drink of champagne and sat back, settling into the chair, as if he had watched the display a thousand times. The girls' bodies brushed together in a gyrating motion, as they mocked pleasure on their faces, all for the approval of these men, who now, it seemed, looked on like wolves.

*Ew.* I felt uneasy, and quickly began to realize that there was a fine line between friendly and flirtatious. And maybe I, being there, right now with these girls, was beginning to cross it.

Anton shouted to Philippe from across the table, "Brother, you say I am hard man to please in business, no? Well, you are wrong. I am not a hard man to please, I am just *hard.*" The table erupted in laughter and I felt Philippe watching me, like he wanted to see my reaction. I feigned ignorance and focused on finishing my meal.

Dessert arrived and I felt my face start to burn after taking a sip of the sweet wine. The drinks I'd had in rapid succession were finally starting to affect me, like I was hitting a wall. The waiter came and passed around a tray full of caramelized apple and pear blossom tarts, with little flowers lining the rim of the tray. I watched in slow motion as Anton looked at the platter and proudly boasted, "Ah, more little tarts!"

Frank, the photographer who'd stayed pretty quiet all night, looked in my direction. He shifted a little in his chair and mouthed, "Sorry."

I started feeling too sick to care.

Natasha and Fiona sat back down and fought over which pastry they would share. Anton lifted a flower to his lips and swallowed it whole, causing the two to explode into hideous screams of laughter. Philippe lifted up a flower and said, "You know, Cat, my dahling, Girard here—" he pointed to the man sitting beside him who had been mostly silent for the duration of the night, "is a — how do you say it? A cul-ti-vat-or of the rose blossom."

"Oh?" I said, looking down at my phone and still having the mental faculties to know that this night was not going to end. If it did, I just might have to extricate myself from under someone's claws.

"He is a gardener," Philippe said. "He reaps, he sows ..."

Girard began to talk. He had a light, effeminate voice. I could barely make out what he was saying above the music and mur-mur of the crowd, but I could tell, by catching phrases here and there, that he was describing the flower in a very clinical nature, describing the layers, the piston, and the pollination process.

I strained my ears to hear him. He was looking right at me while speaking, and I punctuated my smile with a nod or shake of the shake the head, catching little of what he was saying. Then he picked up a flower from a vase at the table and said, "The pungent scent is aromatic."

"Pungent?" I asked, thinking I was following correctly. "But aren't lilies sort of sweet-smelling?"

"I am not talking about the flower," he said, leaning in, cupping his hand around his mouth. "I am talking about a pussy. And I bet yours smells sweeter than any flower."

I laughed nervously, not sure why because what I really felt like doing was crying at that very moment. Naively, I'd thought that maybe, just maybe, going out with "clients," as Clive called them, I would be taken seriously on a professional level. But no, we were just playthings for their amusement.

*Get me the hell out of here.*

I stood from the table, feeling the floor shift beneath my feet, my stomach beginning to churn, and blurted "excuse me" as I staggered toward a dimly lit, wooden stairwell that might take me out of this nightmare. In the restaurant lobby, I could feel the tears welling up in my eyes, the puke bubbling up at the back of my throat. I didn't know where to go, what to do. I wanted to lie down right there on the floor and sleep, but first I needed to purge my insides.

From behind in the dining room, I thought I heard Philippe

calling out my name and cursing Girard. Someone came running after me, and I felt cold hands on my back just as my head hit the floor and everything went black.

# ✦ 11 ✦

In the wee hours of the morning, I opened my eyes to find that I was not in my hotel room. An unfamiliar ceiling fan creaked from overhead, and a television hummed at the foot of the bed where there had not been one before. The foreignness of my surroundings struck me like lightning and I bolted upright from where I was lying, my eyes quickly scanning the room to make sense of the darkened shapes around me.

In one corner of the room, a sliver of dawn peaked between two gold and green window drapes. The tiny w's, for "Westin," embroidered into the fabric told me that I was in the right hotel. Wrong room.

I started to panic, and sprang from the bed, bumping into the corner of a nightstand and falling over a heap of suitcases and pillows in my path. When I finally steadied on two feet, I looked up to see a man lying on the floor in front of me, wrapped in a blanket.

A scream flew out of my mouth before I could silence it with my hand, and the dark figured turned and leapt to his feet, towering over me and lifting his arms above his head in the air. "It's OK, it's OK. You're all right, it's me," he said, pulling the drapes open and letting in the light so that I could see. "It's Frank."

Frank, the photographer, from the night before. But, what was he — what was *I* doing ... *here*? I felt an unusually cool breeze coming in from the window and looked down to see that I was, in fact, bare down to my bra and panties. I gasped, *ohmigod ohmigod ohmigod ohmygod*, and ripped a sheet from the bed to cover myself.

"It's-not-what-you-think," he said, speaking faster than my brain could process, his arms still up in the air.

"Did I ...?" I gasped, panic-stricken, trying to find my footing on solid ground as the room began to spin like a carnival ride. "Did we ...?"

"No, no ..." he said, shaking his head furiously and reaching out to help me find my balance.

"*OHMIGOD!*" I said, bursting into tears, still not grasping — or really believing — the gravity of his words. "DID WE DO *IT*?"

"No, no — absolutely not! I've been on the floor the whole night," he said, the agitation and worry on his face now evident. "I brought you back to the hotel last night after you passed out at the restaurant. I tried to get you to your room, but I couldn't find your key. You weren't doing too well."

At the thought of my incoherent self, I sobbed even harder than before.

"It's OK — you were just sick," Frank said. "From the food, the drinks ... everything."

I stopped to consider the plausibility of this story, but then I looked down, and immediately started crying again. "Then why — why am I practically *naked*?"

"I can explain, I can explain," he said, kneeling down onto the floor beside me, and feeling around on the ground for something. "You got sick in the middle of the night, and threw up. I think your dress — here it is," he said, grabbing it off the floor and handing it to me, "got soiled, a bit."

*Dear God:*

*Please, let me die right here, right now. If you don't kill me, I will kill myself from shame and embarrassment. How could I be such a sick, disgusting mess of a person? How could I let this happen? I promise to never, ever get this drunk again. If I do and you decide to let me live, you can make all of my hair fall out and turn me into a hunchback.*

*Yours,*
*Catherine.*

I grabbed the puke-stained dress from Frank's hands, pulled it over my head, and blurted, through my tears: "So, um, sorry ... I, ah ... gotta go!"

Then I turned and dashed out of the room.

"Poor Frank!" Jonnie said, as I recounted my disaster of a night — henceforth referred to as "the restaurant ordeal" — later that day when she picked me up at LaGuardia. "You probably made him feel like a leper! I mean, crying over the thought of sleeping with him? That can do a lot to a man's ego."

I hadn't even thought about that. I mean, Frank was nice and all — but he could never think that *I* ... that *we* ... oh, no. No, no, no.

"You're feeling sorry for Frank? Feel sorry for me! I was nearly ambushed at the restaurant by the blue-hair brigade." And then, of course, was the inability to hold my liquor. (Note to self: Flirtinis will not make you flirt with wealthy, hairy, old men — but they will make you sick. *Very* sick.)

On the way home, we stopped at Starbucks and I opted out of my regular skinny mocha, choosing instead the bottled water to take with my Tylenol — a suggestion of Jonnie's to make my head stop pounding and my hangover go away much quicker.

For the umpteenth time that morning, she expressed her disbelief at my walking out on Philippe at dinner. "Do you know how many girls would kill for the opportunity to dine with that man?" she scolded while blowing on a steamy cup of green tea. "You're insane!"

"I know ... I know. I can't believe I did it, either," I said. "Things just got a little too ... weird." I started wondering if maybe I just should have stuck it out, but the reality was that if I hadn't excused myself when I did fate probably would have done it for me. And it wouldn't have been pretty.

"Well, I don't think it matters, anyway," she said. "Evidently Philippe still loves you. He sent flowers to the apartment this morning. What did you do to him? He's really wrapped around your finger."

"Are you kidding me?" I jerked, choking as I chugged down my water. "Are you sure they're from him?"

"He signs PB, doesn't he? It's him."

My phone buzzed and I got a text message from Clive, who sounded somewhat annoyed. He urged me to call him as soon as I "made contact with U.S. soil."

I dialed his number, my heart pounding in my chest, thinking that I'd have to explain my actions from the night before. When he answered, even before I could say my name, he was shouting at the top of his lungs.

"EVERYTHING OK?"

"Yes. I'm fine."

"Not you. Philippe! Did you hear from him?"

"No, why? ... but apparently, he sent me flowers this morning."

"Oh, thank god! I guess he's not angry."

"Angry? Would he be angry? With me?"

"Little girl, do you know the stir you've caused? I've been on the phone with Philippe's PR people all morning."

Evidently they went "ballistic," he said, because I didn't show up for a shoot that day.

"Shoot? What shoot?" I panicked. My flight was at 8 a.m. No one said anything about a shoot.

"They were planning to do a few retakes, but, obviously, you didn't get that memo because you walked out at dinner last night," he said with his typical biting sarcasm.

"I know ... sorry," I said. "I wasn't feeling well." Damn it, Catherine! Tell the truth. The *whole* truth! "I was tired from shooting all day." Nope that wasn't it, either.

"Well, the other girls were fine."

"The other girls were wasted the entire weekend!" I snapped. Shit. That was definitely uncalled for. Shit. Shit. Shit.

"What?"

"Well, not exactly wasted, just, um ... hungover."

"Catherine, let me tell you something. Socializing with clients is part of your job. You have a reputation to uphold. As a model, you have to embody the image you're projecting on camera.

You're lucky this time. But I don't want to hear about this happening again."

He hung up.

I looked at Jonnie, still holding the phone up to my ear in disbelief. "I don't believe this. Wouldn't he want me bright-eyed and bushy-tailed rather than strung out or hungover during a shoot? I mean, Natasha couldn't even stand up!"

Jonnie looked away.

"You'd think he'd value my trying to act like a professional!"

"Cat, you need to trust your booker," she said. "Clive knows how to deal with clients. He knows what's going to make them happy and what's not. If putting up with a little bit of crap is going to keep them happy — and renew your contract for another year — then that's what he wants."

"So we're just supposed to let creepy old men grope us and say whatever they want, just for kicks? What are we, prostitutes?"

"No," she said, turning to me, a half-hearted smile on her lips. "We wear better clothes."

# ✦ 12 ✦

Icon's Christmas party was held at the W Hotel in Midtown. I invited Seth to come along, and he promised to meet me there. We planned on meeting in the lobby before heading into the ballroom for festivities.

It was the first time I saw him since the night of our Thanksgiving dinner, since the night he opened up to me about his family. Leading up to it, I was feeling a flutter of excitement in my stomach and a sick, aching pang of near-infatuation, of being on the verge of falling but not quite there — yet.

I'd changed my outfit three times before finally settling on the dress that won him over, that won them all over the night of Gail's party. Jonnie said it was my early Christmas present, mine for keeps. I slipped on the wintry white silhouette and again felt transformed.

I fidgeted with my drink straw as I waited by the bar. Each time I heard someone approach from behind, I caught my breath, hoping that it would be Seth. His tall, lanky, dark frame was stamped onto my brain and when I remembered his face I could only make out his pleasing features, not the cuts and scars from his skateboarding days, the flaws I knew were there. The ones I had traced with my finger.

I looked up at the clock on the wall. It was getting late. A steady stream of people from the agency, girls I knew, Jonnie included, passed by on the way to the ballroom. I pulled out my cellphone and saw there were two missed texts from Seth. The battery was low, and I cursed the thing for failing me at the worst time, but hearing from Seth was still enough to thrill me momentarily:

First message: *Hey Babe – running late. B there by 7:30*

*(Babe. He called me Babe – AGH!)*

*Second message: make it 8*

Humph. I slunk off the chair, feeling slightly deflated. After not seeing each other for two-and-a-half weeks, I couldn't imagine what could possibly be more pressing than this. But since nothing was official between us, I couldn't very well make a fuss over it. I mean, it was *fine*. It didn't mean he didn't want to see me. Right?

I decided to go into the ballroom to find Jonnie. As I walked through the crowd, I spotted Clive. He flitted around the room like a drunken Christmas elf, dressed in red, white, and green. When he saw me, he pulled himself away from the martini bar long enough to plant a solid kiss on my cheek (apparently he was over the minor melodrama that had unfolded earlier that week).

I took my place at our table, looking around at the crowd of reconstructed faces, painted, pulled, and stretched, and began to think that maybe Seth might not have felt very comfortable there anyway. Out of his element. But then I remembered who he was and who his mother was and how this is all he'd ever known. It dawned on me then that maybe *I* felt out of place.

Out of the corner of my eye, I saw a man with a familiar-looking gait, a slow, confident stride, crossing the floor. Clive sprang into action from behind him, like a fox hunting his prey. He directed the man toward our table, and through the crowd I could see the shiny bald head and trademark gray wool suit I knew so well. The blood immediately rushed to my head. I didn't know how to react after what had transpired between us during "the restaurant ordeal."

But if he too felt uncomfortable, he didn't let on. Philippe kissed my hand and complimented me on the photos, which, he said, were up for some fashion photo award and perhaps one of the yacht shots would be used on a billboard. (Yes, *BILLBOARD!*)

"Oh, really?" I said, trying to play it cool, trying to act like I'm a total professional who, naturally, might see herself on a billboard regularly.

"Awesome. Where do you think it might run?" I added. "Run" wasn't that marketing-speak? I think so.

"New York, L.A., all the fashion hot spots," he said.

"Good idea," I said, still keeping my marketer's hat on.

I thanked him for the opportunity to shoot in Aruba, and for the flowers, which I said were *totally* unnecessary (not to mention, creepy coming from a man his age. And with Clive's martini breath huffing down my neck, I told him I "happily" looked forward to working with him again.

"Wonderful, dahling," he said, scanning the room for, perhaps, more interesting conversation? "Because we'd like book you again, next month, for Fashion Week."

"Fashion Week ... you mean, as in Europe?" I said, not quite believing my ears.

"Milan, of course," he said. "Have you ever been to Italy?"

I didn't even have a second to think or respond to this very generous offer, which I would have been thrilled to agree to if only I could manage to avoid being alone with Philippe and his friends, when Clive stepped forward, nearly tripping over his floor-length cape, and said, "I'll have to check her calendar, because she's already had many offers for Milan and Paris next month, but I think she may be available."

"Wonderful," Philippe said, running his finger along the line of my dress, pulling at the fabric. "I have a villa there. If you come, you see it, no?"

"I'm sure she'd love that," Clive said. "Isn't that right, doll baby?"

*Doll baby?*

"You see the whole city from the balcony," Philippe said. "It's *magnifico!*"

"That sounds fabulous!" Clive chimed.

"Yes. You know only my favorite girls get to see my villa, my home away from home," he continued.

"Oh?" I managed to blurt out, after Clive jabbed me. "I'm sure it's amazing there ... in Italy, I mean. I haven't been."

"Then I look forward to seeing you in Milan."

He said "arrivederci" before turning on his heels and getting lost, once again, in the crowd. Clive turned to me, his grin as wide as the Cheshire Cat's.

"That's my girl," he said, reaching over to pat my cheek with his short, chubby hand. "Just let Uncle Clive handle everything for you."

The flutter in my stomach that I'd felt at the beginning of the night returned. But this time, it was for a different reason.

By 8 o'clock, Seth had still not arrived and I began to wonder if something awful had happened. Like my mother, I always jumped to the worst conclusions, thinking that whoever was late was literally lying in a ditch somewhere. My cellphone battery was dead by now, so I made my way out to the lobby to see if I could find a hotel line. On the way, I stopped in the bathroom.

A girl of about 15, with rounded features and rosy cheeks, pushed by me and staggered over to the sink before suddenly losing all self-control and vomiting onto the marble countertop. The woman next to her jumped about 15 feet away, a look of disgust on her face, and the entire bathroom cleared out in five seconds flat.

I decided to brave it and hold my nose because I could no longer hold my bladder, and I ran into one of the empty stalls. In two shakes, a janitor was there, mopping up the aftermath, and an older woman (who I imagined to be the young model's agent) was helping her out.

A petite lady, about thirtyish, emerged from the stall next to mine. When she saw that we were both alone, she looked at her watch and said, "Barely 8 o'clock and that one's already bombed off her ass. She couldn't have been more than 16."

"Oh, yeah," I said, agreeing wholeheartedly, but realizing that just days earlier I had, in fact, been that stupid girl. I shuddered, thinking how fortunate I'd been that it was Frank who took me home that night, and not one of Philippe's henchmen. Things could have turned out quite differently.

"So there's some modeling thing going on down the hall?" she asked.

"An industry Christmas party," I told her while crouching down, trying to fix an ankle sash on my once-in-a-lifetime Christian Louboutins. Stilettos I had gotten on deep discount at a sample sale.

"Well, that's just irresponsible. They need to establish some sort of supervision over these young girls. I've seen way too many end up in a bad place." She walked over to the bathroom sink and started fixing her hair.

"What do you mean?" I asked, wondering exactly what this woman was getting at.

"Oh, the models," she said. "These girls who come from Iowa or a small town in the Czech Republic. There's absolutely no one watching out for them. The agencies don't care ... I mean, if I were a mother–"

I clasped the buckle on my shoe and stood up, joining her at the sink. She looked in the mirror at me perplexed.

"Whoa, sorry," she said. "Didn't realize you were ... one of *them*," she said, looking up at me.

I smiled. "I'm not one of them, per se."

"Yes, you are. You look very familiar, actually. I've seen you before."

I smirked. My first big moment of recognition — in the loo! How glamorous.

"Oh, my god. You won't believe this, but I actually wrote about you during Fashion Week. Cat, right? With Icon? I'm one of the *Times* fashion bloggers. Oh, this is hilarious. I get caught in the bathroom talking trash about modeling to one of the hot young flavors of the month. *Fabulous*."

Ohmigod! What were the odds? This was her. Stacy Goldberg, the journalist from *The New York Times*. The one who called me an It girl.

"You wrote that article? You don't know what that did for me. I got a ton of work after that!"

"No sweat. Just doing my job. But, hey, don't listen to me. I've had a few, and I am feeling way too good right now. Forget what I said."

"Oh, no. Actually, I agree." I said. "About, well, about some of the girls. You really have to watch yourself-"

"Exactly, exactly!" she said. "But what I'm getting at is something more. There's something else that's sort of under the surface. It's something about the industry ..." She stopped herself and eyed me in the mirror.

"Go on. I'm listening."

She looked around before whispering, "I think there's more to these rumors about the business. You know, the fashion industry has existed for years evading scrutiny. The economics of it, the ethics, all of it. To start with, what cut of your paycheck is going to your agency?"

I thought it was about 10 percent, but to be totally honest, I wasn't quite sure. This was pathetic. I was beginning to fit the stereotype.

"Well ..." I said, trying to rack my brain.

"The reason I ask is because I don't think there's any regulation of that. There's no governing agency to make sure that models are compensated appropriately, among other things."

"Really?" This was news to me. I mean, I should know about these things, but — let's face it — they weren't the fun parts of the biz.

"Yeah, I really want to write a piece about it one day, sort of an undercover thing."

"I think that sounds ... interesting," I said. "It could be really good, I'm sure."

"Yeah, well, I'm not exactly an investigative journalist, writing fluff all day long. No offense."

"None taken."

"Well, it was nice talking to you. Good luck with your career. I'm sure I'll see you again, doing your thing on the catwalk."

"Hope so."

She turned to leave but hesitated for a minute before she turned back again. "Hey, if I give you my card, will you hold on to it for me? Just in case, I don't know, you ever hear anything that sounds strange to you. You know, about what we talked about?"

"I'd be happy to," I said.

"Great. I'm sure you'll never need to call. But just in case."

She handed me her card. I slipped it into my purse, knowing that I'd probably never use it. But it was still cool to say that I was on a first-name basis with a fashion reporter from *The New York Times,* and one never knew if there would be an occasion to call her and do a little self-promotion for, oh, I don't know, a fabulous new billboard, perhaps?

On the way out of the ladies' room I bumped into Seth in the hallway. He looked sort of dazed, surprised to see me.

"Hey, sorry I'm late," he said. He was dressed kind of sloppy, to my disappointment, in a pair of fatigue pants and a long-sleeved T-shirt. "I got held up at home, helping my dad with some stuff."

"Is everything all right?"

"Yeah, it's fine," he said, looking around. "Hope you weren't waiting long."

"Oh, no," I said, feeling doubly disappointed. I had hoped something more urgent had kept him away.

"My dad just signed a new band that he's pretty psyched about," he said. "They're on the top of the British charts."

"Cool," I said. Spending time with his dad was probably a big deal for Seth, since they had kind of a rocky relationship. I figured I would be a good girl and just let this one slide.

"Guess I'm not really dressed for the occasion," he said, peeking into the ballroom. "But you look good ..." he said, eying me over. "Mind if we scrap this and head to my place? It's just a few blocks away."

Humph. Now this was annoying. I mean, the whole point was to go to this party *together,* right?

"Awww," I said. "I was kinda hopin' we could stay here a little bit ..."

In the distance, Jonnie threw me a "what the hell?" glance, holding up her watch. I held up my index finger.

"Oh, you see her all the time," Seth said, glancing back at Jonnie and leaning in to me, close enough to kiss. "I thought we might be alone tonight."

I picked up my coat at the coat-check and we headed outside.

Jonnie would understand. After all, how many times had she left me hanging to talk to some guy? Seth put his arm around me, and I smelled a whiff of something strong. Not cologne, but maybe alcohol. This had been a touchy subject with us, so I stayed quiet the whole way down the street, hoping it was just my overactive sense of smell.

But it wasn't. There was no denying the scent of alcohol coming from his mouth.

"Just a few more blocks," he said, sliding his arm down my waist. "I've missed you. Can't wait to get you back to my place."

But now I started feeling uneasy about the whole idea. "Seth," I said, trying to keep my voice calm as we walked along. "Were you drinking tonight?"

"No. Why?" he asked, leaning against me as we walked along.

"Well, it just smells like you have been."

"Mouthwash," he said. "I want fresh breath for you, babe."

He kissed me on the forehead and gave me a sweet, would-I-lie-to-you puppy-dog look. I stopped in my tracks and stared him down. "Are you serious?"

"I couldn't be more serious," he said. "Don't believe me? Watch this."

He extended his arms and walked in a straight line, one foot in front of the other, and then he touched his nose, missing it completely.

I laughed.

"You try that," he said. "It's hard."

I tried it, and I missed, too. I guessed my mother's paranoia was rubbing off on me more than I thought.

"If I'm drunk, then I'm drunk on you," he whispered, grabbing me dramatically and purring into my ear in his best matinee idol voice: "Your beauty is intoxicating, ah, HA, HA!"

I still sorta felt weird about going back to his place, where, he specifically said, his "roommate had vacated." Was I ready for this? Part of me wanted to take things further, but the other part of me wasn't sure that I was ready, yet. Just yet.

"Mind if we stop somewhere for coffee?" I said.

"I've got a better idea," he said.

We went to a place where he knew the bouncer and could get us in for free. It was called, simply, Milk. There were bare-breasted mannequins suspended from the ceiling and graphic images of scantily-clad women painted on the walls. The crowd was Goth-like: girls with black lipstick, guys with piercings on their faces and tattoos creeping up their necks.

"It's a cool place," Seth said as he led me down the cavernous stairwell into the dungeon-like cell.

"Should you be here?" I said, still paranoid. "Thought you didn't like places like this anymore."

He promised to be on his best behavior and ordered non-alcoholic drinks for us. We sat near a booth on metal reclining chairs, like in a dentist's office. Heavy metal music roared through the speakers, and as we tried to hear each other, I inched closer and breathed in the soapy smell of his skin, a scent mixed with the bar's stale stench of beer that took me back to the first night we met at the club.

I studied the lines on his face so that I could always remember. His features were mismatched, slightly irregular. One eyebrow was higher than the other; his nostrils a little uneven. There was a fine scar by his right eye and another near his jawbone. He said he looked like his father. His mother, he said, was the beautiful one. But to me, these flaws made him beautiful.

A rockabilly Christmas song came on the speakers, and the crowd cheered. I looked around to see a couple with matching black lipstick kissing under the mistletoe. I turned around to look at Seth; he was staring back at me.

"What are you doing for Christmas?" I blurted, getting a bit caught up in the moment.

"Probably nothing. My dad will be traveling for work." Even though Seth was Jewish, he still celebrated the holiday since, he said, his father "bought into every capitalist holiday on the planet."

"Wanna come to my house?"

"And meet your family?" he said, raising his eyebrows. "You ready for that?"

Oh, god. Was I moving too fast?

"It wouldn't be a big deal or anything," I said, trying to remain casual about the whole thing.

"Think your religious parents could handle this?" Seth said, raising his shirtsleeve to show off his latest ink.

"Oh, my," I said, laughing. "Probably not."

I told him at my house it was "the more, the merrier," plus, secretly, my parents would be interested in meeting him. But Seth seemed a little worried that my parents wouldn't take to him. If anything, I told him, I was more worried about him thinking they were aliens from another planet.

"Ready to jet?" he said. As we headed toward the exit, Seth saw some of his friends coming in. Theo was there, and as we passed he gave me a peck on the cheek under the mistletoe.

"What was that for?" I asked Theo, playfully.

"You girls throw a kickass turkey day," he said.

"Thanks. I'll tell Jonnie you said so."

"I've been meaning to tell you, I'm sorry about what happened to you back in the summer, when you got sick and all," he said. "That Vincent, man, he's a pig. I never would've let him pull that shit if I knew how cool you were."

It took me a moment to process what "shit" he was talking about.

"Are you talking about slipping me that patch?" I said, my breath becoming shallow. "At Kasbah?"

I looked at Seth. He had a strange expression on his face. "Theo, man, we gotta go," he said, pulling me toward the door. "See ya later."

Once outside, Seth walked ahead of me at a steady pace. In my 3-inch heels, I couldn't keep up with his stride.

"What are you doing?" I called out.

He didn't answer.

"Seth! Wait up."

I caught up to him on the corner. He was stopped dead in his tracks and looked ahead.

"Is this something you knew about, what Vincent did to me that night?"

He looked away.

"So you did," I said. I suspected maybe Vincent had something to do with it, but I never thought Seth knew about it or – *OHM-IGOD* – that he was some sort of accomplice.

"Why didn't you tell me?" I asked, feeling tears beginning to well up in my eyes.

"I was going to tell you," he said. "It just never seemed like the right time. Besides, I was afraid of messing things up with us."

"So you just decided to keep it from me? To lie?" By now, the tears were streaming down my face. How could I be so naïve?

"What would have happened if I didn't get sick that night? What were they planning to do to me, Theo and Vincent?" Jesus, what kind of friends did Jonnie have?

"Nothing, nothing," he said. " ... I wouldn't have let them."

"Gee, that's noble of you," I said, walking into the street and raising my arm to hail a passing cab.

"Where are you going?" he called. "I thought we were going back to my place."

"117 Leonard Street," I told the taxi driver as I stepped into the car.

"Cat, wait," he said. "Don't you think you're overreacting? It's not that big of a deal."

"Oh really? No big deal?" I asked. "So is this some sort of game you and your friends play? Let's see, Seth. Who are you planning to make your next victim?"

"It's not like that," he said.

"Is he coming or what, lady?" the driver yelled, growing impatient.

I looked back at Seth. He stood, motionless.

I wanted him to run up to the car, to say, I'm so sorry, Catherine, I never agreed with what those guys did, they're assholes who don't know how to treat girls. I didn't want to see you get hurt.

But he didn't. He didn't say anything. He just stood, frozen in his tracks, and watched the cab pull away.

# ✦ 13 ✦

I moped around the house all Christmas break. Seth never came. He never called to say he wasn't coming. He never even called to set me straight. Part of me was still prepared to forgive and forget — if given the chance. I know, *pathetic.*

Rehashing the night over and over in my mind, I started to gloss over the bad parts. Like him showing up late, making me leave the party, the alcohol on his breath. I thought I missed him. My mother said I just missed "the idea of him," whatever that meant. She had been blabbering on all week about how reaching adulthood meant that one needed to stop messing around with what she called "experimentation" (i.e., the "bad" boys and start taking things seriously because the decisions we made now would impact our lives forever.

Of course, this was the last thing I needed to hear coming off of a quasi-relationship crisis, but I noticed now that I lived away, my mom tended to squeeze in her parental lectures any chance she got since she could no longer bestow her wisdom on a daily basis.

"You won't believe this, Catherine," my mother gasped, holding up a box of chocolates wrapped in a red velvet bow. "Look what your friend sent us!"

"Nice, Mom," I said, not really paying attention and slightly annoyed that she was interrupting my old-school *Jersey Shore* marathon (which, as a Jersey girl, I must say is not a true representation of how we roll. For example, I don't know anyone around here with 6-pack abs like "The Situation." Now, 6-*packs*? That's a different story.)

"He's such a thoughtful boy!" my mother said, pulling the bow off her package. "I told him Shane's candies in Philadelphia are my favorite. It would be nice if you called him to say thank you."

"What? What are you talking about?" I grumbled, pressing mute on the remote.

She raised her eyebrows and said in her snottiest voice, "Well, Miss Sunshine, I'm sure you don't let your boyfriends see this side of you. I *said* it would be nice if you called Benji to thank him for the chocolates."

"Benji sent those? Why?"

"What has gotten into you, young lady? Don't you listen to me anymore?" She walked over to the fridge, pulling his number out from under a pile of papers shoved beneath a magnet. "Call him and thank him," she said, placing her phone in my hand.

I threw the phone down on the couch, stomped up to my room, reminding her that just because I'm home now doesn't mean that she could give me orders anymore since, after all, legally I was an adult. And then I quietly pulled out my cellphone to call Benji.

He answered on the second ring.

"So," I said, sans identification, "Are you trying to bribe my parents with chocolates so that I'll go out with you again?"

Of course, I was only half-joking.

"Is it working?" he asked. Always ready with a comeback, this one.

"If you want a date with my mom, it is."

He laughed. "Well, then I'll stop."

"Seriously, Benji, thanks for sending the gift, but it was totally unnecessary."

"It got you to call me, didn't it?"

We chatted for a bit — it was actually kinda nice how we could just pick up where we left off, no questions asked. I told him about my trip to Aruba (minus the restaurant ordeal), a little about what's been going on up in New York (minus the Seth ordeal), and about how Christmas dinner was ruined by Aunt Diana announcing at the end of the night that she was leaving her husband for a younger man (hey, maybe she does still have it!). Benji asked me to recite the entire story in painful detail. He loved the family-related gossip, and it seemed to me he'd gotten over his weirdness since the last time we spoke. That was a bit of a relief.

A few minutes later I went back downstairs. My mother, who had evidently been eavesdropping at the foot of the stairs, said, "Well, did he ask you out again?"

"No."

I smiled, just to rub it in.

"Oh," she said, her face falling.

"But he did offer to drive me up to Brooklyn this weekend, so I don't have to lug my stuff on the train."

"What a gentleman!" She clasped her hands. My phone buzzed, and she squealed once again. "Maybe it's him! Maybe it's him!"

For better or for worse, it wasn't. It was the phone call I'd been waiting for — for exactly 7 days, 12 hours, 32 minutes, and 16 seconds. But who's counting?

"Hey, babe," Seth's raspy voice crackled through the phone. In an instant, my knees got weak, my pulse accelerated, my palms began to sweat, my mouth got dry, and I couldn't think of anything smart to say. He said he was sorry he hadn't called for a few days (over a week to be exact). He said he had gotten caught up with "helping his dad" (heard that excuse twice now). He hoped I'd had a nice Christmas with my family (how *dare* he!). Then he told me he was having a New Year's Eve party. Would I come?

There was no apology, no talk of the argument, or the patch, or why he decided not to visit me. At that moment, any girl with half a brain, any girl who knew how to handle a boy and put him in his place, would have said, "Sorry, Seth. Can't make it." *Period.*

But I wasn't that girl.

"What time?"

It was like my tongue was following instructions from a source other than my brain and before I could right the wrong, I was hanging up the phone, feeling all warm and tingly and flushed with the ripe sense of blooming love.

He had said, "I can't wait to see you."

I can't wait to see you.

*I-can't-wait-to-see-you* [thump–thump] *i-can't-wait-to-see-you* [thump–thump]. *I-can't-wait-to-see-you* [thump–thump] *I-can't-wait-to-see-you.*

The allure of Dove soap and sweat and that musky scent that was Seth seeped into my pores, floated into my brain, and fogged my inhibitions. I tried to remember the exact expression on his face the times he had leaned in to kiss me, and I relived the moments over and over.

"But what about *Benji?*" my mother whined the next morning.

"What about him?" I said, hurrying to pack my stuff so that I would be ready when he came.

"Well, have you forgotten that you're seeing him?"

"He's just driving me up," I said, pulling out a few dresses from my closet and trying to figure out which look would be appropriate for New Year's. "What's the big deal? He'll be gone by then, anyway."

"That's not very nice, Catherine, using him like that."

"Mom, it's not *using* him. That's such an ugly word." I was just taking him up on his offer, taking advantage of his *services,* if you will. His car. Well, maybe it was using him. But the point was he wanted to see me. What's the harm in working out an arrangement for mutual benefit?

"I hope you know what you're doing, Catherine," my mother said, sitting on the bed and fidgeting with her watch as I brushed my hair in the mirror. "This Seth boy didn't treat you very nicely over Christmas. And, now, it sounds like he's expecting far more from you than just an appearance at a party."

"Oh, god, Mom, seriously. You have got to stop!"

"A man doesn't just invite you to his home, till all hours of the morning, and not expect something."

"It's New Year's Eve!"

"I just think that he's going to want something."

"He's not like that, Mom."

"Catherine," she said, coming up behind me, placing her hands on my shoulders and staring back at me in the glass, her features softer than I remembered, her hair now streaked with gray, "All men are like that."

Benji didn't say much about the 'Burg. I was expecting the usual right-wing remarks, like my dad's ("You should carry a gun!"), but he kept any comments to himself and dutifully helped me drag my luggage up four flights of stairs once we got to Leonard Street.

As I puttered around the apartment, unpacking while he watched Monday Night Football and munched on Doritos, things felt strangely simpatico. It was as if we had known each other for years.

"Remember to take your mother's leftovers out of the cooler and put them in the fridge," he said, as he lifted his feet while I tried out the new Swiffer I'd gotten for Christmas.

"Thanks," I said.

"And the laundry, your mother said your shirts will get wrinkled otherwise…"

"Yessss, dear," I said, with a saccharine smile.

I heard my phone ringing from the other room, and I walked into the bedroom to answer it. But when I heard the ringtone (Jonnie's clever recording of, "Pick up the damn phone, bitch! It's your man!"), my heart stopped. I sprang onto the bed to answer it but it had already gone through to voicemail. Worried about calling back too soon (and appearing a bit too desperate), I listened to Seth's message. He sounded all groggy and sleepy, like he had just woken up, and was whispering into the phone.

"Hey, Cat," he said, my heart fluttering, "… you're a hard girl to reach. Just wanted to tell you I'm really happy you decided to come up on New Year's. Glad you're not mad at me. I would hate that."

Well, that sounded like an apology to me. Sort of.

"Glad we can get past dumb stuff," he went on.

Past? What are we past? Did we pass anything?

His voice got so low that I couldn't quite make out what he was saying, and as I strained to hear him the doorknob jiggled. I immediately pulled the phone away from my ear and shoved it under the pillow beneath me.

"Feel like getting a bite to eat?" Benji asked, poking his head in through the doorway.

"Sure … um, just give me a minute." I said, feeling my heart pound out of my chest. I really didn't want Benji to overhear Seth's voice. I mean Benji did know about Seth, so it wasn't like I was really hiding anything. But still, it just felt … weird.

We decided on dinner at an Indian restaurant in the East Village (my choice). Benji was interested in expanding his palate (my suggestion) and we figured New York was "better a place than any" (my words) to do that.

Inside the dining room, we navigated through a dizzying maze of beaded streamers and colored lights that hung from the ceiling. The walls were busily decorated with neon idols and gold-plated images of Ganesha and Vishnu.

At first, Benji didn't quite know what to do with the menu selections, but he finally settled on a tandoori chicken platter he referred to as "safe."

"Baby steps," I said.

While waiting for our meal, we watched a television in the corner of the room. There was a beautiful girl dancing on the screen. She was wearing a red sari with gold chandelier earrings and bangle bracelets that ran up to her elbows. She serenaded us from the hilltops until a waiter walked by, cutting her off before lighting candles on all the tables.

"That's it for Bollywood, I guess," Benji said.

"Bolly-what? What the heck's that?"

He shook his head, giving me one of his fatherly, know-it-all looks. "The Indian version of Hollywood. In Bombay, they have a huge movie industry."

"Guess you really paid attention in film class."

"Nah, I'm sort of a film buff, remember?" he said, picking up a piece of naan to dip in a spicy brown sauce.

"Oh, right, of course."

"And actually ... I'm working on a screenplay."

"A screenplay?" If I had a dollar for every time a guy tried to hook a girl with that line, we'd all be billionaires.

He looked up from his dish, "I know it sounds cliché, but it's true. I started writing it my freshman year, just for fun ... but, more and more these days I've been thinking about doing something with it."

"Like what?"

"I don't know, maybe going out to California to see if I could show it to some agents."

"Really? California?" I asked, scrunching up my nose.

"Hey, what's wrong with that? You moved to New York, didn't you?"

"No, that's cool, very cool." *Ballsy,* in fact, I thought. Very. "I just didn't expect it from you. Weren't you the one who said that doing those types of things was 'too risky'?"

"Well, you seem to be proving me wrong," he said, smiling. "Now aren't you?"

"When would you go, this summer after graduation?" I was intrigued.

"Yeah, I'm thinking about moving there for good, though. If I'm gonna do it, I should do it right."

"Moving? But what about teaching?"

"They need teachers out there, too," he said.

The thought of Benji moving all the way across the country made me very panicky. I mean, he was making this decision without even consulting me! Not that, I guess, he needed to.

"I don't see why you need to go all the way out there," I said. "There's plenty of agents right here, on the East Coast, in New York. And besides, the weather in California never changes. It would be a perpetual-"

"Paradise?" he said, looking out the window at the passersby who were bundled up to their eyeballs.

We finished our meal and set off toward Rockefeller Center. I had promised I'd take Benji to see the Christmas tree. That was part of our deal. He drove; I played tour guide. It was nice to go, since I had kind of wanted to go earlier in the month with Seth, thinking it would be all romantic, but then we, ahem, never actually got around to it.

New York looked like a ghost town. The city was so quiet; you could hear the wind whipping around the buildings. I put my arm through Benji's as we walked down the streets and breathed in the cool air — a fresh, crisp, wintry breeze that smelled like snow. As I took a few more sweet breaths, I thought I saw a light flickering in the distance.

"Did you see that?" Benji jerked, nearly jumping out of his clothes. "A shooting star!"

"No way! Not a chance."

"Oh, really, Miss Smarty-Pants? Don't believe me?" By the look on his face, I wasn't sure if he was joking or not. Maybe it was possible?

"Could it have been fireworks?"

"I don't think so. Didn't hear any noise ..." he said, smiling and still keeping me guessing. His cheeks were chapped, and the wisps that stuck out of his hat were blowing in the wind. In his Old Navy pea coat and red hat, he looked just like a character from a Charles Dickens' story, with messy hair and bright eyes.

I played along with this little game. "Well. What do you think that means?" I said, secretly hoping for him to say something sweet.

"It means good luck," he said.

"How do you know?"

"Cause there's our Uber," he said, raising his arm to signal to the only car driving down the deserted street.

At Rockefeller Center, we stood before the largest fire hazard in New York, marveling at its mammoth stature. Then we headed over to watch the ice skaters, making fun of those who were bold enough yet not quite talented enough to attempt axel jumps and other Olympic-style turns.

"Check out those two," Benji said. "Looks like she's got her sugar daddy."

He pointed to a raven-haired girl, about my age, with red lips and a cascade of curls down her back. She was paired with an older, equally handsome man. They looked like they stepped right out of the Burberry winter catalog, dressed in matching plaid scarves, hats and mufflers. The girl, wearing a flouncy skate skirt and tights, kicked her legs around the rink as the older man clapped with delight.

We watched them for a little bit, and Benji reached into his pocket for his glasses. A few minutes later, the pair skated over to the exit. Immediately, I heard a voice.

"Mr. Darling? Is that you?" It was the cute, little brunette.

Benji looked over at her, now with his glasses on. "Miss Rice? God, I didn't even recognize you out there."

Miss Who? What?

"This is my friend, Catherine," he said to her. "Catherine, Miss Rice, I mean Jessica. We're both student teaching this year at Simon Gratz High School."

"What a coincidence," I said. "Nice to meet you."

She was even cuter up close. Everything all tiny and perfect. She reminded me of those cheerleader types from high school, the petite girls with the big boobs, the 22-inch waist and the size 6 shoe. They all wore Tiffany bracelets and carried fake Louis Vuitton purses and leopard-covered cellphone cases. They snickered at you when you changed for gym class, talked over you when you raised your hand in class, and teased you if there was a boy nearby. True to her nature, little Miss Rice sized me up with a quick once-over, smiling curtly with a slight snarl of the upper lip, and then averted her eyes quickly, turning her attention back toward Benji. "Betcha didn't know I could skate like that!" she said, giving him a playful slap on the arm.

"Jessica's quite a talented athlete," the older man said. "She could've skated pro."

"Oh, Uncle Michael, stop it!" Miss Rice protested weakly. "This is my uncle Michael. He lives here in the city."

Guess we got the sugar daddy thing all wrong. But, judging by the artificial tan and perfectly manicured nails, it looked like Uncle Michael had a few sugar daddies of his own.

"Have you done much sightseeing?" Benji asked.

"Well, we went to mass at St. Patrick's yesterday," Miss Rice said, placing her white-mitted hand over her tiny Christmas angel heart. "And, as a devout Catholic — just like you, Benji — I just have to say, it was *ah-maz-ing*."

How dare Little Miss Muffet pull out the heavy artillery right in front of me! For all she knows, we could be a couple!

"I'll have to check it out," Benji said.

"Next time," she said, "You'll come with us! Byeee!" And with that, Miss Rice reached up and planted a rosy, heart-shaped kiss on his cheek, nearly plowing me over with her razor-sharp skates on her way. Then she flitted off to the concession stands, like a sprite little Sugarplum fairy, garnering looks from admirers.

When she was gone, Benji and I exchanged glances. "She's very cute," I said. "Didn't know the teachers at your school were so ... beautiful."

"Oh, yeah, you should see the kids," he said. "The boys go crazy over her. She's got about a hundred 9th grade boys in love with her."

For some reason, I really wished he hadn't said that.

On the way home, we stopped in a cozy little pub off a side street. I wanted hot chocolate to warm me up; Benji ordered a Guinness.

"How about some hot buttered rum? That'll warm your insides," the waiter said through a thick Scottish accent. He was a bearded (and likely blind) old man who clearly couldn't tell that I was nowhere near old enough to drink. Or maybe in whatever time warp he came from someone my age was not only old enough to drink, but old enough to be married with children, too. He pointed to a chalkboard of specials. "Any of them there will do the trick, lassie."

I agreed to try the hot buttered rum, knowing that I would hate the taste but feeling that ordering it was quite right for the moment. We sat in a round leather nook in a corner of the bar that was facing a small crackling fire. The man who waited on us came back over and inserted a few more logs into the fireplace, filling the room with a golden, buttery glow, the fire warming our fingers and toes. Benji and I scooted next to each other so that we could get a good view of the fire.

"This looks like the place where we met," he said.

I glanced around. It was a similar-type Irish pub but had more of a seedy edge to it. A few older men sat slumped the bar, their faces in their drinks. In the background, there was the familiar sound of Bing Crosby coming through one of those old vinyl record players. Every once in a while, it skipped.

"You agree?" Benji asked, picking up his beer and gulping it down.

I looked over at him. There was a froth mustache lining his upper lip. "Don't know how to tell you this, but you have beer foam all over your mouth!"

"Yeah, I know," Benji said, looking at me with a goofy grin. "I'm saving it for later."

I laughed so loud that the half-dead men at the counter turned in our direction.

"So remember how we met that night?" he continued.

"Yeah, you came over to talk to my friends," I said. My drink cooled and I took a sip. It felt like fire running down my throat and into my belly.

"Oh no, no, Missy. You're forgetting the part before that — when you were *stalking* me," he said.

"Stalking you? What are you talking about?" I said. Guess it was shamelessly obvious.

"Oh, come on, Catherine. Don't be embarrassed. I can't say I blame you," he said, blowing on his fingernails and polishing them on his shirt. "I am devastatingly handsome, if I do say so myself."

"At least someone does."

Of course he was joking. But Benji said it with a bit *too* much confidence. And part of me wondered if maybe, just maybe, Benji's whole Clark Kent thing was just an act to get girls. After all, he was cute, confident, and comfortable in a crowd. He told me that he never had many girlfriends, but — after meeting Ms. Rice — I wondered how many *other* girls were throwing themselves at him.

The waiter brought me another drink. By now, I'd lost count of how many I'd really had (if you add in the gulps of Benji's beer). I drank it quickly and cut Benji off in the middle of a story: "You're way more sure of yourself than you let on, aren't you?"

He gave me a weird look. "Where'd that come from?"

"I bet you've never had problems meeting girls. I can tell. It's all an act, your 'aw-shucks' persona."

"What makes you think that?"

"Any man who is as confident as you just can't have problems." He laughed.

It made me angry that everything seemed to come so easy for him. His confidence, his career, he knew what he wanted. I could see it now, flash-forward 15 years: beautiful wife, two charming children, white picket fence, dog in the front yard. It was what he wanted. I could tell. He wanted the American Dream.

*And why didn't I?*

"Well, what about you, young lady?" he said.

"What about me?" I asked defensively.

"You seem to be doing very well for yourself, with a big-shot music producer or whatever ..."

"Music producer's *son*," I corrected him, taking a sip of my drink. I had switched to coffee to keep from sliding off my chair.

"Let's just say, Catherine, I don't always get what I want. I didn't get you, did I?"

Had I stayed silent, I am sure that more, much more, would have come from his lips, but I stopped him. "The alcohol's going to your brain. Let's get outta here," I said. "It's late."

We teetered out of the bar and headed south, hopping up and

down and singing theme songs from TV Land shows, like *The Brady Bunch* and *The Partridge Family*, just to stay warm. Benji attempted to amuse me with lopsided handstands in the blistering cold. We walked so far that we reached the Williamsburg Bridge.

"Guess we better get an Uber now," he said as we looked out over the bridge that connected Manhattan to Brooklyn. "We'll never make it on foot."

But before we could, we found a cab crawling down the street with its light off. Benji made enough noise to get the driver's attention. I slid into the cab while he stood outside, gazing onto the East River. He slid in next to me, with a weird look on his face. "You won't believe this, but I think I just saw another shooting star."

"You're right, I don't believe you," I said. "Two in one night is an impossibility."

He ignored me, slid back into the seat of the cab and lay his head back as we headed toward the bridge. The New York skyline shone in the distance. "Two in one night, a miracle," Benji said. "The perfect ending to my *annus mirabilis.*"

He loved using those 50-cent, English-teachery words. Usually, it involved a vocab lesson, but this time I knew what it meant, having taken Latin in high school. *Annus* meant year, *mirabilis* meant miraculous. A miraculous year.

"And why has this been a miraculous year for you?" I said, laying my head down on the seat next to his. "Because you started teaching? Because you're graduating from college?"

"You don't know?" he said, closing his eyes and reaching for my hand. "It's because of you, Catherine ... because I met you."

We crossed the over the bridge.

# ✦ 14 ✦

The next morning, I could feel his eyes on me, watching my every move.

We slept in separate rooms, Benji on the daybed, me in the bedroom. It was safer that way. It prevented me from allowing anything to happen that I might regret. Lying there at daybreak, I heard a loud clang in the other room. Dismissing it for the noisy radiator, I turned over and fell back to sleep but was awakened about an hour later. This time, it was the smell. Breakfast was cooking, a rarity in my apartment.

I crawled out of bed and cracked the door open. The music was on. It looked like Benji had been up for hours.

"Hello?" I called out.

"Oh, you're up?" he said. "I was hoping to surprise you with breakfast in bed. I make a mean Southwestern omelet."

"You don't have to do that," I said, walking into the kitchen and pulling myself up onto the counter. "I just drink green tea in the morning."

There was a grocery bag lying on the table. He had been out to get bacon, eggs, tomatoes, peppers, cheese, and orange juice.

"You need more than that to get your motor going," he said. I watched him as he stood over the griddle, staring at his creations with pride. He reminded me of my dad when he would cook pancakes on Sunday mornings before we went to church. My mother and I always had to make a big fuss over whatever he made. I started to think what a good husband and father Benji would make one day ... for someone else. It made me happy, but sad, too, like I was missing out on something.

"Guess I'll have a little," I said. "Thanks."

My phone rang. We could hear Jonnie's gansta-fabulous voice announcing who it was — loud and clear — but Benji didn't seem to find it all that amusing. Though it killed me, I let the call go to voicemail. Benji looked up at me, but I avoided his eyes while nervously beating my heels against the kitchen cabinets.

"Catherine, I meant what I said last night," Benji said.

I turned toward the window, knowing this conversation would come but dreading it nonetheless. "You were drinking," I said. "People say weird things when they're drinking."

"I wasn't drunk. I was completely sober."

"Benji, we talked about this, remember? About how we were just having fun last summer ... nothing too serious." I'd said this when I started feeling nervous about things progressing with us. I liked Benji but thought that maybe we were better off being just friends. With me wanting to go to New York and him being away at school, I just didn't see us going in the same direction.

"Catherine, that was your idea. Not mine. I just agreed with you, because, at the time, I didn't want to lose you completely."

He said he still had feelings for me, that he never stopped liking me after we stopped dating. When I moved to New York, he'd thought about calling several times but stopped himself because he didn't want it to seem like he was pulling me back from my new life. Then he said that he didn't know how long he could go on with the whole "friends" thing.

While he spoke, I looked out the window, watching a pigeon on the roof of the building below, trying to build a nest out of cardboard box scraps and newspaper. Everything kept blowing away, but the bird still continued to try anyway. I turned back to him, irritated and embarrassed by this sudden show of emotion.

"Benji, you and me, we want different things. Not everyone has everything figured out like you do. I want time — time to figure out who I am, and who I want to be. That's what I'm doing here right now."

"But do you know what you're getting involved with in this modeling scene?" he said, looking at me, his eyes wide. "Do you realize the track record of these people? They're not like you and me."

The audacity of him to *suppose* to know me to *suppose* to know the secrets of my heart. This is what drew me to Seth. The fact that he didn't know, that he didn't have all the answers. If I stayed with Benji, if I married someone like him one day, I was destined to become my mother. I was destined to live a safe yet uneventful life. This scared me more than fending off any creepy old man, more than battling any bitchy queen bee, more than anything else in the entire in the world.

I looked at him, keeping my voice calm. "I'm sorry, Benji, but I think you've gotten the wrong impression these last few days. I am dating someone right now, someone who I share ... a connection with."

He looked at me, incredulous. "So you deny any feelings for me?"

There was a sound at the front door, and suddenly Jonnie burst into the room. "Sorry," she said. "Doorknob's jammed again."

She walked in and put her suitcases and bags down on the floor, eyeing Benji with a curious side-glance. "So, you must be Benji," she said. "I'm Jonnie."

"Hi ..." he said, trying to appear relaxed, but failing miserably.

"Enjoying New York?" she continued.

The silence was deafening.

"It's fine. Just, ah, fine," Benji said, still distracted. I smiled halfheartedly and offered to help with her things.

"Can you just bring in that garment bag in the hallway?" she said. "I got the cutest dress for Seth's New Year's party."

"Party?" Benji asked.

Oh shit. *Shit, Shit, Shit.* I was going to tell him. Honest I was.

"Yeah, he's having a battle of the bands at a loft in SoHo. Didn't Cat tell y-." She stopped herself, seeing the confusion on his face. "Oh. I'm sorry."

I had remembered telling Benji that maybe we could spend New Year's Eve together, in Times Square. But that was before Seth invited me to the party. In my haste, I had forgotten to tell

Benji about it. It would have been all right to tell him before, but now...

"Ah ... no. Catherine didn't tell me," Benji said, looking visibly upset. "Hey, listen. I'd better go. I've got a lot of papers to grade and lesson planning to do. School starts up again in a few days." He walked over to grab his things.

Jonnie took the hint and quickly escaped into the other room.

I jumped off the counter. "Wait. Please don't leave, Benji. I was going to tell you about the party this morning."

"Guess you've had your mind made up for a while," he said. "Sorry, Catherine. Wouldn't want to get in the way of your *con-nec-tion*."

"Oh, come on, don't be like that!" I said, following him toward the door. "Please stay."

"Guess you're right," he said, ignoring my plea. His face was flushed, red with embarrassment. "I don't know you. You're not the girl I met this summer. That girl was cool and kind and honest. She wouldn't have led me on. She wouldn't have used people."

He pivoted and quickly took off. I called after him, but it was no use. He was intent on leaving. I was left standing there, holding a plate in my hand.

Jonnie walked back into the kitchen. "I didn't mean to ... it just kinda ... slipped out."

I sighed, looking down at the omelet that still sizzled on the plate. It was almost a perfect circle. "It's OK," I said. "I should have told you not to mention it."

"Well, anyway," she went on, "You don't even like him, right? I mean, weren't you trying to get rid of him? Maybe now he'll stop *stalking* you."

It annoyed me how Jonnie could be so insensitive about other people's feelings. I didn't feel that way about Benji. But, to be honest, I didn't know how I felt. I still liked him, and didn't want to see him get hurt.

She reached over me to grab a pan that was in the sink, "Ugh – is this real bacon stuck to the side here? Gross! I'll never be able to use this pan again."

"He doesn't know you're a vegetarian," I snapped. "He was just trying to be ... *nice*."

As I spoke, a steady weight began to bear down on my chest, then a sharp pain pierced my side. I couldn't take a deep breath. It felt like someone was pressing down on me, trying to pin me to the floor. I felt angry: angry about what happened; angry about the things Benji had said; angry about Jonnie's careless remarks. What Benji said wasn't true. I hadn't changed. Inside, I was still the same old Catherine. The good girl. The nice girl.

# ✦ 15 ✦

Seth didn't take his eyes — or his hands — off me from the moment we entered the party. I came with Jonnie, who brought her flavor-of-the-month José. She was off Ian, off Eric, and now, over the past few weeks, infatuated (or as infatuated as a girl like Jonnie could be with someone other than herself) with a hotshot, thirtysomething restaurateur from Midtown. She called him "rebound boy" while she recovered from her long-overdue breakup with Ian, the sometimes boyfriend of two years with whom she finally called it quits after he shaved off his neon faux hawk and adopted an old-school Caesar cut. To Jonnie, this was catastrophic, not to mention the epitome of passé.

"Well, hellooo, sexy," Seth purred into my ear as I walked into the "apartment"— a large, expansive corner loft with floor-to-ceiling windows. A stage had been set up at one end of the room, with the city lights twinkling behind as backdrop.

"Wow ... pretty impressive," I said, giving him a kiss on the cheek. He looked better than I'd remembered. His hair was almost shoulder-length à la Harry Styles doing Mick Jagger (which, come on, what girl can resist?) and he wore a fitted Burberry dress shirt under a black velvet blazer that highlighted the definition in his lean arms. On the bottom, faded Diesel jeans, and the trademark sneaks with the orange laces. "This is your dad's place?"

"One of 'em, yeah. Pretty sweet, huh?" he said, lifting his eyebrows ever so slightly. "Has a spa, sauna, and two master bedrooms."

Interesting he should bring up "bedrooms." He took me by the arm and, as we mingled with guests, introduced me as his "girl," addressed me as "babe." His dad was much different than I had imagined, looking more like a wiry Woody Allen-type than the suave, imposing character Jonnie had made him out to be. His father told me that Seth described me as an old-fashioned girl and how he was glad to hear it. He hoped I'd be a good influence on his son. There was something in his eyes, his expression that looked weary. Broken, in a way.

But Seth, who chatted with some of his dad's friends, was completely in his element. It was like the quiet, unsure-of-himself boy that I'd known vanished and a confident, self-possessed charmer emerged. I must say, seeing this side of him was quite a turn-on...

"Amos, dude, great to see you," he said, as he extended his palm out to a man in dark sunglasses. Behind him stood a slim, willowy blonde who trailed his every step, like an extra appendage. As the man moved past us, Seth whispered to me that he'd just signed a multimillion-dollar record deal with Bad Boy Entertainment.

Before I could smile and say the dutiful "hello," the blond emerged from behind Amos and her platinum curls came into focus. My heart sank. It was Fiona.

"Katie?" she said, squinting her eyes in disbelief. "Ohmigod! Is that you? I can't believe it!"

"It's Cath-" I said, feeling my face flush. "Hello again, Fiona."

"What are you doing here?"

"That's just the question I was going to ask you," I said, gathering back some of my composure.

"Oh, Sethie and I," she said, looking over in his direction as he stood a few feet away, immersed in conversation, "go *waay* back ... our moms were friends. We used to get wasted together. Now he's my hookup when I'm in New York."

"Your hookup," I repeated, not quite following what exactly she meant.

She looked at me and a smile crept over her face. "You're kidding, right?" she said, giddy with delight. "You know, *hookup*. Oh, sorry, you don't know, do you? Shit. Please tell me you're joking!"

"I see you've met Fiona," Seth said, curling his arm around my waist from behind.

"We've met before." Unfortunately.

"Well, don't believe a word she says," he muttered, half-joking, before pulling me into the hallway, away from the crowd. "She's all talk."

We spent the next hour talking to people Seth knew from his father's music business, mostly older than us, sampling the yummy Spanish and Greek tapas that were set up in stations around the room, and dancing when the band played a set. It was fun. I sorta felt special being that my *boyfriend* (could I really call him that?) was the host of this amazing party. Like cosmopolitan royalty or something. If my high school friends could see me now!

We took a break from the dance floor and sat down on small leather ottomans, watching the crowd. Seth leaned in to me, close enough to nibble at my ear, I pushed him away, playfully, embarrassed that his dad might see us. Jonnie threw me a look from across the room, a pleasing, "atta girl" glance. It was definitely in her best interest for us to keep hanging out with Seth, as it was "good for our careers" to travel in such circles, she said. She'd been doing this for nearly half her life, so if anyone knew how to make this modeling thing work, it was Jonnie.

In fact, when I thought about it, Jonnie had been playing the game for so long I don't think she knew how to do anything else. I watched her as she fell all over José — a fool who'd given her carte blanche to eat for free in any of his trendy restaurants whenever she felt like it — and it began to annoy me. How stupid men become in front of attractive women. How like Jonnie to ooze with sticky-sweet nectar — so automatic, as if she was following a script — whenever the situation suited her. More and more, I found I could not bear to be near her when she turned on the charm.

"Follow me," Seth said, pulling me toward him and down a dimly lit hallway and into one of the bedrooms.

"What are we doing?" I giggled, slightly flattered by the idea of him wanting me all to himself, when there were so many other, more important people in the room.

"I can't wait to be alone with you," he said, turning to face me. The room was dark, but I could see his features by the hallway light that shone through the doorway. I reached up to touch his face, the scar on the side of his cheek felt rough and more pronounced.

As he neared me, I closed my eyes and he pressed his lips to mine. I wanted him. I wanted to feel his body on me, to feel the heat of his breath on my neck. He touched me, and my senses heightened. Every word he spoke, every move he made, electrified something within me. But after only a few minutes of kissing, we heard footsteps in the hallway, then nothing. It was like somebody had stopped and was listening for us on the other side of the door. I stood silent for a moment, then pulled away. "I don't think we should do this now," I said, pointing toward the door. "It's early. People are still arriving."

"They're fine," he said. "Relaaax."

In the dark, we stumbled over to the bed, I felt his hands reaching down to places they had never gone before. The music and the murmur from the crowd became louder, and a few people ran down the corridor shouting. I started to worry that his dad might barge in on us. A bottle crashed in the hallway. A guy burst into our room, then fell down laughing. "Oops, wrong door!" he yelled.

Seth continued to run his hands along my skin, oblivious of the chaos around us. His breath became shallow, quicker. He pressed himself against me, pushing down on me as if he was ready to take things further. "Please, Cat," he said, his breath shallow, "Don't make me wait any longer."

He pulled my dress up, reaching his hand down to pull off my underwear. But I stopped him: "No, not here," I said, my heart suddenly beating out of my chest for fear that my first time would be casually at a party, instead of how I imagined it: with candles and kisses and words of love.

"Can't we wait till later? When people leave?" I asked, pulling his hand away. But it was like he in a trance, not hearing me, and bore down harder, stronger, on top of me.

"God, you are sooo *sexy*," he said. His kisses became forceful, and I felt like he'd eat me up at any moment. He began to push me around the bed, forcing me into contorted positions, sucking so hard on my lower lip that I tasted the cold, salty tang of blood.

"Seth, please," I said, trying to pull away and beginning to get scared that he wouldn't slow down. "Seth-"

"Don't be such a tease, babe," he said, pulling me back, and touching me with a gentler hand.

*Am I a tease?* Because I don't want to have sex with him while people are barging in on us? I looked over at the alarm clock. It was not yet 11 o'clock. My mother was right, he would expect something. And sooner than I had ever anticipated.

I managed to get some tread and slide out from under him, stepping away from the bed.

"What are you doing?" he asked, startled.

"I told you, I don't feel right about this. Not now," I said. "Let's go back to the party, *please.*"

"That's not cool," he said, standing up to adjust his, ah, man parts. I reached out for his hand, trying to convince myself that everything would be all right. It would be OK. "Seth, please don't be mad at me," I said.

"I'll be outside," he said, brushing past me, nearly knocking me over as he moved toward the door and shut it, leaving me there with my bra strap torn, my underwear around my knees, my dress in my hands.

"Trust me, you'll never get a piece of that." It was a girl's voice. "She's frigid."

"Shut up, Fi."

Fiona and Seth were on the other side of the door, out in the hallway. I heard them talking through a vent in the bathroom where I was raking through my hair with my fingers, trying to get myself to a presentable state.

"Trust me on this one," she continued. "I've seen her in action, or rather, I've *never* seen her in action!" Her cackle pierced through the wall, ringing in my ears. God, how I wanted to slap her!

"Quit it," Seth said, sounding like he was taking off, walking further down the hall. At least he was coming to my defense.

"Fine, have it your way," she called. "But I still don't know what you see in her. And she doesn't look *anything* like your mother. Your mother was beautiful. This one can barely hold a candle to her. Trust me, Seth, that girl's not good enough for you."

Hot, salty tears slid down my cheeks. They fell into the groove between my lips, then, one by one, over my chin. The words, her words, were those I'd heard a thousand times before on every playground of my life. Not good enough. Not popular enough, not pretty enough, not cool enough. For once in my life, I thought I'd gotten to a place where only I knew that. A place where I could reinvent myself to become anything, anyone, if only I could break free of my own fears.

Footsteps approached, and I heard his voice. "Cat? You still in there?" Seth said. "What's the holdup?"

"Coming," I said, zipping up my dress.

Maybe she was right. Maybe I was *frigid* ... maybe I'd been stingy with my affection because I was scared. Scared of doing something that might not be the most "responsible" thing. Scared of doing something that would mean that ... I'm not a little girl anymore. And that's the moment I decided, right then and there — fueled by anger, fueled by adrenaline — that I would give myself to him. That I would go through with it; that I would break out of myself.

"Be right there," I said, wiping away the tears, reapplying my lipstick and putting on the happiest face I could muster.

"Hey," I said, when I walked back into the bedroom.

We faced each other in the white, unforgiving light coming out from the bathroom.

"Have you been crying?" he said, I could sense the irritation in his voice. "Your eyes are all puffy."

"No, I'm fine," I lied. "Listen, I'm sorry for what happened ... guess I overreacted. I was being immature. But I think I could make it up to you."

He looked at me like he wasn't quite following, or believing, the words that were coming out of my mouth. Neither could I.

I leaned into kiss him, hoping that maybe this would make everything right again between us. Maybe it could be like it was before, before Christmas. Before now.

I wasn't scared anymore, and, in fact, it was like someone other than myself took over my body and I became a passive observer, watching us from some vantage point above the room. I took his hand and led him back onto the bed. He didn't resist, in fact, he came on as strong as before and there was nothing left for me to do but just let it happen.

It hurt, a lot. In the dark, I couldn't see his penis — that thing that I had yet to ever really see on a guy. The thing that (to be honest) scared me the most, because it was so foreign. So alien. I managed to see a dark shadow that felt velvety smooth to the touch. Then, without so much as a warning, there was a dull stabbing of my insides, and a determination to push through.

I turned away from him so that he couldn't see the pain in my face. He asked if everything was OK, if I was enjoying it. I lied and told him it was fine. Good, even. But in truth it felt like someone trying to split me in half. I opened my eyes, and tried to focus on his face, on the part of him that I found beautiful. But in the dark, he looked like a completely different person. His dark features morphed into all sorts of strange faces, his deep panting almost a groan that sounded primal, and a hard look of concentration that seemed like he was looking through me, beyond me. Like I wasn't even there.

*Was this it? What everyone was talking about? This is S-E-X!?!* I think I sort of expected something magical to happen, like angels to be playing on harps and our souls to fuse together in one transcendent moment. But it didn't quite happen that way.

"You were wonderful, babe," he said, slowly pulling off the condom when he was done. "Let's go. Everyone will be wondering where we are."

I wanted to lie in his arms, to be held and told that I was loved, but we had to get back, he said. And it made me feel empty. Strange how something that was supposed to make us feel closer, feel more connected, only made me feel even further apart from him.

From an open window, a draft blew through the room and sent a shiver down my legs. Outside, in the streets, people were chanting, counting down the seconds left till midnight.

"It's gotten cold," I said, covering myself with the sheet, suddenly feeling self-conscious about my body. "Do you have a sweater I could borrow?"

"Top shelf, closet," he answered.

I reached up to a pile of clothes and carelessly pulled down a sweater. As I did, I saw Seth hesitate and turn back toward me. "Shit," he said, under his breath. "I'll get it," he called, anxiously moving toward me.

But it was too late. The entire stack of clothes fell to the floor, and among them was a black canvas bag, the contents of which spilled out onto the rug. There were unlabeled prescription bottles, plastic bags filled with weed, and, perhaps most horrifying of all, a pack of foamy-looking stickers wrapped in a rubber band. They had cartoon characters on them, familiar-looking fat men.

"What's this?" I shrieked. *Please let there be a reason for this. An acceptable explanation for this.*

"Fuck, man," he said. "I was trying to get rid of that stuff."

"What are you talking about?" I asked, looking down at hundreds of pills and bags of marijuana strewn about the floor. *Good god.* "Is this yours?"

He stood silent, averting his eyes. The band began to play in the foreground. "Nah, not really..." he smirked, hardly convincingly.

Suddenly, it all began to come together for me: The missed appointments, the late nights when he was supposed to call and didn't. The time at the Christmas party when I thought he'd been drinking or high on something ... Fiona's "hookup."

"Let me guess: holding it for a friend?" I said. "How naive do you think I am?"

"Oh, come on ..." he said, his voice trailing off.

"You said that you were done with this stuff — that it was

all in the past," I said, still not quite believing what was really happening. I mean, weren't things supposed to be *wonderful* now — after what we just did? Weren't we supposed to be floating around in a state of unparalleled bliss?

"Seth, I've never had sex before. You were my ... first."

"... Sorry things went down like this," he said.

"That's it? Sorry? That's all? You don't care — you don't care that you lied to me about practically everything? About who you are? How am I supposed to trust you after this?"

He sat down in the bed, shoulders slumped. "I tried to change for you ... for us. And I did, for a while. But it's hard, Cat. That's just not who I am."

*Just not who I am.*

The music raged in the other room. A fire raged in my head. I'd been played — the patch, Seth's dealings, his clean persona, everything was a lie. And now, I'd given myself to him. I'd given him the one thing he could never give back. My virginity. I suddenly began to feel nauseated, realizing the gravity of my choice.

"So you're just a poseur, a fake," I said, feeling like a fool for believing him, for who I thought he was ... or could be.

He didn't say anything, and just sort of squirmed around, like an animal in a trap.

I picked up my shoes.

"Where are you going?" he asked, standing up.

"Home," I said, walking toward the door, but stopping abruptly to scoop up the stickers off the floor.

"Oh, come on, Cat. Don't be such a drama queen," he said. "The party's just beginning."

"Sorry, Seth," I said, walking over to the open window, "I'm leaving because, to be honest, *this* is not who *I* am."

And with one simple toss, I threw the patches into the night sky as the band began to play "Auld Lang Syne."

# ✦ 16 ✦

The jet lifted off the tarmac at JFK. I closed my eyes and dug my nails into the felt armrest. The next 20 seconds were the absolute worst part of the flight: up, down, up, down. My stomach rocked from side to side, not sure if I would surprise the person sitting next to me by lurching for the white paper bag nestled snugly in the seat pocket in front of me.

The airplane willfully climbed higher, straining like a baby bird that had just jumped from a tree branch. I held my breath, as if to will this fledgling up to a higher altitude. A few more seconds, some harrowing bumps of turbulence, and we made it onto autopilot. The woman behind me clapped her hands, and I opened my eyes and looked out on a sea-blue sky swirled with white wispy clouds.

*Breathe, Catherine.*

The last few weeks had left me in a perpetual state of anxiety. My chest ached. My stomach churned. My temples throbbed. When the phone rang, my heart thumped. In the middle of the night, I would wake and feel as if someone's hands were wrapped around my throat, cutting off the oxygen to my lungs. Every thought raced through my head, over and over, like a bad song on constant repeat. I started to question everything I did, feeling less and less sure of myself. Sleeping with Seth had turned out to be, quite possibly, the *worst* mistake of my life. If I had been wrong about him, what else could I be wrong about?

"Now when you're in Italy, stay out of the sun," Clive said

the week before my trip. "You're as fair as they come, and I can't have you looking like a lobster like you did when you came back from Aruba."

"It was sun poisoning," I said. "Remember, that dermatologist you sent me to gave me that sunblock that expired?"

"Sweetheart, I don't care what it was," he said, looking up from a magazine. "I can't have one of my top girls running around like a leper."

I rolled my eyes and looked out the window, wondering for a second what it would feel like to fall those 30 stories.

"And thank god you got rid of what's-his-name," he said, reaching for a doughnut from the Krispy Kreme box that sat on his desk. "I don't care if he is Remi Fosgate's son. I was sick of seeing him, always looking so unkempt."

My heart retracted at the mention of Seth. It felt like Clive had reached over and pulled back the scab that had begun to form over that open wound. It had been exactly two-and-a-half weeks since I called it quits.

"Are we finished yet?" I asked, nonchalantly reaching in for a Boston crème, my weakness.

"*Excusé moi?*" he said, batting my hand away.

"It's just … I have an appointment," I said, feeling chastened.

"Missy, you're done when I say you're done," he said, staring down his nose at me through turquoise cat-eye frames. "And as for your boyfriend, well, you did the right thing."

"How would you know?" I said, beginning to lose my patience with him.

"Because, I told you it's good for business. You're too young to be entangled with someone. We need you out *there*."

I didn't know the reach of Clive's influence now spread into my personal life. Not only was he telling me what jobs to take, but now he was telling me who I should and shouldn't date.

"Before you go," he said, opening a drawer and digging down into its depths, "Take these." He tossed a bottle of tablets in my direction. "They relieve water-weight gain."

"Diet pills?" I asked in disbelief.

"Yes, diet pills! Oh, my god! Call the police!" he said, mocking me. "He's giving her diet pills!"

"No, it's just ... I don't think I need them."

"What are you these days? One-thirty-four? One-thirty-five? Have you seen the Italian girls?" Clive said. "An-o-rex-ic."

"Yes, but ..."

"No buts. Take them," he said, dismissing me with a wave of his hand. "Now skedaddle, and get to bed early this week. You want to be fresh for Milan."

Later that night after stepping out of the shower, I couldn't resist getting on the scale. It was an old, clunky contraption that Jonnie had brought from home. She said it often didn't even work (or, when it did, it generously "under-reported"), so I wasn't sure if I could trust it. But at this point, it was all I had. I dropped the towel, held my breath, and tried to step as lightly as possible.

It read: *139 lbs.*

Now, any normal girl who was 6 feet tall would be more than content with that number. But I was not a normal girl. I was not expected to be a normal girl or even look like a normal girl. I stepped off the scale, trying not to panic, picked the thing up, shook it a few times, and then placed it back on the ground.

*Take two.*

But before my big toe touched the scale, I decided it would be best if I emptied my bladder. That would shave off, say, half a pound? (I remember learning in freshman earth science that fluids were actually quite dense! After peeing, I walked back over to the scale, and started to freak. *What if it was right? OMG. What if it was grossly underestimating!?! How could this happen?* Thinking back to Christmas break, I realized that I did inhale quite a few bags of taco chips (my salty weakness while binge-watching Hallmark specials round-the-clock and pining for Seth to call. But, honestly, my diet had never been a problem before. Once again, I opened my eyes and looked down at the scale. Still a stubborn 139 lbs.

"Oh, that began happening to me when I was about your age," Jonnie said later that night, as she sat on the bed and scrolled through her phone while I packed for my trip. "Your body changes every few years, your metabolism slows, and, well, it needs a little help."

"Help? Like, as in ...." I held up the bottle of pills Clive had given me earlier that day.

She looked at me with a little smirk. "You've officially been inducted into the club."

"So you use these things!?!" I gasped. "But aren't they bad for you? Aren't they dangerous?"

"I don't know if they're dangerous or not ... I guess some girls do get sick on them, but I never do. Besides, they work. And that, my dear, means *you* work."

I looked at Jonnie as she crouched over the phone, her tiny vertebrae sticking out one by one, and realized that I, in fact, had a bit more meat on my bones. I packed the pills, knowing that it wasn't right, and it wasn't something I should be doing, but realizing (perhaps one bag of chips too late) that in this business, the normal rules didn't apply.

The doorbell at the models' residence in Milan sounded eerily like the one at my parents' house. Every time I heard it, I felt a little homesick. But it was far from the comforts of home.

Il Fiorellino was a crowded 18th century townhouse, a decaying structure with holes in the walls and a crumbling exterior. Four girls were assigned to one room; some of us slept on mattresses on the floor, while others slept in cots that looked like they were left over from the Second World War.

Our "housemothers" as they were called — Patrice and Maria Vitarelli — were supposedly in charge, making sure we were in by curfew each night and serving a sad-looking breakfast of day-old baguettes with lukewarm café con leche each morning.

For sisters, they were quite a pair. Patrice was a fortysomething Penélope Cruz lookalike who dressed in 4-inch heels and a miniskirt that showed off the legs of a 20-year-old. Maria was a bit frumpy and dressed like my old school librarian. She spoke very little but smiled enthusiastically, eyeing each of us who entered her establishment like a prize.

The first night, I was shown to my "room" - a 12-by-12 foot cell I shared with three other girls. A model from Belgium slept next to me. She stormed into our bedroom at around 2 a.m. the first night, crying hysterically. She had been out on what she called (in broken English) a "date dinner." I tried to understand what she was mumbling about, as she stumbled around the room in the dark. I reached for a light switch, but she screamed, "No!" Moments later, there was a knock at the door.

It was Maria. They spoke quickly in Italian; the Belgian girl able to speak Italian better than English. I was able to understand, with the little Italian I learned in high school, that she had gone out (or, from the sound of it, been *forced* to go out) with a friend of Maria's.

"*Mio buon amico!*" Maria repeated anxiously, over and over.

They said goodnight abruptly, and as I tried to fall back to sleep, I heard the girl's muffled cries in her pillow. I tried to console her, but she was beyond words, so I finally turned over and tried not to listen. But it was hard falling back to sleep. I thought about the next day's go-sees and started to think that maybe the emergency starvation diet I'd put myself on (Jonnie's instruction: cutting everything you're about to eat in halves, and then throwing one half away before you change your mind) wasn't working. In the dark, I inched over to my backpack, pulled out the pills (one in the morning, one at night, as instructed) and swallowed one with every bit of saliva I could muster.

The next morning, I awoke feeling slightly dizzy and assumed it was from being jetlagged. I remembered feeling the same way, years earlier, when I arrived in Ireland (the first and only other time I'd been to Europe) with my church youth group for a week.

At breakfast, I washed down my second pill with a bottle of water and a glass of juice, which seemed to help.

The Belgian girl sat down beside me at the table. On her

neck, I noticed purple welts (hickeys?) that she unsuccessfully tried to cover up with foundation. I wondered if she'd gotten them the night before. She smiled at me, while quietly stirring her espresso, and I guessed she'd gotten over whatever catastrophe had befallen her hours earlier.

Or maybe not. Because when I got back to our room hours later, her stuff was cleared out. The suitcases were gone and her cot was stripped. *Weird.*

Clive was right about the Italian models. Some looked like those skeletons that neighbors sometimes hung on their front doors or placed on porch rocking chairs around Halloween time. Only these skeletons were wearing clothes. And I wanted to be just like them.

My first casting call was in an old cathedral in the center of the city. The church — a dark, medieval-era structure that had once been an operating place of worship — was now used as a space for plays, art exhibits, and the like. As a cavernous, drafty old shell, its crumbling, candle-lit altars and dirty stained-glass windows cast shadows on the floors and walls that made you feel as if you were being followed by an unearthly presence. We could hear bats up in the rafters or pigeons, maybe, flapping around, which sent us ducking for cover each time we heard rustling overhead. It was the perfect space, it seemed, for the Tim Burtonesque, Goth-inspired fashion show that was being held there later that day.

At the start of the call, an unconventional announcement was made: "Mo-dels! Mo-dels!" the Italian casting agent called out in his strained way. "Put away the port-a-folios. This day, you would be judged on le misure. Your measurements."

*Um. Scusi?*

The collection, he said, is for the "very tiny." A few girls winced and we all looked at each other, dumbstruck, then quickly sized up the competition. I was definitely one of the taller girls. But I knew, I KNEW, judging by the skeletons around me that I was not the skinniest. Or close to it.

*SHIT. Shit, shit, shit.*

As I waited for the demoralizing task of being "weighed in," I started to feel anxious and fidgety, like I'd just drunk an entire case of Red Bull. This feeling had been coming and going all morning long, but now — with the situation at hand — it got worse. My heart raced, but it wasn't like a normal steady beating, more like an irregular thumping that came and went.

The girl in front of me in line seemed equally nervous. She already had that pale Goth thing going on — the dark under-eye circles, the black hair — and nervously paced from side to side. She began doing these bizarre repetitive movements: cracking her knuckles, rocking on her toes, clearing her throat over and over again.

"Shhh!" an Italian girl ahead of us, irritated by the bodily noises, snapped.

The girl glared back, revealing blood-shot eyes, and shouted, "Stronza!" Her pupils, wide as saucers, sat deep in their sunken sockets. Small beads of sweat dotted her forehead. This girl was not well. Not well at all.

"Well, you're scary enough for this show," a Brit girl said under her breath after Goth Girl's response.

"*Freeeak,*" another called out.

Goth Girl, at 5'10," weighed in at an emaciated 52 kilograms, which is about 113 lbs. I, on the other hand, weighed in at 63 kilograms. *Ouch.* I could have sworn the girls around me were looking on, secretly pleased, and I panicked. Losing out on a show like this at Fashion Week could be a career-ender, for sure — not to mention the hell I'd get from Clive.

Without much thought, or reason, I grabbed hold of the measurement sheet and — as the director stepped away for a smoke break — switched my measurements with Goth Girl's. Most of the girls had left the room so it was just me and another girl, who was thankfully distracted by her cellphone. Immediately, I started to feel guilty, but quickly convinced myself that I was doing myself, everyone else, and really, Goth Girl *herself,* a favor by getting her outta there. I mean, the girl was sick. She needed a doctor, not a new free pair of shoes.

The casting agents broke for lunch and told us to come back an hour later to see if we made the cut. I returned wearing my new pair of Spanx that I'd brought from home, which worked amazingly well to shave an inch or two off my middle and thigh area. I closed my eyes and held my breath as the names were read out, but before I could even start to feel sorry for myself, I heard "CAT!" ring out clear as a church bell in that drafty old sanctuary. Maybe God was on my side?

The thing about doing a show in this country, other than the fact that I could only understand like every third word that anyone was saying to me — yes, even with my trusty English-to-Italian app — was that everything moved at a much slower pace. We were kept at the venue for the entire afternoon waiting, if seemed for hours, to get our hair and makeup done. There was no sign of Goth Girl, and I guessed (slightly guiltily) that my little plan had worked.

Someone decided we should do a run-thru, sans designer duds, and I teetered down the runway on 4-inch platforms during a freakishly garish musical homage to Michael Jackson's "Thriller." How retro. Trying to stay in a straight line had become increasingly difficult for me as the day went on. Whether it was due to the jetlag, the combo of bread, water, juice, and my "secret helpers" (as Jonnie called them), or the fact that my lunch consisted of a croissant and espresso, I wasn't sure.

"CAT!" the director suddenly screamed as I returned to the beginning of the runway, his face twisted into knots with veins popping, and motioned for me to come talk to him. As I walked down the runway steps, I saw Goth Girl standing behind him, glaring at me through a tear-streaked face.

*HOLY MOTHER OF JESUS.*

She knew. She KNEW. *I am caught. I am soooo caught! I am going to get fired. And I'm going to hell for lying in a church!* (To be quite honest, I was more worried about what Goth Girl might do to me than anyone, or anything, else.)

I walked over and smiled, prepared to plead ignorance.

"Yes? ... um, Si?" I said.

"You need more — how you Americans say — vestuario, clothing?" he asked, in a thick accent.

"Um," I said, looking down at my street clothes and not quite following where he was going with this. I tried to eek out "I don't understand" in Italian ("non capisco"), but with my horrible accent, for all I knew I was ordering fries with that.

He shook his head, looking even more frustrated than before.

Goth Girl, who was still glaring at me from over his shoulder, softened a bit and stepped in with her own broken words: "He want you to model more looks. More sets," she pointed to a rack of clothes that had just been wheeled in.

"Oh, si, si!" I yelled, grabbing the extra outfit he handed me to put back on my rack.

*SAFE!* I was safe. I let out a sigh of relief. No one, not even Goth Girl, had a clue I'd forged my measurements. (And, thanks to my new best friend, Spanx, they might never know.) But I still wasn't sure why Goth Girl was making an appearance. And it made me nervous.

After I turned to go, she immediately launched into a tirade in Italian, holding up the tape measure that was used during the casting, and screaming at the director what I could only make out as "demanding a recount," if you will. He measured her a second time, and minutes later she was standing next to me in line for hair and makeup, clearing her throat over and over again. *Humph.*

The show started at 7pm. Church bells chimed, and spooky music piped through the organ. Helpers got us into our looks, which were like nothing I'd ever seen before, not even in avant-garde fashion magazines like *W*. They were more like costumes, or wearable art. Definitely not commercial or "ready to wear." My first look was a cross between a skintight spacesuit and a bumblebee, complete with bee-striped black and yellow glow-in-the-dark reflector patches, and a 2-foot long antenna headpiece. The second was a variation of that, only this time I was lowered down into a chocolate brown bee-striped funnel skirt, complete with a 5-foot train, that I was only able to move across the floor with 6-inch platform moonboots for extra height. In my hair was some sort of twig sculpture apparatus, with (faux) bats nesting inside, to make it look, one can only imagine, like a moving tree somewhere in Death Valley. Good thing I was on the other side of the world at this moment, otherwise I'd die if anyone I knew saw me like that!

As we paced up and down the runway, we were directed not to smile, arch our backs, or move in any traditionally "model-y" way – but rather slump-shouldered and stiff like zombies. As I walked into the candle-lit room, I could not see the crowd but saw the outline of heads against the stone walls. The stained-glass windows, which glowed from the streetlights outside, added to the ominous effect.

For the finale look, the girls were all paired up. Karma being the you-know-what that it is, guess who got stuck with Goth Girl? The other girls breathed a sigh of relief when they weren't placed with her. But, by this point, I didn't really mind. In fact, I sorta felt sorry for her. She kept to herself and, other than the insults hurled at her earlier in the day, no one said much of anything to her. She was the outcast and, in many ways, not unlike me in my former life.

Right before the finale, I felt around for her in the dark, trying to feel her furry bat-like moonsuit so we could line up.

"We go? We go?" I said when I felt her, trying to speak in the simplest English words I could find.

But she just looked at me with an empty stare.

"Now? We go, we go!" I repeated, pointing to the runway entrance.

Again, no response.

Ok. *What the heck?* She was totally coherent an hour ago, it had seemed.

Her wardrobe helpers were nowhere to be found. I was going to have to get this girl to the runway MYSELF. I took her hand

and led her out onto the platform. She was easy to pull along, since she weighed next to nothing.

"You're late! You're late!" the runway coordinator scolded in an irritated whisper. "I just sent the next girls down instead."

"Sorry!" I mouthed. "We're ready now ... I think," I whispered looking at Goth Girl, who was now doing her perfect zombie look for the runway.

We got the shoulder tap and, before I could begin to traipse down the long, wooden platform, Goth Girl stopped me.

"No," she said. "Can't do it."

"What?!" I panicked, suddenly feeling hot and breathless, and reaching down to feel her hand, which was holding something. "Yes, you can. You just did. Just go, it's easy. I'll be right there behind you."

She placed one foot in front of the other slowly and walked out. I tried to keep up behind her in my moonboots, a dead tree following a slow-moving moon-bat. *Oh, god. Oh, god, oh, god. Please let us get through this. Please let her make it down and back.*

As we neared the end of the runway, her gait became increasingly awkward and uneven. I reached out to steady her, but before she could utter a word, her whole body began to convulse, right then and there. Her breathing turned into loud, heavy gasps as she struggled for air, like she was having some sort of asthma attack. I froze, not quite sure what to do, waiting for someone to come to her rescue. But no one in the crowd did. Instead, CAMERAS FLASHED!

"Bravo! Bravo!" one person cried out, clapping.

*Did they just? Do they think? Oh, no. No, no, no!*

"Help! Help! I screamed at the top of my lungs, wrapping my arms around her. "Assist ...assistenza!"

Everything happened so quickly after this, like in a dream, that I wasn't sure of the sequence. A man from behind the runway area rushed, fell to the ground, and began to administer CPR. A mob of people from the crowd encircled us, and — standing there in that sacred space — some began to pray. And for a moment, I prayed. If I hadn't forced her down the runway, maybe she would still be all right.

The paramedics worked quickly. They placed her on a stretcher, with an oxygen mask over her face and a heart monitor attached to her chest. One of them mentioned something about cardiac arrest — or quite possibly, a heart attack — and a few of the girls around me started to cry. *I* started to cry. As the medics took her out of the church, I placed her things on the stretcher beside her feet, grabbing her wrist as it fell limply to the side, and held it. "I'm sorry," I whispered, and squeezed her hand. Curled up inside, I felt something hard. I uncurled it and a small blue bottle of pills fell out. When I picked them up off the ground, I recognized them right away — they were the same ones I'd been taking.

# ✦ 17 ✦

That first show in Milan was enough to permanently scare me off of medicine, pills, aspirin, Flintstones vitamins, coffee, or anything that might even hint at altering my biological state. After the runway show that evening, I proceeded to race home to the models' apartment, flush the entire bottle of poisonous pills down the toilet before sticking my finger down my throat (in true model fashion) and forcing myself to throw up whatever vile toxins remained in my system.

From now on, it was lean proteins, carrots, hummus, and celery for me, and of course my favorite Starbucks mochas. And, oh — of course — my trusty Spanx.

The next night I was invited to informal cocktails at our models' apartment, hosted by our housemothers as sort of a welcome event for newbies. On the way home from fittings — during which I managed to fly under the radar and escape with just minor injuries (a scratch here, a pinprick there) — I rode a shuttle bus back to Il Fiorellino and sat next to a New Yorker named Ashley, whom I'd met that morning. We gravitated toward each other after hearing a familiar accent and had been inseparable the entire afternoon.

Ashley was in the know. She had been present for the Goth Girl spectacle, and, rumor was, the girl (who had a name, it was Belladonna something-or-other) was recovering and out of the hospital. That helped me sleep a little better.

"Can you believe that freak?" Ashley went on. I put two-and-two together and quickly realized Ashley had been the girl who called Goth Girl a freak at the casting the day before. "She had a nasty diet pill habit. Who would get caught up with that shit?"

Clearly, Ashley hadn't been at this modeling thing long. She had just started modeling while pursuing acting in Los Angeles, and, it seemed, wasn't quite used to the way things went in this business. Her second violation: Not knowing that models were to be seen and not heard.

"They are smoking something if they think I'm gonna strut around in a thong," she said, complaining about one of her wardrobe changes on the ride home.

"It's a string bikini," I said, laughing at her histrionics. "Besides, it's what everyone wears around here. The beaches are practically all nude. It's perfectly normal in Europe!"

"Well, I told Donatella what's-her-name that there's no way she's getting that thing on me, hells no! Not in this universe!" She flipped her long, red ringlets over her shoulder and narrowed her translucent green eyes as she heaved a deep sigh. With this attitude, however noble, Ashley would not be long for *this* universe.

"What are they making, a peepshow or a fashion show?" she continued.

"Good point," I said, stopping to question whether, sometimes, there was really much of a difference.

We pulled the door open to the townhouse and were greeted by a scantily clad Patrice, holding a tray of hors d'oeuvres. The white cotton apron she was wearing barely covered her behind. Ashley turned to me, whispering, "And here's the star of the show!" and laughed.

"You are first to arrive!" Patrice gushed, as she lead us through the foyer into a candle-lit drawing room swathed in thick draperies, lined with fraying antique rugs, and adorned with dead animals on the wall. Ashley looked at me, "Was this the set for 'The Addams Family'?"

The doorbell rang and three old men arrived. We looked at

them in their tailored suits, slicked-back hair, and manicured hands and wondered which one was Patrice's boyfriend and which was Maria's. I wondered why they weren't already married for two women their age.

The front door slammed, and I heard the click-clack of pointy heels on tile. Two girls who were rooming upstairs entered, one saying she was too tired to stay and the other giving excuses as to why she couldn't attend. I felt kind of foolish, being one of the only girls who actually made it, but I knew accepting the invitation was the courteous thing to do. I sort of felt sorry for Patrice, offering to help her in the kitchen, but she refused, ushering me into the sitting room to sit with Ashley.

Two more girls came down to join the little soirée; they were from Brazil and had just arrived that afternoon. Maria put a record on an old-fashioned player and began to dance with one of the men. Patrice placed shots of homemade pear liquor on a table for each of us to try.

"*Alla vostra salute!*" she said. Each of us lifted the sweet liqueur to our lips. It tasted like candy. As soon as we placed our glasses down, Patrice filled them up again. Since the drinking age was 16 in Italy, it was nice to be able to drink in public without fear of getting caught.

Patrice took a seat next to me on the sofa, cupping a glass of wine. She curled her legs beneath her body and leaned her head on the pillow by my head. The record was playing traditional Italian music, and we watched as Maria and one of the men begin to dance a tango. I could see Patrice watching me from the corner of my eye. She leaned in, and I got a whiff of her perfume, felt the warmth of her body as she pressed against me, whispering in my ear, "Enjoying Milan?"

"Oh, yes, very much." I said. "It's so different from the U.S. Your oldest buildings are five times older than ours! And the landscaping is so beautiful."

"Beautiful, yes," she said, dangling an arm in the air, and gently placing a hand on my head.

OK, um, slightly creepy. But maybe she's just friendly?

"My child, what beautiful hair!" she exclaimed, lifting it up to smell a strand. "And so nice smelling."

I glanced over at Ashley, whose expression at that moment was one of horror. Her eyes bulged, and her face was wrinkled up as if to say, "What the f-?"

I managed to pull a little away from Patrice, and blurted, "Suave."

"Su-a-vé?" she repeated, sounding out the vowels.

"It's, ah … shampoo," I said, inching away. *Good lord, Catherine. Is this the first thing you can think of to say to get this woman away from you?* "For my hair."

Ashley was all ears. She leaned in from where she was sitting across the room, stifling a laugh. "Do tell, Cat. Do tell us of this Suave you speak of."

By now, every stranger in the room had caught on to our not-so-engaging conversation about discount American hair products. "It gives you salon-quality looks without the big price tag," I said, in a high-pitched voice, shaking my head and flipping my hair like the girls in the Suave commercials.

Ashley burst out laughing.

"I must get this Salve," Patrice said, in all seriousness, reaching out to touch my hair again. "Where can I get this wonderful Salve?"

"Suave," I corrected, rising to leave. "You can find it in fine grocery stores everywhere."

As I pulled away, Maria, who was now sitting on the other side of me, pressed her hand firmly down on my thigh. "Stay, stay. There's no rush, darling."

"Oh, I have to be going," I said, hoping to remove her claws from my leg.

"But you haven't yet gotten a chance to dance," she said, pointing to the men at the end of the room who had been giving the rest of the girls tango "lessons," which I later discovered involved grabbing every body part they could reach.

"We need to get to bed." Ashley said, coming to my rescue. "Gotta be up at 6."

"Yeah, big day tomorrow," I said, breaking free of Maria's grasp. "Thanks for the invite."

"Yeah, *thanks*," Ashley snickered, walking ahead. "Quite a show."

In the morning, I overslept, missing breakfast, and rushed to catch the shuttle bus outside on the corner. I found a seat next to Ashley again, but before I could say anything about the night before, she grabbed me by the arm and said, "Sorry I forgot to warn you about Patrice."

"What? What are you talking about?"

"Did you feel strange, like she was hitting on you last night?"

I had tried to put the entire event out of my mind. But now that she mentioned it, Patrice was a bit ... friendly.

"Is she gay?"

A smile crept over her face.

"Get outta here!" I squealed in delight. At home, the only lesbians I knew looked like Ms. Bart, my 8th grade gym teacher, otherwise known as "the linebacker."

"It gets better," she said under her breath, looking around to be sure none of the other girls would hear. "I caught her hooking up with some girl in the back room my first night here."

"What! Are you kidding?" I screamed. "A model?"

She nodded her head. "Uh-huh."

My eye scanned the bus, wondering who it could have been. "Who was it?"

"I couldn't see her face, but she was just a kid. Couldn't have been older than 15."

"I don't believe it!"

"You wouldn't believe half the stuff that goes on around here," she said.

When I returned home that night, a small ivory-colored envelope lay in front of my door. My name was inscribed on the front in gothic letters.

Looking down at it, I was a bit hesitant to open it. My fingers ran against the sealed edge. *Please, don't let this be some sort of sick love letter from Patrice.* I couldn't get what Ashley told me out of my mind. I gently tore open the envelope and pulled out a vellum card. In the same hand, it read: "Sig. Alfredo Angeloni requests the honor of your company this evening."

I turned it over to see if there was anything else written, but there wasn't.

It couldn't have been for me. I'd never met Signore what's-his-name. I threw the card on the bureau and flopped down on the bed, dreading the nightly removal of my stage-worthy makeup. But before I could stand up to head to the bathroom, I heard a loud ringing in the room, coming from — of all places — the closet. A bit fearful, I opened the door and was shocked to discover an old rotary phone attached to the wall. What else could I do but answer it?

"Um ... hello?"

"Ka-tar-in." It was Maria. She was the only one around there who pronounced my name that way. A feeling of dread rose up from the pit of my stomach. "Yes?" I answered, adjusting my tone to very serious and stern to match hers.

"Did you receive the calling card from Sig. Angeloni?"

Calling card? What is this, the 18th century?

"Oh, that was for me?" I said, wryly. "I didn't realize that was for me. I don't know a Sig. Angeloni."

"You met him last night! Don't you remember?"

I stopped to think.

"He is tall with black hair. He was wearing an orange silk shirt," she said.

I thought hard and finally did remember a man who fit that description. I realized that I had not even talked to him the entire night and made the mistake of expressing this fact out loud.

"Well, that's exactly why you should use this opportunity to get to know him," she said, matter-of-factly.

Get to know him? *Get to know him?*

*Oh. My. God.* I started piecing things together and vaguely remembered the Belgian girl who stayed with me the first night had had one of these cards on her bureau when she arrived. I noticed it because of the beautiful calligraphy on the envelope. *Had last night all been a set-up to get us to go out with these men?*

"Sorry, I don't really think I can," I said to Maria, somehow finding the courage to speak these words. "I'm completely exhausted. I have a long day again tomorrow."

"Oh, a few drinks won't hurt you. It will relax you on the runway."

"Maria," I said, deciding I needed to be more direct. "Please tell Mr. Sig. Angeloni that I thank him for the offer. But I really don't think so. Besides, I ... I have a boyfriend."

Little white lie but completely appropriate under the circumstances.

"Boyfriend? What does that have to do with this?" she asked, irritated. "This is not improper. You are merely enjoying the companionship of a friend."

She went on angrily, "You American women are so uptight. Everything is so black and white. You cannot enjoy the simple joys of life."

And with that, she slammed down the phone.

I put down the receiver and called Clive on my cell. I had to call my agency and get my living arrangements changed. There was no way I could spend another night in a place like this.

While I was leaving a message on his voicemail, Ashley burst into the room with an envelope in her hand. "What is this? What the hell is this?" she screamed, waving the card around in the air. She stopped short when she noticed I was on the phone and covered her mouth.

I left a message for Clive at the office, then another on his phone. When I hadn't heard from him a few hours later, I texted *911*, hoping he'd sense the urgency. The last thing I remember was waiting anxiously by the phone, dozing off here and there, until awakened by the buzz of the alarm clock the next morning.

With my blurry morning vision, I thought I saw yet another paper slipped under the door. Perhaps an eviction notice? I certainly was taking up a warm bed that plenty of other, shall we say, *agreeable* girls could be sleeping in, I thought to myself, laughing weakly. As I neared the door, I saw that it was, in fact, an envelope. My heart quickened.

I tore into the letter, but thankfully it read:

*Cat,*

*Sorry I had to leave without saying goodbye. I have gotten another room at the Hotel Hosanna, off Via Pier della Francesca. My agency was shocked at the conditions here, and they got me in right away. Please join me.*

*Ash*

The next few nights, I stayed with Ashley. We bunked in a hostel that had nice, clean rooms and a (thankfully) hands-off staff. It was a pleasant relief from the uneasiness I felt staying at Il Fiorellino, where it seemed one always had to watch her back. But the third night there, we were woken up by a violent pounding at the door.

"Who's there?" I called out, jumping out of bed and placing my hand firmly on the deadbolt. I looked over at the clock. It was 1 a.m.

"Hello?" I called again.

"There's an urgent call from America," a man said. It was the nighttime guy from the front desk. "Is there a Catherine Watson there?"

"Yeah, yes," I stammered, not wanting to believing my ears and, as usual, fearing the worst. Could something have happened to my parents? I'd given them the emergency number there, in case they couldn't reach me on my cell.

"Be right there."

I grabbed my robe and slippers and told Ashley, now sitting up alert in bed, to stay put. The innkeeper led me down to a phone at the front desk. I gripped the plastic receiver with my sweaty hand,

"Hello? Mom?" I said.

I heard the echo of my voice and no response on the other end. Then a man's voice, in delayed response, shout out: "Nice to fucking hear from you!" It was Clive's raspy growl. "I've been calling all over the European continent for you. Were you planning to check in?"

"I did!" I cried. "I left you several messages! I've been trying to reach you all week!" Tears started spilling from my eyes. *Not this again.*

"You just don't learn, Catherine, do you?" he said. "Gotta have a mind of your own. Well, it's not gonna get you far with me, babe."

"Clive, if I told you what was going on there at that place!"

"What are you talking about?"

"They're running an escort service or something. They're practically prostituting out the girls who stay there!"

"Sure ... our girls have been going there for years with no complaints. Suddenly Mother Teresa comes along and there's a problem. You're unbelievable."

"I'm not lying, I swear to God. You've gotta believe me. There's other girls, too."

"Cat, do you know how many girls would die to be in your position, would sleep with every fucking photographer in New York City to be in your position? To be picked up from obscurity, hailed as the next big thing? I don't know how much longer I can put up with your disobedient bullshit."

By this point, I was sobbing in waves, and I didn't even care if he could hear.

"Wanna screw things up? Fine, but not on my dime," he went on. "Now, you listen to me, and listen good. If Philippe didn't want to sign you on so bad for another year, I'd have dropped you long ago. He might fall for your innocent angel crap, but I don't. We're on the cusp of something big, here, Cat. Screw it up this time, and I'll fucking kill you."

# ✦ 18 ✦

"Girl, you were on fire on the runway — on *fire!*" Manuel, the hair and makeup artist I'd met back in New York during Fall Fashion Week, shouted from across the room as I entered Philippe's Italian villa. "Go on, Miss Thang!"

We were there for an after-party. It was the last one I was to attend, after a whirlwind week of shows and parties. Any girl's dream, right? I knew this was one I couldn't miss after my conversation with Clive earlier in the week. He had called later to apologize and smooth things over. But it was too late. I knew where I stood.

"My-ah love, come with me," Philippe said, ushering me toward a group of journalists who were lingering near the bar. "Someone want to speak with you."

Another reporter, no doubt, who wanted to hear me say the same rehearsed statements Gail had prepped me for: Philippe is back "with a vengeance." His sportswear appeals to the "modern generation." His clothes are "fun and comfortable, but sexy, too." My favorite? "Oh, Philippe's signature layering tanks, of course. I have one in every color."

As I spoke, Philippe stood beside me, holding my hand. At one point, he lifted it and kissed it. It was all for the cameras, of course. He had been acting like we were a couple the entire night. The entire week, actually. He had gotten to Italy after I had left Il Fiorellino, and he had treated me to dinner and taken me sightseeing. It was all very surreal. During his runway show today, he hadn't let me out of his sight.

The cameras flashed again, and Manuel, who had migrated over to our side of the room, pulled on a lock of my hair, sniffed it, and said to the crowd, "She smells so good, I could eat her up!"

His date, a very glamorous drag queen he'd picked up in Lombardy earlier in the week, shrieked with delight as Manuel and his friends surrounded me like vultures, pulling at my hair, pinching my ass, and running their hands along my dress — a $5,000 creation on loan from Philippe.

Philippe disappeared into the crowd to greet some visitors, and Manuel whispered, "People say Cat was plucked from obscurity, discovered by Philippe. But it was me, not the 'Master of Cloth,' who discovered her. She was just a sad, skinny little bitch sitting in my chair and I gave her killer hair, lips, and eyes. She was transformed from an ugly duckling to a swan!"

"Was that the way it went?" I said, laughing weakly.

"And now," Manuel said, turning to his friends, "She's gonna to be huge! She's gonna be the face of Philippe's entire label ... you *mark my words!*"

His words and excitement should have inspired something in me that felt like happiness, pleasure ... contentment. But all I could do was keep down the bile that bubbled up in my throat. I excused myself, walking through Philippe's villa — one, which, made Gail's apartment in New York look like a storage closet. Massive oil paintings hung on the walls, giant neoclassical statues depicting Roman gods decorated the rooms, and an atrium had fountains that spilled water into marble pools, what Philippe called his "Roman baths."

I ducked into a bathroom that was larger than my entire apartment. The walls were taupe with bronze accents. Goldplated busts on miniature pedestals were placed strategically throughout the room. The bathtub was filled with floating candles and scented with rose petals bobbing on top. I locked the door and stood there, motionless, catching my breath in the dark. I watched a sliver of dusty moonlight creep through a cracked window, listened to the hubbub of the crowd on the other side of the door, listened to the people laughing, mingling about. Philippe's voice came into earshot. I heard the clinking of glasses. There was a toast.

I walked to face the mirror above the sink, resting my hands on the cold marble countertop. *This is it, Catherine. The tomorrow you've been waiting for.* The same pain I had felt the morning Benji left me, New Year's Eve day, when we'd had that terrible fight, began to bear down on my chest. I thought I was going to falter, to crumble under its magnitude. I held on to the counter and looked into the glass, into my eyes, to see that confident person who I'd supposedly become. But there was nothing there. Just the cold, hard stare of a girl, no, a woman, I had not known. She stared back at me, overdone, her face a mask of makeup, her hair sculpted into artificial Barbie doll curls, her lips fire red, eyes filled with fear.

Someone knocked on the door so I slipped out, walking into the great hall and circumventing the partygoers to search for the balcony Philippe had raved about — a limestone plateau that overlooked the city. I was alone for a second before a couple walked out onto the balcony. They stood a few feet away. A strong wind swept through, and the man put his jacket over the woman's shoulders, shielding her from the cold.

They reminded me of a couple I'd seen earlier that week. Both so in love. They stood behind me in line at a little breakfast nook next to the hostel where Ashley and I were staying. The woman waiting on us at the counter was a small, hunched old lady. She wore a starched white apron and white cotton cap, her gray hair tucked neatly inside. The woman greeted me politely and handed me a cup of espresso with a slice of dark chocolate on the side. The couple behind me, who knew the old lady by name, ordered and watched as she fussed with the percolators and kneaded dough to put in the oven. She looked content existing in her own little universe, humming to herself as she wiped down the counters. I could tell she had been doing the same thing for years, decades. It was ingrained in her ... everything so automatic. I wondered how she could be happy doing what seemed so insignificant. She wasn't conquering the world, she wasn't loved by millions, she wasn't gracing the cover of magazines or surrounded by new cars, clothes, or tech, but she seemed happy.

*Oh, to have such simple, uncluttered bliss.*

The old woman handed the couple their breakfast and they took a seat by the window. Deep in conversation, they stared fervently into each other's eyes, enamored, one could tell, by the other. The man leaned over to kiss her lips, and I felt embarrassed sitting there watching, like some sort of a voyeur. As they cooed over each other, pangs of guilt rose up in me. *I could have this. I could have this with Benji.*

An old-fashioned payphone in the back of the shop rang, and the old lady walked back to answer it. As she spoke on the phone, I thought about calling Benji. Just to say hi, just to see how he was doing. He couldn't be mad at me if I called him all the way from Europe, could he?

When the lady was off the phone, I skipped down the hall, my heart falling in sync with my footsteps, and climbed into the old wooden booth and closed the door where I could talk in private. Why was I suddenly nervous? My hands got clammy, and I pulled my cellphone from my pocket, gripping it like it was a lifeline. Benji answered after the first ring, and my impulse to hang up almost ended the call right there, but the worry in his voice prevented me:

"Hello? Hello? Catherine, what's wrong?" He sounded alarmed. I realized it was nearly 1 in the morning where he was. Damnit, this was gonna be a whopper of a roaming charge.

"Benji ... hi. It's me."

"What's wrong?"

"Nothing ... just calling to say hi. I'm in Italy."

"Christ, do you know what time it is?" He sounded irritated. Very irritated. Brilliant, Catherine.

"Look, I'll just get right to it," I said trying to sound very diplomatic and grownup. "I'm sorry for jerking you around on New Year's Eve. I realized I made a mistake, and I should have hung out with you, in Times Square."

"So you're calling *now* to tell me *that*? Couldn't it have waited till morning?"

"Please don't be mad at me."

"Well, I guess that's water under the bridge now," he said solemnly. Ah, now that's the Benji I knew and loved. It always killed me when he used those old-fashioned phrases. "Water under the bridge," so irresistibly Benji.

"So we're cool again? Just like that?"

"I didn't say that, Catherine. Look, it's late, lemme go."

"No, please. Don't go," I begged. "I need to talk to someone."

Before I could control the intonations of my voice, I began sobbing, harder and louder than I could have expected. I cried so hard that I began to hiccup uncontrollably. Luckily, the couple had left and the old lady was outside talking to a deliveryman. I tucked myself further in the phone booth and knelt down on the floor.

"Benji, it's been a nightmare here. I don't know what I'm going to do. My agency is ready to drop me."

"What? Why?"

"It's complicated ..."

He asked me what happened, and it all came out: the hard time Clive had been giving me lately, the diet pills, the models' apartment that ran an escort business on the side, all of it.

"Did you get out of there? Have you found a place to stay?" he asked.

"Yes, yes. I'm safe," I said, glad to hear the concern in his voice, even if he was still mad at me. He asked if I could find another agency when I got home. I wasn't really sure if that would be against the rules — breaking my contract with Icon. *I should have never signed that damn contract; I should have listened to my parents.*

Benji listened patiently, but it became increasingly clear that he didn't want to talk, because his responses became shorter and shorter. I told him that once I was back in New York, after I got things straightened out with my agency, maybe he could come up. I'd make up for New Year's Eve, for what we missed.

"I don't know, Catherine," he said in a small voice.

I rambled, "And maybe, if you have a long weekend off from

school, you can come up and we can go back to Rockefeller Center and go to the Natural History Museum and maybe walk through Central Park ..."

"Catherine, I really don't think I should," he said, with bit of reluctance. It sounded like he was about to say more, but there was a pause.

"Ah ... remember that girl you meet at Rockefeller Center? Jessica Rice? Well, I'm sorta seeing her. We've been out a couple times."

Immediately my cheeks got hot. I couldn't decide if I was more angry that he had (a) found an interest in another girl, (b) waited until this point in the conversation to tell me, or (c) was dating that cute little b!#%$, who was probably ready to pop out two kids for him if he so chose.

"That girl I met?" was all I could eek out.

"Her name is Jessica."

"Oh." Now he was defending her honor?

"Were you dating when we saw her in New York?" The thought of him falling for her fake, syrupy-sweet crap made me want to stab someone's eyes out with a pencil.

"No. Are you crazy? We barely knew each other then. Remember, I told you she had just started teaching at my school. Besides, what do you care anyway? Aren't you still dating what's-his-name?"

Silence.

"Well?"

"We broke up," I mumbled miserably, feeling more pathetic than ever.

"Sorry to hear that. But let me tell you something, Catherine. You're probably better off. That guy was a creep."

"How would you know?"

"I could just tell. From what you told me, he sounded like a shady character. Never held a job, had a troubled past, just bad news."

I remained silent. Benji was right. He knew this all along. And he knew me. He knew what I needed more than I did. I needed to tell him that.

"Benji ..." I began to speak, but was cut off by the sound of a high-pitched voice. A *woman's* voice. And then I heard a muffled sound, then no sound. Was I on mute?

*Ohmigod! Was it her? Little Miss Muffet?*

Benji got back on the phone.

"Is that her?" I couldn't help myself, feeling ready to be physically ill. The worse part was I knew I had no right to feel this way. He wasn't mine.

"Look, we just got back from a late movie. I'm sorry," he said.

"Fine," I spat. The poison just poured off of my tongue. "Go have fun with your perfect little future wife. I know that's what you want, Benji. Martha Stewart to cook in the kitchen and Carol Brady to bear perfect children for you."

This struck a chord.

"Is that so terrible, Catherine? Why is that so bad? What's wrong with doing what other people do? What's wrong with living a normal life?"

He went on, whispering into the phone so that the ice queen wouldn't hear. "You'd never be satisfied with me, Catherine. You were right; we *don't* want the same things. You're *not* my type. You want to hang out with druggies and poseurs? Fine, then, do it, but don't pull me into it, and don't call me from the next continent over when something goes wrong in your perfect little world."

I was back in Philippe's bathroom, feeling lightheaded. I thought the cool night air would help clear my head, but it did more harm than good. I sat on the rim of the bathtub, wondering what it would feel like to slip into that pool of water, to submerge myself and never come up again.

Benji was right; I didn't belong in his world. But I didn't belong in this world, either. I held a glass of wine in my hand, the bitter taste still lingering on the tip of my tongue. Drinking wine was like so many other things in my life ... stylish, sophisticated, and something I pretended to like. The glass teetered precariously on the rim of the marble basin. I let go and watched it tip over onto the tile floor, crashing into a thousand tiny pieces. Drops like blood splashed on my pale legs, chards of glass lay everywhere. It felt like suicide.

"My love, are you still in there?" Philippe asked, tapping lightly on the door.

I hesitated, hoping that he'd think someone else was in there and just leave. "All right, *bella,*" he said, "I'll be out here waiting for you."

It was nearly 3 a.m., and most of the party guests had cleared out. Empty glasses were littered throughout the house. A small mirror had been taken off the wall and placed on an end table in the living room. Lines of coke were still dispersed across it. Gail laid next to it on the couch, slumped in a coma, a frail, hollow version of herself. Philippe roused her. "Time for bed, *mi bambina.* Let's go."

He called for a maid to come and help Gail to her room. I, too, was ready for bed, I said, ready to go back to the hostel.

"Just a second," he said. "Follow me."

We walked into a design studio off the kitchen area with drafting tables and sewing machines. He pointed to a mannequin in the corner that was partially clothed. "Everything is going to be blended knits next season," he said.

He pulled out a few sketches and showed me some of the designs he was working on for the following year, clothes, he said, that I had helped to inspire. Whatever that meant. To me, I was nothing more than a walking coat hanger. A puppet for others to pull the strings of...

"In this," he said, grabbing a cotton jumper, "you'll bring back the fresh, girl-next-door feel. Americans love that. It was the look Remi did so well in the '80s. You can do it, too. The camera loves you."

He asked me to try it on, handing it to me as if I were to strip down right then and there, in front of him. "Oh, I'd love to," I said, forcing a smile, "But can it wait till tomorrow? It's really late."

"I insist," he said. "I need your measurements."

*Screw it up this time, and I'll fucking kill you.*

"Of course," I heard myself saying as I took the garment and walked into a bedroom across the hall. The door had no lock, so I stepped into a large walk-in closet. While standing there in nothing but a thong, I heard a tap on the door. "How are you doing, dahling?"

"Fine," I called. "Just a minute." But then I heard soft footsteps padding through the room, and before I could run for cover Philippe stood there before me.

"Excuse me," I blurted, springing toward a clothing rack to grab my dress. But he lunged at me, pulling me into his arms.

"Where are you going, my love?" he said. "Oh, do not give me that face. You act so naive, but you know very well what you are doing here tonight.

"You really are, ah — how do they say it?—an 'old-fashioned' girl, aren't you?" he continued, staring down at my bare breasts. "It's so refreshing in this business. Modesty, purity ... those are your virtues. But, come now, you have played that game for too long."

He was strong for such an old man and I didn't have the strength, or the energy, to pull away from him. He reached down with an icy hand to touch my breast and I closed my eyes while his lips moved over me. They covered my breasts, my shoulders, my neck. *This is what Clive was talking about. This is what being a "good girl" really meant.* I fell limply in his arms, scared that resisting might set him off in a rage, scared that making one false move, one wrong decision, would ruin everything I'd worked so hard for.

He led me out of the closet and onto the bed, with the intention, I knew, to take things further. I was scared to go through with it, but I was also scared not to. I felt unsure of what the right thing to do even *was* — and then, of course, there was that part of me that just didn't care anymore. When we came into the light of the room my tears — my one sign of rebellion — were all over my face.

"Oh, dahling, are you crying? Please don't," he said. "There's no need for that." He rose from the bed, walked into the closet and returned with my dress. "Perhaps this is too soon. Perhaps you are not ready for what I have to share with you."

I looked up at him, not able to vocalize my sudden curiosity.

"Come — get dressed and freshen up," he said, handing me my dress. "I have a *proposta*, ah, proposition, that just might change the way you feel about me."

Five minutes later I found myself fully dressed and standing across from Philippe at a drafting table in his design studio, as if nothing out of the ordinary, nothing sordid or demoralizing had just occurred between the two of us.

I settled into my chair and held my breath.

"Dahling, let me explain something to you," Philippe said, leaning on the arm of a chair and folding his hands on his lap. "When you become of a certain age, you start to lose your ... how do I say it? Your *mojo*, as the young people say today. You start to see death in the face, when those around you, your peers, start leaving this life, to meet the next. You start to wonder how much time you have left and what you realize, what I realize, is that I don't want to die alone. Companionship. I want companionship." Um ... ok. So this man was asking for sympathy, for "companionship," after just trying to grope me in a walk-in closet.

"And I am prepared to pay," he said. Very matter-of-factly, he pulled out his checkbook from the inside pocket of his suit jacket.

"What? Why me? Why now?" I winced.

"Being of the moment is everything in fashion. And every model has a moment, Cat," he said with a very dramatic sweep of his hand. "It's the girls who can take that moment, who can *seize* that moment, and turn it into a career ..."

I looked down at the floor; the worst was yet to come.

"Dahling, if you don't take advantage of the gifts you've been given, the opportunities you've been awarded, well, then, you will lose them. You will lose them all," he said. "Just like Remi. She wanted to do things her way. She thought she knew better, she turned people off, no? And when she started losing work, she sank into a deep depression. And look what happened."

He pulled out a pen. "So, let's get to it," he said, very business-like. "In exchange for your companionship, I am willing to offer you your own apartment, expenses fully paid, in any part of the city you desire. You want to live in the Village, live in the Village. You want to live uptown and shop at Bergdorf's, do it, dahling. The world is your oyster."

*Ohmigod. Is this happening? Is this really happening?*

"Your monthly allowance will be 20,000, and, in addition, you will sign an exclusive contract with me for the next five years."

He stood up, as if this final icing on the cake was to send me off into orgasmic praises. "You, Cat, will be the face of Philippe couture, commanding nearly 1,000,000 dollars a year!"

If the last 10 minutes of my life had been a played-out modeling cliché, this was like a script for a *True Hollywood Story*. He stood before me, as if waiting for me to accept right then and there.

"The *face* of Philippe," he repeated, both arms extended for further dramatic effect.

What happened to youthful innocence? I thought the "face" was that of an unsoiled, all-American girl. He wanted an angel in his advertisements and a whore in his bedroom. What a farce. What a lie everything in this business was turning out to be. Nothing was as it seemed: not in the pages of the air-brushed magazines, not in the looks on the runway, not in the hallways and meeting rooms and studios and agencies, and, as I learned in Milan, not even in their own homes.

*"You walked out on Philippe Borghetta? Are you crazy?"*

*"Come on, babe. Don't be such a drama queen."*

*"Screw it up this time, and I'll fucking kill you."*

The thoughts swirled through my mind, adding to the crushing weight that bore down on my chest. It was the fantasy, what I'd wanted all along. A departure from the norm. An exclusive contact. A place in the city. Success. Status. Money. More money than I knew what to do with. I could have it. I could give myself up. What did it matter anymore, anyway? No one cared who I was on the inside.

"I'll think about it." The words filtered out of my mouth as I rose to leave. I thought it would hurt, but it didn't hurt that much. I'd become numb to the pain.

# ✦ 19 ✦

"My goodness, to what do we owe this honor?" my mother gasped in delight as I stumbled through the front door, dragging my suitcases and bags from my trip abroad.

She sat in the family room, with her feet up on the couch, reading an issue of *O, The Oprah Magazine,* as my father sat in his easy chair and flipped back and forth between ESPN and *60 Minutes.*

"I thought you were going to be in New York this week. When did you get back from Italy? Why didn't you call me?" She hit me with a barrage of questions, rising to grab my things.

"Change of plans," I said, not wanting to get into it at the moment.

"What happened? Did something go wrong?" she asked, following me all the way into the kitchen.

"Mom, I'm really tired," I said, feeling like telling her the truth, and setting her peaceful little world off-kilter, would be an incredibly selfish act at 7 p.m. on a Sunday night. "I'm just ... jetlagged. I'm going to bed."

She looked at me with a terrified look. "You're not on drugs are you, Catherine?"

*Ha, if only.*

"Oh, god, Bill, she's on drugs," my mother said, bursting into tears. "I knew it! Look how skinny she is — she's barely visible. There's nothing left!"

I sighed with the last ounce of energy I had in me. It even hurt to laugh.

"I'm NOT on drugs," I barked over her hysterics as I dragged my feet up the stairs, past the newspaper clippings and framed magazine covers, past the mini shrine of some girl who was supposed to be me.

I closed the door to my room and fell into bed, into a dark oblivion that lasted for days. I couldn't eat. I couldn't rouse myself from sleep. There were hours, days that seemed to escape from my memory. My mother stood over my bed, on the phone with the doctor, talking to my aunts, worried sick. Night terrors rattled me. I would wake in a sweat, tangled in sheets. Night after night, I found myself in Brooklyn, in the dark, dank subway tunnels, the catacombs of New York.

I was waiting for a train. My mother's voice would call out in the distance, "*Catherine!*" I'd follow her voice, but just when I thought I had found her, she would suddenly sound further away. As I weaved through a mob of people, I'd come upon a small crowd collected at the end of a platform, near an idling train. They were looking down at something on the tracks.

*"Step away from the platform," the automated conductor called over the loud speaker.*

*I thought about stepping away, but something pulled me closer to the scene. The crowd parted, leaving a small gap for me to enter. I inched forward.*

*"Poor thing," a voice said.*

*"She's been like this for days," a woman moaned.*

*Oh, god, what had happened? Was there a girl on the tracks? Just when I thought I was close enough to catch a glimpse, a head or shoulder would appear, blocking my view.*

*"I think the worst is over, but she needs to stay here for a while," a man said.*

*The curiosity was killing me. I pushed through the crowd. My arms wobbled, like they were made of rubber cement. When I got to the ledge, all the people were gone and I was alone. I took a deep breath, preparing to look down. But when I did, there was nothing there.*

*I scoured the train's underside, seeing something up ahead: a shoe. Somebody's shoe. A girl's shoe. My shoe. The black and white saddle shoe that I wore in elementary school. I knew it was mine, because there was* a smudge of red marker on the left side that my mom could never quite cover up. The shoe dangled ever so slightly against the rusty underbelly of the train car. Above it was a leg. A navy and green plaid schoolgirl skirt. I heard a cry. It came from my mouth. My eye was drawn further upward. Caught within the metal links that held the cars together was a girl. She was slumped over, her brown hair caught in the chains.

"She's fallen between the train cars. When the train starts, it's the end of her," a voice said.

I was petrified to know if the girl was really me. I stood frozen, not able to move. My mother and father ran onto the platform, hysterical. My mother was crying as she knelt down beside the girl. I tried to run toward her to comfort her and let her know that I was OK, that I was still really alive, but suddenly I felt her cold hands, her wet tears touch my face, then an aching numbness down below. I reached down to touch my legs, but there was nothing there.

"Catherine, wake up, wake up!" my mother said, rocking me back and forth. I opened my eyes and immediately felt for my legs.

"You were having a bad dream," she said.

My bed sheets were soaked, my pillow drenched with tears. A few feet from me stood a large man in a lab coat with a stethoscope dangling from his neck. It was Dr. Barroway, my old pediatrician.

"Wasn't it nice of Dr. Barroway to make a special trip here to see you? No one makes house calls anymore," my mother said, batting an eyelash or two in his direction.

"Cathy," he said, placing his hand on my shin, "I think you've got a case of mononucleosis."

"You know, the so-called *kissing* disease," my mother said, with a somewhat comical look. "Dr. Barroway says you'll have to stay in bed for three weeks. Better call your agency and tell them. No work or running around, young lady!"

That night, I got up to go to the bathroom and never made it, fainting half way there. The 12 steps were too far to go. I dreamed that I was walking down the runway, with people all around me watching me, waiting for me to trip and fall. The girls from my junior high cafeteria sat in the front row. I heard them snickering as I walked past. Seth was there, too, all in black. When I neared the end of the catwalk, I saw my mother sitting in the audience. Her face was in her hands. I looked down and saw that I had no clothes on. I stood there, naked, as the cameras flashed.

*"Catherine would never have done something like this."*

"Honey, I talked to your agent, Clive, today," my mother said, bringing up a tray of soup the next afternoon. "What a charming man! He doesn't seem so bad to me. He was very concerned about your wellbeing. He told me to tell you to take as long as you need to recover."

The music in the nightclub was loud that night. I remember that. This is the way it was. No, I think the ceilings were higher. The draperies were gold. Red, green, and gold. Jonnie and I started dancing. Then, from the corner of my eye, I saw Theo and Vincent walk over and talk to some guy. He was tall and wiry, with messy brown hair, sneakers with orange laces. He was cute, definitely cuter than Theo or his friends. We could tell they were watching us. Jonnie loved the attention, so she pulled me closer to her, dancing all sexy and grabbing me by the waist, thrusting her pelvis against mine.

He had a book bag slung over one shoulder, that guy, the cute one. From the dance floor, over Jonnie's shoulder, I could see him pull something out. Vincent reached for it and they shook hands. A few seconds later, Vincent was behind me, running his hands along my body...

"Bed sores can form if you lie in bed all day, Catherine. So, Dr. Barroway said it's important for you to switch positions from time to time," my mother said, helping me readjust. "Atta girl, that's it. Pretty soon you'll be back on track."

*"Do you realize the track record of these people? They're not real, they're not like you and me."*

"So the other day I was watching my soaps and," my mother prattled on. "Catherine, are you listening to me? What's the matter? You've been staring out the window all day. I told you, it's too soon to go outside. So, anyway, there's this new cute girl on *Days of Our Lives*. Her name is Payton, well, on the show it's

Payton, but in real life it's Kimberly Something-or-other, but anyway, I saw her interviewed the other day on *Access Hollywood* and, turns out, she used to be a model with your agency. Isn't that funny? She's a real nice girl."

*"Nice girls with no edge get nowhere in fashion."*

"Turns out she's from the Deep South. Anyway, I just was thinking that maybe if this modeling doesn't last, maybe you would like to try acting? You had that part once in your 5th grade play, remember? You were one of the five food groups? Whole grains, I think it was. Sweetie? Are you listening to me? I swear you never listen anymore. Sometimes I think I'm just talking to hear myself talk."

*Mirror, mirror on the wall.*
*Who's the saddest girl of all?*
*Thought you knew which way to go,*
*Thought you were running the show.*
*Now you've got to figure out*
*What your life is all about.*

"Eat, you have to get your strength up," my mother said, placing a carb-laden plate of pasta in front of me on a tray as I sat up in bed. I tore into it like a rabid dog. I hadn't eaten more than tea and toast in days. "That's right," she said. "Dig in, you need to get some nutrition in you."

"Thanks, Mom." The words came out of me, unexpectedly. I said it again, louder. And I meant it. It wasn't her duty, this motherhood. It was a choice. A choice she had made for herself when she just a little older than I was now. How wrong I had been about her wasting her life. Who was I to presume to know what made her happy? I couldn't even figure out what made me happy.

"I'm sorry."

"What for, sweetie?" she asked, glancing up from a pile of laundry she was folding, a surprised look on her face.

"For judging you."

"What on earth are you talking about, honey? Is something bothering you? You've been so despondent these last few days."

I couldn't tell her. I couldn't tell her that my world was falling down around me. That I had gotten myself into a complete mess. That I was one camera click away from being a high-price call girl. That's what it was — not what he said, not a "companion," but someone who'd be paid for, among other things, sex.

I thought about my first time with Seth, and it made me sad. Not because of how emotionless it was, or how things didn't work out with him. Part of me knew, all along, that he wasn't who he said he was. I was just lying to myself ... because I wanted it to be so. I wanted someone who was different from other guys, other people, I'd known. The sadness I felt was more from regret ... regret that it wasn't Benji. It should have been him.

I'd made mistakes in the past year. But I was not going to lose any more of myself, of the girl I had been, and the girl I was finding out I wanted to be. The problem was, I didn't see any way out of this mess with Philippe and Clive, other than to limp away, bruised and battered. What I wanted to do, what I dreamed of doing, of fighting back, could never happen. A girl like me could never win against a force like them. An institution like that.

We sat at the kitchen table. It was the first day I was able to get out of bed and make it further than the bathroom down the hall. My mother was telling me about a ceramics class she had been taking at a local art studio. She held up her first project, a dainty, bone china vase with tiny Irish clovers spotting the edges.

"That's beautiful, Mom," I said. She had fired it in the kiln herself. "I'm glad you're taking a class and doing something for yourself."

"Yes, well, with you gone and your father barely around, I have to fill my days with something," she said, with a hint of pride. "I think I'm going to take another class this summer."

She pointed to a cup and saucer set at the end of the table that was sitting on newspaper. "I was just going to glaze that for tomorrow," she said. "I have to leave it dry overnight. Want to help? It will just take a few minutes."

I sat at the table and she pulled the newspaper over to me

before grabbing a couple of clean paintbrushes. She showed me how to put just the right amount of glaze onto the brush to get a full, even coat.

For a few minutes, we sat next to each other in silence. It was a calm, peaceful silence, the kind that I despised as a child, filling it with meaningless words and phrases. But now it was a much-needed, yearned-for connection that I had missed. As we sat in silence, I tried to keep my thoughts from going over to the dark side. I tried but couldn't quite find the calm my mother now so readily enjoyed. I felt restless and put down my brush.

"Mom, I don't know what I'm doing," I said.

"Oh, it doesn't have to be perfect, dear," she said, bending her head around the rim of the cup. "You can thin it with a little water."

"No, Mom," I said, staring down at a dried drop of glaze on the newsprint. "I mean with my life, with my career. I don't know what I'm doing."

"What do you mean?" she said. "I thought you enjoyed modeling, being in New York?"

"I do, I mean, I did. It's just that I don't know if I'm really cut out for this."

"Well, dear, you knew it would be a challenge," she said. "Your father and I warned you. But I thought you said that it was different."

"It was in the beginning, but now ..." I couldn't tell her the truth of what had happened. She would be horrified. She would try to fix it all for me. She wouldn't let me ever go back. "I just feel like I'm ... failing at it."

"Failing!? You just finished traveling all around the world. Right now, your face is plastered all over I-95! You've reached your goal, honey. Isn't this what you wanted?"

"Maybe." I said weakly. "But I can't help feeling frustrated." And angry. It wasn't supposed to be this way. This wasn't supposed to happen. I tried, I really tried to keep my boundaries intact. But I wasn't strong enough. I'm being forced to be someone I'm not.

"I'm not a model," I said.

"You're a beautiful girl!" she protested. "Those people are crazy."

"That doesn't matter!" I said, raising my voice. "A girl like me gets eaten alive up there! Mom, all the things you've heard, or thought, about modeling — they're all true. A nice girl can't be a model; a 'good' girl can't work. You have to *do* things ... *sleep* with people ... you can't be smart, you can't show weakness ..."

My voice ran and ran in circles, finally ebbing down to a hard cry. My mother held me like a doll. Here I was, all grown up — a woman, technically — crying in my mother's lap. I couldn't stop. I couldn't stop once she looked into my eyes. All I could do was cry. I shook with grief and with fear for myself, with fear of what I needed to do to set things straight. To hold on to myself.

She stroked my head, and I bubbled over. There was something in her, in all mothers, that doesn't let you keep up your shell, your façade. A mother always knows. I could never hide from her. Even now, I couldn't lie to her, because she knew, she knew the secrets of my heart.

# ✦ **20** ✦

One afternoon while lying in bed, I sat up out of my psychological stupor and realized that only one thing was clear: Benji was right.

He was right about everything. It killed me to think that he lumped me in with the rest of these people. I am, and will be, nothing like them. I couldn't stand for one more second that he would consider me a shallow, callous, self-absorbed, New York socialite who valued image over intellect. That he thought of me as a fast girl more concerned with partying and sleeping around made me feel even more depressed. I needed to see him one more time, to set the record straight.

By now, he was probably blissfully committed to Miss Rice in happy coupledom. I knew I'd lost my chance with him. But we had always made good friends. And I could use a friend right about now.

While my mom was out running errands the next day, I managed to escape from the house. It was an unusually warm March day, and the flowers in the neighborhood were just beginning to bloom. It had been a mild winter, and now spring seemed to be approaching quickly. Everything, including me, seemed to be waking up from a long, foggy dream. I felt like Snow White as I padded down the sidewalk, spotting butterflies and wild flowers; squirrels scurried to clear a path for me. It put pep in my step.

While on the commuter train into Philly, I came up with a plan: I'd surprise Benji at his teaching job. That way he wouldn't have any other alternative but to talk to me. I called an Uber to Simon Gratz High School, the school where he student-taught in an underserved part of North Philly. Surprisingly, I made my way into the school pretty easily, sidestepping metal detectors by entering through a back entrance. Classes were in session, and as I walked through the quiet hallways, I felt the all-too-familiar dread of high school. I found the main office and entered, feeling like an awkward ninth-grader on her first day of class.

"Mr. Darling, please," I said, as the receptionist suspiciously eyed me while fielding phone calls. She gestured for me to wait a moment. I took a seat in the waiting area, beginning to wonder if coming to Benji's work was maybe the wrong thing to do.

*Oh, god, am I a stalker?* Whatever happens, please, please, God, don't let me run into Miss Rice. It would be mortifying—

"Don't I know you?" a woman called from behind me.

I looked up from an old copy of *Chicken Soup for the Teenage Soul* to see a fresh-faced Jessica Rice. Goddarn it.

"What are *you* doing here?" she asked, looking around curiously at the secretary. The bell rang and students began to change classes.

"I came to see Benji. I was in the, ah, area and I just wanted to say hi." Shit, shit, shit. Why did I have to run into her?

"You were in the area? In North Philadelphia?" she said, knowing full well that few skinny white girls walked around these parts.

"Actually, yes," I said. "Charity work, you know. I do quite a lot these days, through modeling." God, you're an obnoxious liar.

"Ah-ha." She said, clearly not convinced. "Well, Benji's not here. Didn't he tell you? His student teaching ended. He's done."

"Um … oh, yeah, he mentioned something about it." Smooth. "But I didn't get all the details. We've been playing phone tag for weeks, you know …." Good girl, keep her guessing.

"Well," she said, folding her arms and rolling her big baby blues as she glanced down the hallway. "Benjamin turned down a faculty position for next year. He's leaving Philly to go god-knows-where. Says now he wants to be a 'screenwriter.'"

As she said the word, she held up her fingers to air quote the profession he had chosen, which evidently did not sit well with Miss Do-Right.

"Really?" I said, elated, yet disappointed that I would not get to see him. "Wow, I can't believe it! That's great."

"Great!?" she scolded. Uh-oh. Trouble in paradise? "He'll be living off of ramen noodles for the rest of his life. That doesn't sound so great to me," she said sharply and turned on her heels. "I'm late for class."

"Hey, that's not always the case," I said, calling after.

Little Miss Rice stopped in her tracks and snapped her head around like a tiny Chihuahua. "Really? Well, not *all* of us are willing to sacrifice everything to become superstars like you, Catherine.

Ouch. That hurt. Seeing the look on my face, she softened a bit. "It's just that, well, he's new to it all ... and sometimes it can be scary out there."

Alas, the ice queen does have a heart.

"He'll be OK," I said. And at that moment, I knew I was right.

Benji was following his dream. He was going out on a limb, taking a stab at fame. To be honest, I didn't think he had it in him! But I was thrilled — maybe he'd reach his goal. Maybe he'd find what he was looking for. Maybe he'd have an easier time than me. Whatever happened, I wanted to see him now more than ever.

I took a cab to Benji's place, an old brownstone he'd been renting, not far from the school. His car was gone, and from the outside it looked like no one had been there in weeks: flyers stuck in the door, weeds in the sidewalk cracks. A cat meowed at me from a neighbor's step next door.

I walked up to the front window and stood on my tiptoes, trying to get a good look inside, but a film of dust covered the glass. I couldn't see more than a blurry pile of newspapers stacked in a corner.

*What if it's too late? Oh, god — what if he's decided to move to California before graduation?*

I felt a lump in my throat. The thought of Benji leaving, never to be seen or heard from again, was too much. Even *I* gave my forwarding address in New York. I sat down on the step, thinking about all the opportunities Benji had given me that I'd blown. Last summer, I wrote him off pretty quickly, thinking what a dork he was for dressing all preppy in his khaki Dockers and short-sleeved Polo shirts. And I couldn't see past what I thought was his old-fashioned view on life, his inability to stray from the path of what he had been taught. Then, in New York, when he told me that he liked me and thought we could be more than friends, I secretly scoffed at him. I pushed him away.

Why shouldn't he leave? What was keeping him here on the East Coast? It certainly wasn't me. It certainly wasn't a girl who turned down his advances, who laughed at him, a girl who had misjudged him. Misjudged his authenticity. His ambition.

I boarded a standing-room-only SEPTA bus back to the train station and looked out the window, feeling like I could cry at any moment. Someone spotted me and asked me if I was the girl on the billboard on I-95. I said no. The bus dropped me off at Market and Front Streets in Old City. I started what seemed like a grueling seven-block walk up to Eighth Street to catch the train home, but had to stop along the way because I felt light-headed; a symptom Dr. Barroway said would come from doing too much too soon. I found a bench on Second Street to rest, with the strong smell of yeast and hops coming from a brewery a few doors down, next to the pub where Benji and I had met. I thought about walking by, but, really, what was the point now? Going there wouldn't bring him back.

When I felt I had the strength to make it a few more blocks, I stood up and slowly started to walk toward the corner, but before I could turn, something caught my eye. An old, beat-up Honda with Pennsylvania plates, like the one Benji drove. It had a faded blue bumper sticker on the left side, like Benji's had, that said Big Brothers, Big Sisters of America.

*Oh. My. God.*

I stepped closer to get a better look, and when I was sure it was his car, I ran down to the pub, my heart pounding against my breastbone. I poked my head in the door. He was easy to spot, standing at the end of the bar, in the exact position he had been on that cool, rainy summer night when we met. My heart fluttered at the sight of him, my chest tightened. This was my moment of redemption.

"Hi."

He looked up from his paper, doing a double take before his brain could process who was standing before him.

"Mind if I sit down?" I asked.

I could tell the gears in his brain were moving, but he still didn't speak. I pulled out a barstool.

"How did you find me here?"

"Intuition," I said.

He looked at me curiously.

"I knew that you wouldn't be teaching right now, since you're off to bigger and better things —"

His puzzled look persisted. "What are you doing here? I mean, on this side of the pond? I thought you were in Italy?"

I diverted my eyes, trying to catch a glimpse of what he was reading.

"Oh, well, um, I'm sort of taking a little break from all that."

"Oh," he said, his eyes softening. "Guess it's been a hectic last few months for you. But, hey, you're famous now. I saw you on a billboard on the interstate the other day. Nearly drove right off the road."

We laughed.

"So ... you're off teaching?" I asked, trying to change the subject.

"How do you know that?"

"Psychic."

He asked me again, expecting a serious answer. I told him that I'd been to his school and saw Miss Rice.

"She told you? Really?" he said. "I didn't even tell her. I didn't tell anyone — other than my principal, but I guess word gets around."

"Wouldn't you have told her anyway?" I asked, prying gently enough to get a definitive answer on their status.

"Well," he said, looking over at the dartboard on the wall, "I sort of broke things off with her."

*There is a god.*

"Oh?" I asked nonchalantly. "How come? I thought she was, I thought you and she were ... you know ..."

"She's no Cat Watson," he muttered under his breath, turning away.

"Good for each other," I finished.

Wait, what? "What did you say? Did you say that she was no *me?"*

He had a sneaky grin on his face, the kind where I didn't know exactly if he was joking or not.

"Does it always have to be about you, Catherine?" he said, shaking his head, the smile still on his lips. "What's the real reason you're here? It's more than just to get the dirt on me and Jessica, I suppose."

"Yes, well, um," I said, taking a slow breath. "I wanted to tell you that ..." This was hard. I struggled with my words, knowing that the real reason that I came here wasn't only to apologize to him about things I did earlier. It was to try to get him back. I loved this guy — as a friend, as a person, as a living, breathing human being. He was wonderful to be around in so many ways, and I was just beginning to see it.

"I just wanted to apologize ... for that really inappropriate overseas phone call. God, it was totally stupid of me to wake you up in the middle of the night—"

"No, listen, Catherine," he said, cutting off my words. "I'm the one who should be apologizing. I was a total ass. I never should have said those things to you."

"No, you were right," I said. "I haven't treated you right. I took advantage of our friendship. I assumed you'd always be there, waiting for me, when I needed you. I started to become someone who I didn't like, someone who was only thinking about ... herself."

He looked up at me, his eyes kind, knowing.

"But you were wrong about who I am," I continued. I told him that I wasn't that sort of girl. I wasn't a "fast" girl, as he put it.

Maybe at one point in my life, I pretended that I was, or at least thought I could be. But now I realized that it was all an act. It required a lot of faking on my part to become someone I wasn't.

He sat there for a very long time, listening very intently to everything I said. Shaking his head, pursing his lips here and there, making me feel like he really understood that I had seen the error of my ways. That I almost let the most important part of me slip away.

"And that's why I've decided to stop modeling."

"You what?" he asked, suddenly taken aback. "Why?"

"I ... I just told you why," I said, finally verbalizing the decision that had been accumulating in my mind over the past two weeks. There was no way that I was willing to sacrifice more of myself for that pitiful fame and glory. The frightening thing is that I knew deep down somewhere out there was a girl who would. That's why it was so easy for Clive and Philippe to proposition me. Because there were, as Clive said, "hundreds" of girls just waiting for an opportunity like I had. Just waiting to "seize the moment," as Philippe put it.

"But you can't," Benji said, exasperated by my revelation. "Catherine, you're not the kind of girl to give up. Look, I know that Italy was hard, but you're making it, you're living out your dream. You can't cop out now. It's not like you."

"Benji," I said, finding his response refreshing, charming even, "It's not my dream. I told you, it's not."

It was as if he didn't even hear me.

"Catherine, years from now, after you're, say, married with children, grandchildren, you'll be glad that you followed this dream. You're never going to be one of those people who say, 'What if? What would have happened if I hadn't had the courage to say: Screw it all! Screw my parents, screw what society says, what I'm supposed to be doing. It's now or never. If I don't do it now, I'll never do it. I'll never know.'"

Was this the practical boy I had grown to love? The one who stood for stability, for everything that was dependable in the world? What had happened?

He went on, "I just know that if you don't give it your all, you'll regret it." There was something very telling in his words, in the way he said those words out loud and how impassioned he became. It all clicked now.

"Is that what you're doing? Is that why you've decided to stop teaching?"

He looked down at the bar, slapping his palm on the counter. "You know what? Yeah, it is. I knew that if I started teaching full-time, I'd never have the courage to leave."

"But you did, you did have the courage to leave."

"Thanks to you," he said, looking up from the counter. "I thought if you did it, if you had the courage to do it, why not me?"

"Really?" Had I done something for him? Had I helped him in some way?

"You know, Catherine, before I met you, I was content. At least, I tried to convince myself that I was content with leading the sort of existence that was safe. But there was always this dull ache, this feeling that I ignored. A feeling that maybe, just maybe, there was more to life."

This certainly was flattering. I sat there, a smile on my lips. I had somehow helped him find this newfound joy, this opportunity he had granted himself. But I couldn't help but feel a teeny bit sad at the thought of our paths diverging. Just as I was coming down, he was rising up. And, on top of that, he was moving away, clear across the country.

"That's why, Catherine, you should never give up," he said.

I looked down at the countertop, running my finger along the rounded edge, shuddering at the thought of reliving my moment in Italy with Philippe.

"Benji," I said, hesitating slightly, "There's something else you should know. I haven't told you everything. Well, I haven't told anyone."

It all came out. The attack in the closet. The proposition. That fact that I thought my agent was in on it. By the look on Benji's face, he was horrified, furious.

"Aren't there laws against this!?" he asked.

"It's my word against theirs," I sighed. But still, I hated the thought of going out on their terms. Of letting them get away with this and possibly doing it again to someone else. "I wish there was something I could do, something to prevent it from happening to other girls."

"There is," Benji said, looking down at his rumpled newspaper, a sneaky grin on his face. "Remember that journalist you told me about?"

And so, that afternoon over stale pretzels and burnt coffee, we hatched a plan.

# ✦ 21 ✦

The only way I could do this — and do it right, without getting hurt in the process — was by getting someone influential on my side. That reporter. What was her name? Stacy Goldberg from *The New York Times*. I dug through one of last season's purses to find her business card, crumpled up, with crumbs and lipstick blotted all over it. Though smudged, I could read the phone number. As I picked up the phone to call her, my mouth went dry.

Can I do this?

*Should* I do this?

I put the phone down, remembering what Benji had said about not telling her who I was until she agreed to meet me in a public place and write an exposé that would not cite me as the source. Of course, I would need to give her enough proof so that she thought this story was worth her while. Calling right now, then, I had nothing to lose. If she wasn't interested, I could shop this story around to others. There were plenty of papers in New York City.

She answered the phone right away. Without telling her my name, I told her that I had some "very interesting" information about some very unusual "practices" in the fashion industry.

"Are you directly involved, or is it just hearsay, something you heard?"

"It's happening to me as we speak," I said. She asked how I had gotten her phone number; I told her we had met months ago at a function.

"What's your role in this? Are you an agent? A model?"

"You'll know soon enough," I said. "I can meet you tomorrow on Fifth Ave. Go to Zara's clothing store. When you get there, go upstairs to Women's Contemporary. I'll be standing next to the shoe display, near the fitting rooms. Two p.m."

"All right, but this better not be some wild goose chase. I need some serious proof if you want me to pursue this."

"You'll have it," I said. "What I need from you, though, is a promise that if we move forward you won't reveal who I am."

The next day, I walked through my favorite clothing store (designer-looking duds at discount prices, who can resist!?) wearing a pink mohair boho cap, a matching pink scarf wrapped around my neck, and enormous Jackie O sunglasses. I made sure that my hair was tucked neatly inside my hat so it would be even more difficult to determine who I was. I felt like a Bond girl as I took the elevator up to the second floor and walked toward the display of 3-inch suede booties in pastel spring colors. I lingered by the area, glancing through a rack of wide-leg, denim sailor pants, trying to act nonchalant even though I felt like I could just start screaming at the top of my lungs and bouncing off the walls at any moment from the surge of adrenaline ripping through my veins.

A woman about fortyish, looking quite out of place in a pair of ill-fitting mom jeans, appeared in the elevator and made a beeline for the shoes.

For a moment, I thought it was the reporter and my palms started to sweat. My heart fluttered. But then I remembered the reporter, Stacy, was much shorter and a bit younger.

"Meeting someone?" a girl's voice said from behind me, coming out from the fitting room. It was the girl I had noticed downstairs when I first arrived. She had been looking through the clothing racks and had come upstairs to try something on. I gave her a strange look.

"It's Stacy. Are you ... my afternoon date?"

"Stacy Goldberg?" I asked her, taken aback.

"Yes. Hope you don't mind," she said, pointing to a dress she had tried on. "I'm in search of the perfect little black dress."

I breathed a sigh of relief. This would be easier than I had thought. She was a regular girl. I gauged her to be a bit younger than I remembered, in her late twenties. She looked as excited and interested to be there as I was. She said that while it was her dream to do investigative reporting, she was still climbing the ladder, waiting for her chance to prove herself.

She was intrigued by my hinting. What she had seen at shows backstage had whet her palate. She thought there was a lot that went on that the public didn't know about and got the feeling that the industry was sort of put on a pedestal, managing to evade scrutiny. "I know for one thing," she said, "commissions for models who work aren't regulated. In the '70s, commissions were capped at 10 percent. But, I know today…"

"It's at 20 percent, sometimes higher, and there's nothing that models can do about it," I said. "I know, I've heard girls complaining and those who say anything—"

"Get blackballed," she said.

This girl knew her stuff.

"So, whatcha got for me?"

"Well, before we go any further," I said, pulling a boot off a ledge and sitting down to hold it up against my foot. She sat down beside me. "I need you to promise not to use my name. It's very important for my … safety that my identity isn't revealed."

She looked at me. "Are you in danger?"

"Well, not really. But things could turn very ugly if someone finds out I'm telling secrets."

"OK, you have my word," she said. "But I can't promise that anything will come of this meeting if there's no story here."

"Oh, I think you'll have a story," I said, pulling out a small phone tap from my bag that was cued and ready to go.

"What's this?" she asked.

"You'll see," I said, handing her a small earbud for her ear, which she hid by pulling up her collar. I held the tap in my hand and pressed "play" as I asked the salesgirl for a pair of light pink suede summer sandals in a 10.

This is what Stacy heard:

"Hello, Stacy. Thanks for meeting me here today. I am a model who has worked under contract for a very prestigious New York modeling agency for the last six months. In the last few weeks, I have become aware of some very inappropriate — and possibly illegal — practices within the industry. Most recently, I have been directed, pressed really, by my agent to accept an offer from a client who I had been working for almost exclusively. As I have been told this is a turning point in my career, I feel that I am being forced to make choices that will secure me in this profession indefinitely. This is a recent conversation between me and that client — a very high-profile, multimillion-dollar account whose brand graces the pages of every fashion magazine. This designer has been hailed as the leading European designer of the 21st century. The following conversation was taped days after he invited me to his home and forced himself sexually on me. When his advances failed, he offered a so-called 'business' proposition: a contracted proposal of a 20,000 dollar a month allowance, a five-year contract, a fully-paid apartment in the city, and the opportunity to make 1,000,000 dollars a year in exchange for not just modeling for his campaign but also providing sexual services. This first call you will now hear is a taped conversation we had over the phone, following that incident."

I made the call from Benji's parents' house, using the phone tap we purchased at Best Buy. The portion of the conversation that Stacy heard is after we began talking and names had been exchanged. I couldn't have her hearing who was involved without first promising full anonymity for me and disclosure of Philippe's identity much later. (Static.)

A man's gruff voice: "Dahling, where have you been? I was worried when we didn't hear from you."

(Shuffling around, breathing. You could almost hear the sound of my heart beating out of my chest. My voice came out faintly, like I had just run up a flight of stairs to answer the phone. My anxiety caused a breathy, barely there voice. "I've been at my parents' house."

"Oh, you don't sound well," he said.

"I guess it was all that traveling. I got sick. I've been home recuperating," I said, clearing my throat and regaining some of my composure. "What I called to talk to you about was the, ah... thing we discussed before I left Italy."

"Oh?"

"I'm ... I'm sorry that I left like that. It was really wrong of me. God, I can be such a drama queen sometimes, you know?"

"Oh, *mi piccolo bella,* you know that you're my favorite girl. You know I would never do anything to hurt you."

"I know, I know. Look, if it's OK with you, I'd like a little more time to think about your very generous offer."

"Sure, baby, but I really would like to know ... soon."

"There are some things I wanted to ask you about it. First of all, thank you. I know it's a great honor that you've chosen me."

"There is no other. You're my Remi. She lives through you, dahling."

I saw Stacy's eyes widen as she turned to look at me. Shit. She knew it was Philippe.

"About the offer," I said awkwardly. "Can you remind me of the, ah, specifics, again?"

"Oh, no, over the phone? These things should be discussed in private. It's safer for both of us."

"Oh, right. I'm sorry. It's just that I'm a bit confused about things."

"What are you confused about?"

"Well, would I be working exclusively for you? Would my agency get a cut of it?"

"Unfortunately, I don't think we can bypass your agents, sweetie. They would still get their commission on the contract. The other portion of it, your apartment allowance, the rest of the money, we may be able to proffer something so that they don't see that and the money goes straight to you."

"What do you mean? You're talking about the money that I get for promising my exclusivity of ... myself? Promising to be with just you and no other men, to stay in the apartment you would provide for me, separate from the work I do for you through modeling?"

"Yes, dear. I'm not sure how we will work it out. Clive will indubitably want his cut from somewhere."

"Maybe I should talk to him, then."

"We'll work it all out. Wait to talk to him after you have decided what is right for you, for your career. Just remember, this could solidify you in fashion history. You could become a living legend, my love."

"I know," I said, trying to force every ounce of bile that was bubbling up from my stomach to stay in my throat. "Thank you, again. We'll talk soon."

I could tell that the first conversation had ended when Stacy's jaw was down on the ground and she looked strangely at the girl who brought me a pair of cork wedges to try on.

Next victim: Clive. I called him just to get a feel for how deeply he had knowingly, willfully been involved with this proposition.

"I'm still kinda sick." I said. "The doctor says I need bedrest for three more weeks. But with the spring season approaching, I know there's no time for that."

"That's my girl," he said. "Just take off the rest of this week, rest up, and you'll be fine. So ... how did the fitting for Philippe go?"

"Um ... fine. It was fine."

"Really? Just fine?"

"Yeah. Um, did he tell you he wants me to sign an exclusive contract with him? For the next few years. Did he mention it?"

"We talked."

"I thought you would have talked to me about it first. It's a pretty big deal."

"We thought, considering the delicacy of it all, that he should be the one to pass it by you."

"Oh. So you know about what we discussed?"

"I have a good idea," he said. "I think you'd be crazy to pass it up."

"You mean, pass ... everything up?"

"Everything, yes. I mean everything: the contract, the

apartment, the exclusivity of it all. Cat, this is your ticket, handed on a silver platter. You'd be crazy to pass it up. And don't play Little-Miss-Innocent. I think you're finding out, Cat, that role will get you nowhere in life. Success is not for the pious."

There was a long pause as I was pinching myself over the trap he had so carelessly walked into.

"Yeah, you're right. How many girls get this opportunity?"

"See what I told you months ago? Stick with me, kid. I was worried about you for a while, but I think you're turning out all right. You're gonna make it in this business, and you have the potential, if you play your cards right, to become a household name. Maybe even with your own reality show! Let's talk next week when you're back in New York."

The tape ended, and Stacy turned to me, holding out her hand to shake. "You've got a deal," she said. "This stuff's unbelievable."

I smiled. "This is going to be tough."

"It's worth it," she said. "Even if it just gets people talking. This story needs to be told."

I pulled up pictures from Icon's holiday party that I had taken as I waited for Seth to meet me that night. A few teen models had passed out on couches in the lobby of the hotel. One girl, lying in a see-through cami with a drink in her hand, was awoken by one of her bookers, who helped to get her to her feet.

"I knew that underage drinking was going on that night, though the agencies told me these girls were always chaperoned," she said, looking at the images.

"Yeah, guess who's doing the chaperoning? The people supplying the liquor and drugs," I said, remembering the girl in the bathroom with us who couldn't have been more than 15. She had been snorting something that I saw passed out at a table by some agency reps.

She looked at me. "So are you prepared for this?" she asked. "Becoming my 'Deep Throat'?"

The moment she said it, we both laughed.

"Hey, it's the modeling industry, not politics or even the porn biz," I said, realizing, that in fact, those lines had blurred.

That day, I left Zara's comforted by the thought of a kindred spirit among all the madness. I walked out of the shop with my phone tap and a new pair of cork wedges. Before turning the corner, I pulled out my cell and called Philippe at his New York studio to tell him that his offer, which I had been mulling over for quite some time, was just too good to pass up.

# ✦ 22 ✦

I came home that afternoon, giddy with excitement, to find Jonnie standing in her nightgown bent over a lopsided chocolate cake, icing with a steak knife. Pots, pans, cake mix, and icing were strewn all over the kitchen counter. The cake mix box was crumpled up and mashed into the floor with droplets of batter.

"Jonnie?"

"Oh, hi," she said softly, not lifting her gaze.

I put my bags on the bed and noticed a magazine lying open. It was the current issue of *Glamour* magazine, the one that was to have a center spread of Jonnie on the beach in Thailand, where she had been while I was in Italy.

"Ohmigod!" I shrieked, picking it up.

"Didn't make it," she said, lifting her head to look straight ahead at the wall.

"What?"

"The issue. I was cut. Didn't get in."

"What? That's crazy! What happened? You said it was a great shoot."

"It was." She teetered over the cake, not picking her head up to look at me. I walked over to her and leaned against the counter. Her eyes were red and puffy.

"I'm sorry," I said. "You know it's just part of the business, it happens to everyone," I said, pulling a strand of hair out of her eyes.

She laughed a little, shrugging her shoulders while holding the knife intently over the cake. "Does it? Didn't happen to you

... well, it doesn't matter anyway. I'm going to get old and fat. So now I can have my cake and eat it too, right?"

She licked her sticky fingers. "Never could have cake."

I looked down at her tumbling masterpiece, wondering if this blow was too much for her ego. She had always been the lucky one, the one everyone was drawn to, the one for whom this business was created. But perhaps Jonnie wasn't quite as strong as I'd thought. Perhaps none of us were.

"And now," she said, placing the knife on the counter (to my relief) and slumping down onto a rickety stool, "No agency will take me. Said I'm getting *too old*. Too old at 22."

"That's crazy, Icon would never drop you," I protested.

"Oh, really?" she said. "They already did. Shall I play the message from Clive?"

My jaw almost fell to the floor. Jonnie was once one of the highest earning girls at Icon. Why would they do this? It was ludicrous! Unless, of course, they thought they'd be making more money somewhere else...

"Oh, god!" I blurted, barely able to contain the force of my words. *Was it because I accepted Philippe's offer? Did Clive think he didn't need Jonnie anymore now that he'd be making a fortune off of me?*

"My contract was up for renewal," she said. "Didn't think I had anything to worry about."

"Jonnie, I'm so sorry," I said, the wheels still turning in my head. That's probably what happened. Clive thinks there's more money to be made elsewhere. And now, since Jonnie is getting "up there" in her years, he thought this was a perfect time to ditch her. *Unbelievable, that scum!*

"But you will totally find another agent, don't worry," I said. And I meant it.

I crouched down next to her and told her that even if things seemed like they were at their lowest point — as they often did these days — they would improve. I said it not just for her but for me as well. We were destined to find our way. If not in modeling, then in something else, something better that life had in store for us.

"There's nothing else for me to do," she cried. "There is nothing else I know *how* to do. I'm not like you, Catherine. I was never a good student, I barely even finished high school. No college would want me ... it's too late."

"What are you talking about? Our lives are just beginning! We're young! You could take night classes for college credit — it's not too late. Or what about opening your own café, your own vegan restaurant? You cook the best Tofurky I've ever had!"

"The only one you've ever had," she said as she broke into a smile.

"See? There's lots of other things you could do," I said. "Hey, maybe this turns out to be a good thing. Maybe Icon has given you the push you needed. You knew you couldn't model forever, right?"

She got real quiet and looked down at the floor. "Of course ... but Cat," she said, biting down hard on her lip as a tear ran down her cheek, "I've been modeling since I was 13. Leaving the business is not as easy as it sounds."

"Just don't let them defeat you. Don't let them win."

"Right," she said, weakly. "But I just wish I could show them that they can't go around ruining people's lives on a whim, throwing people away when they think they're all used up. I wish there was something I could do."

"There is," I said.

Over the next few weeks, I met with Stacy three or four more times. Once it was in front of the TKTS booth in Times Square, which was so crowded with tourists that no one would have singled us out. Another time it was down on Canal Street, surrounded by a throng of merchants selling knockoffs.

Each time, I brought a new tidbit of information. While I wasn't able to get a copy of Icon's accounting records, I was able to get paycheck stubs from a bunch of girls Jonnie knew who were quietly inquiring with a lawyer about the discrepancies in their take-home pay. And then there were the diet pills. Prescription ones, narcotics. Little did I know, but Jonnie had been put on and off them since she was 14, even though by medical standards she was considered *under*weight. She had promised to speak to Stacy about her experiences, as Stacy preferred to talk with Jonnie directly to get her side of the story. Stacy had already been doing a lot of research, and she had talked to a few other models who agreed to have their names published, which would add credibility to the story.

On one particular day, Stacy told me that the lead I gave her about the questionable practices of some model homes in Europe lead to a string of testimonials from girls who had (or knew someone who had) been forced into prostitution. Others were coerced into accompanying sleazy old businessmen to dinner, a setup they later discovered some of their agents were well aware of.

"Know any of them?" Stacy asked, pulling out her phone and flipping through some composites.

I looked through the pictures, not recognizing any of the girls at first. Most of them were with agencies I had never heard of, which probably meant their ethics were even shadier than a well-established agency like Icon's. They were able to fly under the radar more easily.

As I got to the end, I noticed someone. It was my roommate from Italy, the Belgian girl. "I know this girl! I know this girl!" I said, aghast.

"You know her? She stopped modeling a few months ago, after a really bad experience. Seems she was almost raped by some guy she was set up with in Milan. Said his name was Angeloni-something-or-other."

The name rang a bell. And then, it all came back to me in high-def: The vellum card. The fancy script. Maria's panicky phone call. *This was the man they tried to set me up with!* Knowing that I was just one dinner date away from being covered in purple hickeys (or worse, possibly much worse) sent a shiver down my spine.

I thought about the girls who hadn't been as lucky, who had a harder time than me, or those who kept coming back for more, over and over, thinking that maybe, just maybe, this time it will lead to a big break. This person, or this photographer, or this go-see would get them on the cover of that magazine. The belief that their dream would come true. It was all an endless, meaningless search. Fame at all costs. It was like a drug, this desire.

It came back to me in waves. The yearning, the will to make it. To *be* something. To *be* someone. Why didn't I listen to my parents' warnings? *Naive thinking at best, hazardous at worst*, my father said of my desire to be a model. Why did I think I was different, that what happened to other girls wouldn't happen to me? That I was somehow exempt from any suffering?

Looking back, the signs were all around me. "You don't want to end up like Remi," Philippe had said. Envied by all around her but sad on the inside. Miserable. *Dead*. Remi may not have had the courage to change her fate, the courage to leave, but I did, and I would.

It was then that I knew there was something I still needed to do.

A fierce wind whipped through my trench coat and singed my exposed ears like a thousand tiny bee stings. I shuddered, turning my collar up as I walked ahead. An ominous storm cloud hovered above, eerily appropriate. I wondered if maybe I had made a mistake by venturing all the way here to the outskirts of Queens by myself.

I found the stone pretty easily. It was nothing fancy. Gray-and-white fleck with black lettering. Simple. Understated. Not at all what I expected.

### Regina Allen Fosgate
### 1969–2003
### Devoted Wife, Loving Mother

I placed the flowers at the base of the stone, feeling a calm quietness wash over me. A sort of a reverence. This was the first time I'd ever been in a cemetery. I had never known anyone who died other than my grandfather on my mother's side, and

I was really too young to remember him when he passed away. How strange to be treading on the grandfathers of others now, the mothers, fathers. I shivered. A family in the distance walked somberly, while a child shrieked behind and chased after a squirrel.

*Devoted wife, loving mother.*

It hit me then that Seth's mother was lying, still as stone, beneath my feet while mine was somewhere in New Jersey. He would never be able to call her. He would never be able to count on her for anything. She would never take care of him when he was sick, she would never listen patiently to his stories, his complaints. It struck me then how badly he'd been robbed.

How final. How absolute.

"I'm sorry." I said. For Remi, but also for Seth. Maybe I had been too hard on him. Expected too much. Maybe he did the best he could with what he had been given. And if I were truly honest, maybe I expected too much from myself, too. I couldn't be Seth's mother. I couldn't save him. It seems one can only save oneself.

On my way back home to my apartment, Clive buzzed my cell. It was getting tougher and tougher to stall him. He was anxious to get me back in the swing in time for fall photo shoots. My stomach was in knots each time he asked how I was feeling, each time the phone rang (this season's ringtone? Kelly Clarkson's *Stronger* — "what doesn't kill you makes you stronger" — to pump me up). The doctor's note, which gave me a total of four weeks' "bed rest," was running out.

He tried to pin me down, at least once a day, to sign the contract. I told him that my acceptance was contingent on getting everything in writing. This would buy me more time, I thought, until the article came out. Clive conceded to my wishes and said he would make it so the "mutual agreement" with Philippe (i.e., illicit sex-trade component) was left out of the document.

"You're a smart cookie," Clive said, referring to my choice to proceed with Philippe's offer. "You are becoming a business-woman. I'm impressed."

Before we hung up the phone, agreeing that I would be in the following week to sign papers, he told me that a Philippe shoot scheduled for May had been pushed up to April, three weeks early.

"I'm assuming he'll be back in town this weekend, so I think the shoot's scheduled for a few days after his arrival," Clive said.

My heart fell to pieces. The thought of seeing Philippe again, face to face, was too much to bear. I think Clive could hear the worry in my voice. "But ... but ... he wasn't supposed to be back for a few more weeks ... I, I mean, that's what I was told," I said.

"Is there a problem?"

"No, no," I recovered. "Just needed a little more time to pamper myself before he arrives in town."

Two weeks before the story was set to run, I got three panicky text messages from Stacy. Jonnie refused to talk, and another interview, someone from the Counsel of Fashion Designers of America who had agreed to meet her for an interview, canceled at the last minute and wouldn't return her calls. Possibly worst of all for me, the article would run one week early. The story would print on the last day of my Philippe shoot, something I wasn't at all prepared for.

Fortunately, Philippe had postponed his arrival and I had managed to escape from meeting with him — albeit at the price of a few delicate phone calls in which I appeared to be joyful at his return. He said he "could not wait" to get back to New York to see me. The words sickened me. I began to feel I was in too deep and feared that something would go terribly wrong. After all, who was I to think that I could blow the whistle on a whole industry of people, a way of life that had existed this way for decades?

"Just hang in there," Benji said. "You haven't signed anything, and your old contract expired. You can't lose, I promise you."

"Yes, but it's the wait that's killing me. I could walk away from it all right now and never—"

"Have to see those creeps again," he finished for me. "I know." He knew exactly what I was thinking. We each finished each other's sentences more and more often. "If that's what you really want, Catherine..."

But, he continued, it was probably better for me that the story was coming a week earlier. Now I wouldn't have to suffer another week with my stomach in knots. He was right: The sooner things were out on the table for everyone to see, the sooner I could bow out of this nightmare. That is, if everything worked out as planned. It was a big *if*.

When Jonnie came home that night, I confronted her about the interview. She said that she was too busy, that she didn't have time. Then she came clean with the *real* reason: She was in talks with a new agency.

"I think I've finally got an agency that's interested in me and I'm not going to jeopardize it now," she said.

"But what about our talk?" I asked. "What about looking into schools? I thought there were other things you wanted to do."

"Oh, that can wait," she said, cutting out an advertisement for Botox from a fashion magazine. "Think this would work for me?"

At that moment I realized there was no breaking through to her. There never really had been, after all. She was lost. This world that had sucked her in at such a young age had shaped her destiny. She no longer had a choice. She would continue to be swept up, to ride a big wave, where, every now and then, she would soar. But eventually, she would wipe out. It would happen again. But who knew if next time she would have the strength to get back up.

That night, I lay in bed staring at the New York skyline, and I thought about Jonnie and all the other nameless beauties. The fragile ones, the ones who couldn't keep their heads above water and didn't have anyone to guide them, to support them. Someone to keep the monsters at bay.

# ✦ 23 ✦

"Darling! How fabulous to see you!" Gail shrieked. Her taut face twisting into odd contortions as she tried to exact a look of pleasure, which, had she been able to, would have still looked like a cross between Edvard Munch's *The Scream* and a circus clown heaped in pancake. Guess that's what a lifetime of drugs and plastic surgery will do to ya.

I thought she was talking to someone else, perhaps someone right behind me, because this was the first time I had gotten such a greeting — in fact, any greeting at all that didn't include a scowl — from the woman.

"It's been sooo long," she continued. "Milan feels like eons ago."

She pointed to a director's chair next to the makeup area that faced the photographer's backdrop. On the back of the black canvas chair in bold white letters, it read "CAT." Gail motioned for me to sit in the chair — in *my* chair — next to Philippe's chair, which she was keeping warm till his arrival.

I awkwardly perched myself on the seat. *Oh, what things I had to do to get this chair! What things I'd have to do to keep this chair!*

"San Pellegrino?" she asked, holding out a bottle for me. "Ever since I left Italy, I just can't subsist on anything else. The bottled water over here is pure sewage."

She placed a bottle in my lap, and for the rest of the day we sat on our foldout thrones overseeing the mini kingdom that lay before us. The makeup artists scurried in Gail's presence. She wasn't known for being easy to work with. She would make them redo a face, over and over, until they got it "right." The lighting crew, the photographer and his assistant, even the caterers cowered to her — "Yes, Gail!" "Oh, that's an excellent idea! I never would have thought of that!" — full in the knowledge of her reputation for tantrums, not to mention the fact that, as vice president of the House of Philippe, her signature was what would ultimately let them pay their rent that month or put their kids through college one day.

And I, her newest protégé, was consulted on all details of the shoot, however minor.

"Don't you think that lighting is too yellow?" she asked me as the models got into place to shoot the ready-to-wear looks.

"*Oh. My. Lord.* What on earth are these prop people doing? I asked for white doves, not black and white! For god's sake, we cannot release black doves for a winter shoot!"

She continued: "Is someone wearing perfume? What is that god-awful stench? It must be the makeup girls. I told you, ladies, you cannot wear perfume around the designs. We can't have our clothes reeking of *Glow.*"

Since I was with the taskmaster, I, too, was treated with kid gloves. "Hello, dah-ling" and "hello, beautiful" and smiles and people stopping what they were doing to let me pass; googly eyes watching me from every corner of the room and hushed whispers when I entered someone's workspace. I was no longer invisible, yet not exactly an equal, either. I'd suddenly been thrust onto a higher plane, placed on a pedestal that I had no intention of lingering upon any longer than absolutely necessary.

The second day of shooting went the same, but as the day dragged on I felt the panicky, hives-inducing feeling I had on the day I moved to Brooklyn. I tossed and turned for hours. Images of old-fashioned newsreels cycled through my brain. I imagined those vignettes from old movies — the ones where you see the papers running on a printing press, then a little boy shouting the next morning on a street corner, "Extra! Extra! Read all about it!"

I bolted upright and jumped out of bed.

*That's it. I'll just call out tomorrow, saying that I'm sick. No, wait, THAT would look too suspicious. Would that look too suspicious? They would know!* AGH! I'll just have to go to work and face Philippe for the first time since Milan, like everything is fine. I'll pretend that I didn't even know, didn't even read the news. Besides, models aren't supposed to know about current events anyway. I mean, for this job, we're not even required to know how to *read*.

11:45 p.m. Obsessively checking the newspaper's site to see if the story has posted.

Midnight. Only 5 more hours until the newspaper lands on everyone's doorstep.

1:50 a.m. AGH! The story is posted but I can't read it unless I get a subscription! Who the hell charges for the internet!?!

2:32 a.m. Do I still have time to break into the printing press and pull the fire alarm?

4:02 a.m. Aghh! Where did the time go?

5:17 a.m. *OHMIGOD OHMIGOD OHMIGOD.*

By 5:22 I was sitting on the toilet battling the worst stomachache of my life. I thought I was going to die. I hoped I was going to die. *Please, God, let me die. Or at least, let everyone else die in a meteor crash or something.* One may think it was selfish of me to wipe out most of the world just to escape my own personal hell. But no one would know if they were dead. It would be like they went to bed last night and never woke up. It would be like a very long, peaceful dream...

BEEP. BEEP. BEEP. BEEEEEP. 6 a.m. The alarm blasted through my eardrum like a rocket, exploded like grenade in my heart.

Judgment Day.

My fingers trembled as I wrestled with the newspaper. I walked 10 blocks to get it at a little convenience store on Lorimer Street because the newsstand near my apartment was closed. As I stepped out my door, I half expected to find a wasteland of epic proportions, something out of *Apocalypse Now*, but, alas, everything was just as it was the day before. Birds were softly tweeting. Pigeons were flying overhead. The burnt-out car that had been sitting in front of my apartment for days was still there. Even so, I knew my world had been turned upside down. It was a strange feeling, sort of like on Christmas morning when you look outside and everything looks the same, only it's not. Things are different. Changed. There are wonderful presents sitting under the tree, objects that you'd dreamt about for months. Only this time the surprise was for someone else. And, oh, what a gift it was!

I found the lifestyle section and pulled the pages apart, nearly ripping the newsprint with my voracity. There it was, in black and white. It was grander and more horrifying than I had imagined. The photo I had given Stacy, which Seth had taken of Fiona on her 19th birthday a few months back when we were still dating, took up half the page. In it, Fiona lay motionless on a couch with a line of cocaine on the table in front of her. Beneath, the headline read:

### Glamour Gore: The Ugly Truth of the Beauty Biz
*What's Happening to Our Young Girls?*

The words that followed made all the blood drain from my face: "five-part series," "investigative report," "corruption," "underhanded practices." I ate up every word, trying to see, perhaps, if my identity could be derived from any contextual clues presented. It would be hard to hold me accountable, I thought, because Stacy did a very good job of disguising my identity while padding my comments with either hard evidence or testimony from other girls who had had similar experiences. And then there were the industry quotes. They made some pretty bold accusations: tax evasion, fraud, unpaid wages, underage drinking, sexual assault, prostitution. This would instill great paranoia in those select untouchables whose way of life had been stable but now would be as shaky as a house of cards.

"Jesus Christ!" Raphael, my hair stylist, screamed as I blew through the door at half-past eight. He threw down a copy of *Time*

*Out New York* and I froze. A wave of panic washed over me. "They're demolishing the old Studio 54 building! Those bastards!"

"Pure sacrilege," his assistant snarled with a lisp.

"That's too bad," I eeked out.

*Thank god.* No one had seen the *Times* yet. I sat in the makeup chair and held my breath, waiting for the other shoe to drop. There was the TICK, TICK, TICK of my watch. The clearing of the throat, AHEM, AHEM, AHEM, from the woman carelessly fastening hot rollers in my hair. The turning of magazine pages on my lap. RIP. RIP. RIP.

RINGGGGGGGGGGGGGGGGG!

A phone ringing nearly jolted me out of my skin. A few feet away, the photographer picked up his cellphone. Beep. "Uh-huh. Uh-huh. Yes. Hmm. I see. Well, OK, we'll be here." Beep.

Philippe's flight had been delayed. Gail was nowhere to be found and hadn't shown up at her office yet. The shoot wouldn't start until almost noon. Three more excruciatingly long hours.

TICK, TICK, TICK.

By 1:30, I felt like I'd lost 10 pounds just in sweat. If something didn't happen soon, I was going to lose my mind. At 1:45, we finally got word from someone in Philippe's camp. They said to go ahead with the shoot — something had come up. My heart raced; I had just two outfits to model before it would be a wrap. I figured that if time was on my side, I could hurry and get it all done before either Philippe or Gail showed up.

But time wasn't on my side. At 2:32, Gail appeared in the doorway, her left arm interlaced with Philippe's. Dangling from her right hand was a copy of *The New York Times'* LIFESTYLE section.

And just like that, all hell broke loose.

From the tops of the rafters, she wailed and he moaned.

"When we catch the people who did this — who slandered us — it's over for them!" she screamed. "Don't think my lawyers don't know about this!"

They spouted vitriol like two screaming babies confined to their cribs. They threatened, they cursed, they condemned those who had prospered from their "power," their "vision," their "talent." The fear, the fear, the loss. Their grand empire had suffered a blow. A compromised structure, the façade now cracked, and from it tumbled its fragile mortar.

They raged for what felt like hours upon hours. Just when you thought you could make your escape, they descended. Accusing all yet no one. There was no one to blame but themselves. And yet they cornered each of us, the helpless prey. "Who knew? Who knew!?"

The photographer. The stylists. The makeup girl. She could talk — oh, she could talk. The seamstress we fired. What an ungrateful cunt.

And Cat? Oh, no. She's one of us now; she has too much to lose.

Besides, I'm just a model. A no one. A nobody. I smile and nod and turn my head in pretty pictures. I make other women feel worthless with my art. I make myself feel worthless with my art.

It was nothing more than a glance. A nod, a gesture in my direction. In that split second, it all could have, it all should have, come together in his mind. Could the fire in her eye be more than just the gleam of youth? But there was no fire. There was no gleam. There was no spark of life, only the flat, blanket stare that I had perfected for him, for them, for everyone on the street. That dead, empty stare that incited envy, projected superiority. Oh, what a perfect look; it served me well.

Vapid beauty saved me.

# ✦ 24 ✦

"And we're back," the bobbled-headed lady said. "Talking with Catherine Watson, former top model Cat, and one of the first to come forward in what has now become known as 'Modelgate.' Catherine left the modeling industry and spoke out against the notoriously underhanded modeling business. She's really helped to open our eyes to the harsh realities. So glad to have you here today."

"Thank you for inviting me to the show, Joan," I said, still unclear as to which of the three cameras in the studio I was supposed to be looking into.

"Tell me," she said, in her most serious newscaster voice, "It must have taken a lot of courage to do what you did, at such a young age. How did you do it?"

"Well, Joan, it was hard at first, but I needed to share my story. After I quit modeling, I got the courage to come forward and reveal myself as Stacy Goldberg's main source in the *Times* exposé. I did it because I wanted other girls to learn from my experience," I said.

"That's wonderfully admirable," she said. "And now, tell us about the new project you're working on. I understand you're trying to reach out to other young women, who were like yourself?"

This was it. My moment. The first time I would be able to reach a large enough audience. Well, large enough to reach all five New York boroughs, which was a start.

"Yes, Joan — in fact that's why I'm here today. I want young women and men who are struggling like I was, trying to 'make it' in the modeling world, to know that they're not alone. They can connect with others who are facing similar challenges."

"So, are you talking about a support group of sorts?" she pressed, asking the scripted question as if she didn't know the answer.

"That's exactly right, Joan. It's called Model2Model — it's a group where models can ask questions, get answers, and talk to more experienced models who provide guidance and insight on navigating the system so that new models can avoid some of the pitfalls."

Joan tried to cut in, but I wasn't gonna get off my soapbox yet.

"Listen, Joan, the truth is that unlike many other talent groups in the country, models have no rights. They have no protection, like actors have the Actors Equity Association. Every agency's policies are different, and their practices vary greatly. Even some with well-known names like Icon have been known to engage in unethical practices."

She cut in quickly, not wanting me to steal the show. "I understand the average age of a model beginning her career in this industry is usually around 13 — just a child!" She cried into the camera.

"That's right, Joan. And, let's face it, girls this age don't possess the decision-making abilities, the reasoning skills, or the maturity to make adult decisions. Often, their parents — like mine — aren't familiar with the business, and are just as unprepared or unqualified to make the right choice for her."

"Pity," Joan said, giving her most insincere, distracted newscaster look, like she was pouting over the third run-over kitty cat of the day. I could tell I was losing her.

"But I believe that by having a system of checks and balances in place, we can avoid the problems that we've all heard about or read in the papers," I said, my heart starting to race faster at what I was to say next. "That's why I want to start a model's union of sorts, where everyone can benefit from regulated commissions, overtime pay, labor laws, and protection for minors. This would not only clean up the image of the industry, but it would make it a lot safer, and ultimately, more profitable for all those involved when they're not dealing with legal bills."

"Brilliant!" Joan winked, signaling the end of the show. "Best of luck!"

The applause track rolled, and the camera lights stopped blinking. As I gathered up my belongings in the green room, my cellphone buzzed. "Wonderful, darling!" my mother chimed through the phone. "We're so proud of you."

"Really, Mom? You don't think I seemed too nervous? Was I too heavy-handed?" I asked sincerely.

"I should think not!"

Since the scandal in the papers, my mom had been calling me nonstop. Who could blame her, really? Her baby was at the center of an industry crackdown that had made worldwide headlines. And since she couldn't watch the show on local cable, she went online to view the real-time webcast — a setup my mother had arranged herself, thanks to the computer classes she was now enrolled in at community college (along with everything else: pottery, cooking, genealogy, you name it).

I hoped my mom's anxiety would die down, but, understandably, she was still concerned about what was going on in my life. After things dissolved with Icon, I was able to come clean and fill her in on some of the more PG-rated details of the last 12 months.

Cutting ties with Icon was much easier than I had thought it would be. A few days after Philippe and Gail's tirade, Clive called to say that Philippe wanted to wait till things "cooled down" before we proceeded with any aforementioned deal. I was almost off the hook.

"Oh, yes, that's fine," I said. "God forbid we get caught up in those horrific accusations," I added, feeling slightly uneasy about treading that close to something that was on everybody's minds but nobody's lips.

Clive paused for a moment, then said, "What accusations do you mean?"

*Oh, god.* Did he catch an inkling of the uncontainable joy in my tone? He wasn't stupid. No, sir. He was not stupid.

"Um, well ... oh, I don't know. It really doesn't bode well for the, um, industry."

Clive didn't wait to hear those last few words, "Cat, I think you'll agree that all dealings between us and our clients have always been nothing but ethical. How dare they try to pull us down with them, those sleazy, B-rated agencies that operate in back alleys? That's what those torrid stories were about, Cat. Nothing more. There's nothing for us to worry about."

Three days later, Clive was gone. Just like that. A man who had been working in the fashion industry for 25 years just slunk away, into the shadows, quietly placing all his items — the Christmas cards that hung on his door year round, the tourist tchotchkes, like the little macadamia nut man who sang, "Aloha from Hawaii" on his desk — in a cardboard box sometime after 7 p.m. on a Tuesday night.

The next day, I received an unusual phone call from Philippe's lawyers. With so many strategically placed words, they tried to bribe me to keep my mouth shut about all aforementioned "arrangements." But I didn't need the money, thank you very much. I was already getting what I wanted.

Each day in Stacy's report, I read more and more about the industry, things that, had I known them before I started my career, I probably would have hesitated to step into this world. We watched the television reports and, in time, the court cases. I was called to testify in the agency brothel ring fiasco — an operation that spanned from New York to Miami to Milan to Tokyo. Stacy went on to win a number of journalism awards for her investigative work, and rumor had it she was up for a Pulitzer Prize. She was finally reaching her dream, she said, and perhaps in a way I was reaching mine, too (or at least figuring out what it *really* was).

Soon after Clive left Icon, the agency hired a yes-man whose sole purpose in life seemed to be to get me to finally sign that contract. After weeks of being hounded, I finally told him that that phase of my life was over. They would not get one more penny out of me. Seeing what I could do with just my one voice gave me a greater sense of purpose than any photograph, magazine spread, or catwalk jaunt ever could. Me, Catherine

Watson — meek, mild, invisible Catherine — could make her mark on the world in a way that was helpful to others. Not in a selfish, self-centered way that only helped to validate my own existence. I didn't need that anymore. I knew I was alive, I felt the blood coursing through my veins.

I pushed through the studio doors, the late September sun blinding me, and reached in my backpack to grab my shades. They were a small reminder of my former life: a pair of $300 Versace sunglasses I'd gotten in a gift bag after a show. Across the street, a bespectacled boy leaned up against a subway entrance with his face hidden in a book; he looked up and waved me over. This person didn't have a cool hairdo, a trendy outfit, or the newest pair of Diesel jeans, but the sight of him made my insides go all mushy anyway.

"Hi," I said, as I approached.

"How'd it go?" he asked, placing a kiss on my cheek.

"My parents said it went really well. I think it did, too."

"That's my girl," Benji said. "Catherine, the fearless warrior, fighting for the rights of beautiful people everywhere!"

"Yeah, too bad I can't fight for you. Ha ha," I said, tugging on his earlobe. "Ready for class?"

It hadn't been hard to change Benji's mind about moving out to California. He agreed that New York was as good a place as any to work on his screenplay. What I didn't know was that after graduation he'd gone ahead and enrolled in NYU film school — a decision that was made easy by my having enrolled at NYU, too. Yes, it's true: Catherine, the girl who wanted adventure, excitement, a life less ordinary, was opting for the more conventional path. But it was the only way to accomplish my long-term goals. The plan was to major in pre-law, and then go to the Fashion Law Institute at Fordham Law School.

Looking back, I'd realized many of the things I encountered in modeling wouldn't have happened if there'd been rules and regulations in place. Maybe with a law degree I could advocate for better practices, or at least help girls who'd been wronged. I wanted to start Model2Model as a way for models to protect themselves, but maybe one day *I* could help protect them, too. That certainly didn't sound like such a ho-hum existence, now did it?

Plus, I wanted to be an undergrad in New York because I'd still be where all the action was (and besides, where else can you throw a rock and hit a bona fide fashion model?). My parents, happy that I was finally getting my degree, quickly got over the fact that I was not going to Penn, my dad's alma mater. And it helped that, according to my dad, I was "following in his foot-steps" as a lawyer. But, deep down, I sorta felt like I was taking a path all my own.

It would be an uphill climb, for sure. And difficult to take on the modeling world, but I'd already seen what a few articles could do, and I knew that one person could make a difference. But, of course, I had help. I wasn't doing it all alone. A few days after Jonnie moved out to work for an agency in Miami, I got a phone call from my old roommate Ashley ("Girl! You've been causing a lot of trouble!"). The West Coast girl was moving back to the East Coast to take a role on a new soap opera — and she needed a place to stay. The timing was perfect, and soon after Ashley moved in, she helped me recruit a few models from her old agency and those she'd come to know through acting. People loved the idea of Model2Model and thought it was great to help out the newbies — and besides, who didn't like getting together over coffee to commiserate about one's love-hate relationship with the beauty biz? Our first meeting was held in our apartment at the end of July, and the rest, as they say, is history.

"Follow me," I said to Benji, after we'd taken the subway back to NYU, and were walking toward Washington Square Park.

"Back to my place again?" Benji asked, as I led him toward graduate housing. "Haven't you got enough of me yet?"

"Very funny," I said. "This is a surprise."

We'd been practically inseparable since his move to New York in late August. And while we'd come very close, I hadn't yet let things get as far as they'd gotten with Seth. That's because this time, I was going to do things when I was ready, on my own terms. And you know what? Benji was just fine with that.

He followed me down a small alleyway off of Washington Square where, across the street, a King Kong–sized version of me was plastered across the side of a building. I was wrapped in one of Philippe's oversized trench coats and wearing a pair of Jackie O sunglasses. When I first saw it, I had to look twice to make sure it was actually me, the girl looked so foreign.

"Whoa — when did that go up?" He asked, looking over at me with an incredulous grin. "You sure you're ready to give that all up, missy?"

I got a whiff of his sweet-savory Old Spice and glanced at this clean-shaven boy, looking quite like the person who'd made my chest tighten more than a year ago, and saw something different in his eyes, something … wiser.

"Couldn't be more sure."

And it was at that moment, standing on the south side of West 4th Street, that I knew I loved Benji. That I was *in love* with him. The studious one, the fuddy-duddy. The only guy I'd ever met who had more patience with me than my own father. Who, after all the ups and downs I'd put him through, was still here, ready to hold my hand. It was he who helped me believe I could leave this industry with my head held high. It was he who helped me realize I had the strength to do something that was greater than myself.

I turned away from him, lest these feelings of adoration run away from my senses and turn into all sorts of wild thoughts that included houses and babies and SUVs and something that looked quite like my mother's life.

Benji smiled at me, all too knowing. "So, I guess this year has been *your* annus mirabilis after all," he said. "Your miracle year."

"Has it?" I asked, playing along. "Why so?"

"Well, because it led you to find your true calling."

"Yes," I said. "You're right. This year has been my annus mirabilis." But it wasn't entirely for the reasons Benji thought. It was also because this year, quite simply, had led me to him.

# ACKNOWLEDGEMENTS

Thank you to my husband Eric, who without your inspiration, support, and guidance this book truly would not exist.

Thank you also to my dear agent Jennifer Byrne, a "sister-in-spirit," best friend, and writing accomplice who has stuck by me these 20 years. Here's to many more! Thanks, also, to Debra Moffitt, friend, writer, and therapist whose wit and wisdom (and baked goods) have bolstered me in hard times (hello quarantine!). Thanks to you both for reading early versions of *Catwalk* and supporting me in this writing life.

A big thank you to those who helped me along this publishing journey, including editor Donna Brown and Lily Wilson at Lily Catherine Design. A shout out to my supportive beta readers at Wattpad who gave me so many insightful comments and helped me to see, first hand, what this story could mean to many. Special thanks to writers Liz Durano, Shelley Burbank, Monica Kuebler, and Ashlyn M. for their votes of confidence early-on, and to the Wattpad Ladies on Life (LOL 35+) community for their support.

Finally, thank you to my mother Cyndee and the many family members who read early versions of the book. Your support means so much to me. Love you all!

Kelli Wilke Photography

# NICOLE GABOR

is a published author of more than twenty children's picture books and an award-winning health writer and editor. Her debut novel *Catwalk* is inspired by her experiences living and working in New York City as a model. Nicole is a senior editor at *KidsHealth.org*, the Web's #1 most visited site for children's health. She lives in Delaware with her husband, three children, and their Goldendoodle named Ginger. Learn more at www.nicolegabor.com.

Made in the USA
Middletown, DE
04 March 2022